Dimorphic

Cy Wyss

Nighttime Dog Press, LLC
P.O. Box 816
Zionsville, IN 46077
http://www.nighttimedogpress.com

Contents

Contents iii

1 Bleak October 1

2 Brain-Dead 11

3 Freefall 17

4 Sidekick 25

5 The Iron Menagerie 31

6 Bungalow 38

7 Chin's 47

8 The Blond Smoker 53

9 The Hawk 61

10 Engagement 68

11 Liberation 78

12 Hospital 80

13 Protection 99

14 Suspect 102

15 Missiles 109

16 Spirits 117

17 White Room 127

18 Line Up 135

19 The Prodigal Daughter 144

20 Dragon 151

21 Warehouse 157

22 Captured 174

23 Black Room 180

24 Mission 185

25 Hard Drive 189

26 Safety 207

27 Hide 221

28 Breakfast 232

29 Decoy 234

30 Breakout 237

31 Message 247

32 Raveland 254

33 Exchange 258

34 The Wolf and the Fox 261

35 Mail 270

36 Disclosure 273

37 Nibble 291

38 Memorial 295

For ten years I have been polishing this sword;
Its frosty edge has never been put to the test.
Now I am holding it and showing it to you, sir:
And I ask, is there anyone suffering from injustice?
—Jia Dao, *The Swordsman* (Translation J.J.Y. Liu)

— 1 —

Bleak October

♀/♂

It would be unfair to blame that crazy year on Batman. Yet who can say how much my love for the Dark Knight was responsible for the whole murderous mess? At the very least, I blame DC Comics for my lifelong hero complex and fanatic ability to take random violence personally.

Throughout our youth, my twin brother, Ethan, gallivanted around Atlanta, branding its towering facades with fantastic graffiti. He was a wisp of smoke dissipating in the night air, leaving behind a spray of hieroglyphic taunts. I, on the other hand, spent life in a tent in our backyard nibbling cheese puffs and devouring the Justice League's latest escapades by an upended flashlight.

He grew up into a wiry beast of a man, while I grew up into a buxom klutz of a woman. How fair was that?

By twenty-one Ethan was big in the XGames and had scored a lucrative sponsorship for professional daredevilry. I, on the other hand, had dropped out of law school a week before graduating to join the police academy, from which I was ejected a mere two weeks later due to irreconcilable clumsiness and an unfortunate inability to defer to authority.

It didn't matter. If I couldn't be a police officer, then I'd be a bounty hunter. Or, a private detective. Or, a fireman. I would be something heroic, even if it killed me—reality be damned.

But reality had other ideas. October descended, and the worst happened. In global events, 500 million dollars of U.S. sky supremacy suddenly vanished over Afghanistan; in regional events, Atlanta underwent a freak drought, which was promptly declared apocalyptic; and, in personal events, my beloved twin died.

It wasn't a hero's demise. He simply miscalculated on his motocross. By the time they airlifted him to the trauma center, his cerebral cortex was lifeless. A day later, on October 31, Ethan was declared brain-dead by the presiding neurologist.

I was there. I sat in an armchair next to Ethan's bed and stared at his spiritless body. None of this seemed real. I watched his stomach rise and fall as lingering breath filled his muscular chest. Inside, his organs hummed right along, unaware they no longer constituted life.

A hospital representative wanted to know if I was available to discuss "arrangements." He was an obsequious, odious man with a hooked nose and close-set dark eyes. I followed him from Ethan's antiseptic-smelling room into a dim, sterile hallway. We passed a nurses station where a blond woman sat at a computer. Carved pumpkins crowded the counter and Halloween decorations hung from the ceiling, streamers dangling above the typing woman like Damoclean swords.

"I'm truly sorry for your loss," the representative said, waving me into a room painted lilac. He sat behind a large oak desk, and I slumped in a winged armchair before him. I couldn't bring myself to speak. Behind the man, a glass-framed print held daisies in an out-of-focus field of green. Bile rose in my throat and I choked it back, swallowing heavily.

"Well, Judith," he said. "May I call you Judith?"

I nodded weakly.

"In terms of options, there's a local hospice that does end-of-life care. I can give you their contact information."

I frowned. Surely this was some kind of cruel joke. Ethan wasn't dead, only sleeping. Doctors, even neurologists, were wrong all the time. Weren't they?

"Alternatively. . . " He cleared his throat. His eyes crossed for the barest of moments. "We can arrange for him to be taken off life support. In this case, perhaps you have a funeral home that you can work with to be there."

I glowered at him. He wasn't getting it. Ethan wasn't dead. He breathed, he even twitched. How could a dead man twitch?

"He still moves," I said.

The man took up a pencil from his desk and flipped it over repeatedly between his long fingers. "Autonomous reactions are not uncommon, even for patients in irreversible comas. I'm sorry to keep repeating this, but your brother's MRI clearly showed all activity has ceased in his cerebral cortex, which is the seat of consciousness and one's higher functions."

"Of course it's ceased. He's in a deep sleep. Who's to say the activity won't come back?"

"I'm sorry, Judith. We simply can't keep your brother here for long. You have forty-eight hours to make arrangements for his care, whether you decide to pay for a hospice or—"

"Or, a funeral?"

He swallowed. "Again, I'm sorry. I realize it is difficult to believe. But you must know that over ninety-eight percent of patients with your brother's symptoms never recover."

"What about the remaining two percent?"

"None of them recover enough to lead functional lives. It's a pity, but the accident that spared his body did no such thing to his mind."

"Meaning he'd be better off if he was mangled too; then at least he would have died properly?"

He stared at me. "I know this is a lot to absorb. Perhaps you should go home and talk it over with other loved ones."

He didn't know there was no one else. It was only me now. I alone would decide. Having control over Ethan's life support in my hands didn't make me feel super-powered; instead I felt helpless. Helpless and ineffectual.

I rose from my chair. The man sat up straight. "You'll be in touch?"

"Yeah. Sure."

I turned from him without another word and exited his lilac office. The hallway was chartreuse, a contrast I didn't appreciate. Why were hospitals so hopelessly institutional? I pushed through double doors into the emergency receiving area. It was nearly empty on this late Sunday afternoon.

I trudged through the hospital grounds, insensitive to the bitter wind and looming chill. Dark clouds gathered on the horizon and murmured of an end to Atlanta's drought. Towering mourners in shades of russet and purple surrounded me, their black dead leaves dropping through the twilight and swirling around my feet.

I barely noticed the subway ride and the walk to our house; they passed in a tear-stained blur of foul wraiths and noxious traffic. It was after sunset when I made it home, exhausted. The rain began, a great sheeting deluge from the sky. I curled up in bed, dead inside, and hoped I'd never wake up.

* * *

The water's surface shimmered above me. I shot through its skin, kicking and coughing. Why was I choking?

I was choking because a monster was sucking on my face. I clawed at it, breaking its suction and ripping it off. I gagged on an oily tentacle and pulled on the slimy length until at last it came out. I rolled to the side and chucked the whole evil beast onto the floor.

I was unable to interpret the insistent red light flashing before my face. Agony swelled in my throat, and I laid back against a hard pillow and closed my eyes. I felt like I hadn't slept at all. I opened my eyes and stared at a ceiling of gray squares.

It wasn't my ceiling.

My head grew heavy as I stared at it, and I couldn't keep my eyes open. I succumbed once more to the dark water surrounding me.

* * *

My heart pounded furiously, and a cold covering of sweat lay under my pajamas. I looked up at my ceiling. Popcorn texturing stared back. This was my room, this was my ceiling. Why did I feel like I had just been somewhere else? I shook my head. The blue glow of my clock said 1:13

a.m. Reality came back to me. Ethan was gone. My brother, my idol—gone. I got up and stumbled out of my darkened bedroom.

The black paper cat Ethan had hung near our front window mocked me, its orange streamers slowly twisting in an invisible current. The jack-o-lantern Ethan had carved sat on our coffee table. I paused to strike a match and lower the flame laboriously into the pumpkin, as if a moment's somber ritual could bring him back from the dead. Incandescence poured through narrowed eyes and a toothy grin, then followed me across the dining room to Ethan's bedroom. I swung open his door.

The first thing I saw was the gentle glow of a large habitat. Inside, I knew there was a large corn snake, whose name was Fred. I wandered over to the glass enclosure and looked inside. Fred was nowhere to be seen—probably she was ensconced in her hidey-hole.

As my eyes adjusted to the dimness, the next thing I noticed was the big black garbage bag with Ethan's effects that I had hastily dumped into his room. I swallowed. I supposed I'd have to look through it sometime.

I dragged the bag over to Ethan's bed and opened it. Inside, his nylon suit was in gritty shreds, the armor plates and helmet that had failed him having settled to the bottom of the bag. I pushed the ruins of the outfit around, looking for his wallet or his watch or anything else small and hidden.

Silver winked amid the refuse. I gasped. It was Ethan's pendant. A gorgeous piece—a coiled serpent in sterling silver with obsidian chips studded throughout. He had worn it all the time on a thick pewter chain. My hands shook as I placed it around my neck. It was surprisingly warm against my bare collarbone.

Tears ran down my cheeks. What was the point? Ethan's life had been sexy and exciting, a life of speed and success. My life was clumsy and frustrating, a life of dreams and depression. Now the real hero was gone, and there was only me, the abandoned failure. Who would I live vicariously through now?

I laid down on my brother's bed and bawled. After several minutes, my head grew heavy and Ethan's scent surrounded me as I drifted off into a merciful slumber.

***

I coughed and choked, struggling to sit up. I only managed to hang my head off the side of the bed. It wasn't Ethan's bed. Where was I?

The flashing red light was back. I squinted at it. It was a respirator, warning me of some kind of connection problem. Below me, the face mask sat in a puddle of sour-smelling bile on the floor. I could see how that might constitute a connection problem.

I looked around. I was in a hospital room, at night. Rain splattered against the windows. I wiped my mouth with the back of my hand and saw that it wasn't my hand. I held it up and stared at it. My hand was too broad, and there was hair on it. I clapped those foreign hands to my face. Someone else's stubbly jaw pulsed under my touch.

I rolled out of the bed onto unfamiliar legs. In front of me was a sink in a small alcove, illuminated with a dim night-light. I whacked my knee on an armchair and stumbled over big feet on my way to the sink. Nothing seemed to be where it was supposed to be.

When I finally made it over there, I slammed my forehead into the squat mirror above the faucet on my way down to the tap. I drank voraciously, shoving my head into the sink and letting the water run over me. Some water got up my nose, and I sneezed and backed off, sputtering and rubbing my face.

When my hands parted, I saw the face staring back at me from the mirror. It was my face. Or, at least, as close as possible—for someone of the opposite sex. A more prominent brow, a more angular chin beneath the shadow, darker shades of blue eyes and brown hair…

I was Ethan.

My eyes rolled back in my head and my knees buckled as I fainted.

***

Back home, I started awake and nearly fell off Ethan's bed. My hand…I raised a hand to my face and stared at it. My own hand, my slender, manicured hand—it was back. What on earth had happened? It must have been a dream. How bizarre. I couldn't remember ever dreaming I was my brother before. And what a dream it was: intense and realistic. In spite of the unease, I smiled.

I wandered back into our living room, sat on our battered couch, and flicked on the TV. All I could find was late-night television with supercilious comedians and the news with stories of vigilantes in black supersuits running around the city beating up muggers and rapists. I switched off the TV and yawned.

The snake pendant was heavy at my throat as I went back to my room and climbed into bed again. I willed myself back to sleep and could only hope I'd have visions of my brother again.

* * *

I returned to the dream that seemed too real to be a dream. I was kissing the linoleum beneath the hospital sink, sprawled in a heap. I struggled upright. I ran my hand over my chin. The foreign stubble was there. I moved my hand to my chest. No boobs, only taut pectorals. Odd lips tightened, and I laughed.

I looked at the hospital gown, stretched over hairy thighs. I didn't seem to feel anything out of place beneath it. Shouldn't I be able to feel it if I had a penis all of a sudden?

I ran my parched tongue over the cracks in my lips. I lifted the gown to my chest. There it was.

I pulled the gown back down and smoothed it over my knees. Now that I'd seen it, I thought I could feel it—a faint but sensitive presence between my upper thighs.

I laughed again, which turned into a coughing fit. My insides were on fire, and there was blood in my spit. I chortled and coughed hysterically for what felt like ages.

After my shuddering subsided, I stood uneasily on legs that were far too brawny to be my own. I stared at myself in the mirror for several minutes, rubbing the face I saw there. Ethan's face.

After staring at my new self for a while, I moved to the exit, careful to keep my unfamiliar size in mind so I didn't stumble or whack myself on the furniture again. My big hand closed around the cool metal lever. The door opened easily and I stepped into the pale green hall.

The first nurses' station I found was as empty as the hushed, dim hallway. Jack-o-lanterns winked at me across the counter. Above, a familiar black cat with orange streamers lazily circled in the conditioned air. I nodded at the cat. She turned away, saying nothing.

I followed exit signs to double doors at the far end of the hall. As I neared, I saw moving figures and strobing red lights through narrow windows. I pushed through the doors into chaos—into hell.

Emergency workers ran helter-skelter bearing casualties on rolling gurneys. Those not injured enough to warrant a wheelchair sat stiffly on benches and slumped on the floor. Blood was everywhere—its dank, ferrous stink cloying and oppressive. I covered my mouth and nose with my hand and almost retched.

On my left lay a woman with Elvira hair, her beautiful red velvet gown drenched with a darker red. On my right lay a fangless Dracula in a black-and-vermilion cape, the lump of a bloodied head at his side. Vacant eye sockets stalked me as I moved away.

It seemed that Ethan had ended up on the wrong side of heaven in the afterlife. It might have been the occasional reefer he enjoyed on our back porch, or all those oversexed fan-girls he cavorted with. In any case, I was awash with remorse. I floated slowly down the corridor as wave after wave of mortally injured broke against me. Suddenly, the current parted to reveal the overlord himself.

Satan was a pale, fat guy with bushy white hair circling a bald crown. His eyes were eclipsed by thick, gold-rimmed glasses reflecting the soulless fluorescence of the ceiling. His ashen face seemed to be flaking apart, and he wore the suit of a harlequin that sagged over him in stripes of crimson and purple and ended in bulbous red feet. He was directing the scurrying demons, meting out this gruesome triage.

Double glass doors banged open, making me jump. Two EMTs rushed in with another casualty and a crest of bracing air.

While Satan's back was turned, I gritted my teeth and stepped around the new arrivals, treading into the cold shallows of an autumnal Atlanta night. Drizzle slid from the portico. A frigid, wet wind hit my exposed backside, and I scuttled away from hell.

Before me, mist parted to reveal the shape of a familiar yellow vehicle. I quickened my pace. When I reached the taxi, I hesitated. Thin fog filtered from beneath the car. I steeled myself and pulled open the door, then passed through the amorphous wisps, plopping myself into the plush embrace of worn leather. A last vaporous curlicue brushed my leg as I slammed the door shut.

The driver's close-cropped black hair was streaked with white. From what I could see of his profile, he was wearing the same flaking white face paint as Satan on his dark, heavily folded skin.

"Be with ya in a sec."

We were silent for some time while the driver attended to his clipboard, slowly and deliberately tracing each line, silently spelling the letters with his broad, chalky lips. At last he twisted around and looked at me. His mouth stretched upward into an abashed smile.

"Love the costume. Real authentic and all."

I was too astonished to speak.

"I be an angel," he said. "See my wings?"

I leaned forward. Large shapely cutouts with yellowed feathers rested on the front passenger seat next to him. He wore a thin white robe over his clothing. I sat back. The driver's appearance was distinctly cherubic in spite of his time-worn face and shabby costume.

His gaze returned to the watery night beyond the windshield. "Heard there's a big accident tonight. Tour bus or something, from a party. Bet it be crazy in there."

"That's too bad." Ethan's voice reverberated in my head.

"Uh-huh." The man contemplated the powder dusting the pale half-moon cuticles on his fingertips. "So where we off to, buddy?"

How odd to be called "buddy" instead of "ma'am." I contemplated the rain outside, which was now a downpour, enclosing us in a roaring waterfall. Where would the angel take me? For all I knew, the river Styx lay beyond the gloom, with Hades yawning thereafter. Even so, what choice did I have? Besides, it was only a dream. Right?

I gave the angel my address, and we pulled away from the curb.

— 2 —

Brain-Dead

♀

Our dad's call came early the next morning. Technically, Julian was not our father, but he'd been our guardian until we turned eighteen. Julian had done three things when we turned eighteen. First, he'd severed all legal ties with us so we were officially on our own. Second, he'd seduced me. Third, he'd taken off for Texas, leaving me broken-hearted with only my brother to pick up the pieces. Saying our relationship was a little strained was like saying the arctic was a little chilly.

I ignored my cell phone the first time it rang since I was still in bed. The second time, I looked at the caller ID. The third time, I finally answered.

"What do you want?" I asked.

"The bureau is sending me to Atlanta for a few weeks," he said.

I sat up straight. My gut twisted. "You're coming here?"

"Yeah. I've got a house rented in Decatur, only a few blocks from you."

"Great," I said. I swung my legs off the bed and yawned silently.

"Don't sound so enthusiastic," he said.

"Why are they sending you up here?"

"I requested a transfer."

"You're coming here permanently?"

"I don't know. This is temporary, but I'm hoping it'll turn into permanent. Their SAC will retire within a few months."

Julian had been an FBI agent for a decade. Before that, he had been a detective in Atlanta's police force along with our real father. The firefight that took our biological dad's life had injected new vigor into Julian's applications to the bureau and he was picked up that year—the same year he was appointed our guardian.

"You only transferred to Texas three years ago."

"I know. And, now I want to come home. I can't stop thinking about our time together. I know I left abruptly, but if you can find it in your heart to forgive me, I'd like to start over."

My throat tightened. Part of me desperately wanted him back. Another part of me was indignant. How dare he assume I'd just been sitting around waiting for him?

"I don't know if I can do that," I said.

"Give me a chance, Judith. Think of how good it was between us."

"A relationship is more than just the physical part," I said.

"I know. But, we fit together like hand in glove. I know you still have feelings for me."

"How do you know that?" I asked.

"Ethan told me. Just last week he chewed me out because you were still moping around without a boyfriend."

"Ethan is dead."

Silence. I didn't say anything, either. A few moments later, Julian spoke.

"What do you mean?"

"I mean, Ethan is dead. Or, braindead anyway. He had a motocross accident. They want me to pull the plug."

"You're shitting me. Ethan is in the hospital? Why didn't you call me?"

"Well, first of all, it just happened yesterday afternoon. Second of all, what could you have done?"

"Jesus, Judith. You need support. Where's Blaze? Get her to come and stay with you."

Blaze was my best friend, and some kind of distant cousin to Julian—close enough that they shared the same gold-flecked sienna eyes. Where Julian's hair was jet black, Blaze's was dyed shades of crimson and canary, like long multi-chromatic flames framing her heart-shaped face. I didn't even know what color her hair really was. I'd only ever seen it red.

"I want to be alone," I said.

"Come on, Judith. It's the holiday season now. Nobody wants to be alone for Thanksgiving."

I walked through our living room on my way to the kitchen to make some coffee. I stared at the Halloween decorations Ethan had put up. A black paper cat with orange streamers dangled from the ceiling. A jack-o-lantern sat on our coffee table. He'd even pinned orange and purple leaves to our samurai poster, making the dude's armor oddly sinister. A new movie with that samurai was due out soon, and we'd been planning to go see it together. Usually, the poster spoke to the vigilante spirit not far beneath my surface. Now, it just made me sad.

The door to Ethan's room was ajar. I stopped and stared at it. I was sure I had closed it last night. Hadn't I?

I stepped closer and my foot squished something cold and soggy. I looked down. A hospital gown lay scrunched up on the floor. Suddenly, my dream came back to me: the emergency room, the man dressed up as a clown I had thought was satan, and the taxi driver with yellowing wings. It was all just a dream. Wasn't it?

"Judith. Are you still there?"

"Uh," I said. "Yeah. Look, I just woke up. I'm going to make some coffee and take a shower. I'll call you back later."

"Promise?"

"Yeah."

"When?"

I stared at the hospital gown, my mind racing. "I don't know," I said. "An hour?"

"All right," he said.

I clicked my phone off, moved to Ethan's door, and pushed it gingerly so it slowly opened. Gentle light spilled from Fred's habitat. Laundry sat scattered around the floor and books were piled on his desk. Nothing was out of place, except for the fact that, on his bed, lay a dead man.

* * *

I stared at my brother's lifelike corpse for quite some time, frozen in place. I reached into the room and pulled the door closed. I turned and began to pace near our coffee table. I ran my fingers through my hair.

"Okay," I said to myself. "I've got a live dead body in my brother's bed. I'm a big girl. I can handle this."

I opened the door again and went into the room this time. I stood next to the bed and marveled at the fact his chest rose and fell with obvious breath and his color was much better than it had been at the hospital.

"Ethan?" I asked.

I poked him. He didn't move. I shook him. Still, nothing.

"Ethan, get up," I said. "This isn't funny."

From her habitat, Fred the snake watched me with glittering yellow eyes. I wished I could talk to her and ask her what had happened. Did he get here by himself? Or, had someone moved him for reasons unknown, possibly to make me think I was going crazy?

I reached over and pinched Ethan's nose shut. Nothing happened. After a few seconds, I got nervous. If he was alive, I certainly didn't want to kill him again.

Ethan snorted gently and his mouth dropped open. I jumped as if I'd been stuck with a cattle prod. Holy shit. He was alive.

"Ethan," I said. "I know you're in there."

I sat on his bed next to him and thought about the dream I'd had. In the dream, I'd been possessing my brother's body. Was it possible that had really happened? No. How could that even be a thing?

I thought about everything we'd been through together. The death of our mother was traumatic, but not nearly as much as the death of our father six months later. Our mother had been away on assignment most of the time anyway. Our father was the main caretaker. When he died, it was Ethan and me against the world. At least, it was until Julian stepped in. Then, it had been the three of us against the world.

Ethan had always been with me. When I lost my first molar and cried because I was convinced it had been a permanent tooth and I was going to be an empty-mouthed freak. When I had gotten my period unexpectedly for the first time in grade seven and was too afraid to ask the school nurse for a pad so Ethan had run to the store for me and bought some, risking the undying ridicule of his friends. When I pushed him off the roof of our garage in grade ten while he held an umbrella, because we wanted to see if it really would break his fall like in cartoons. It didn't.

My eyelids drooped. I took Ethan's hand and held it. I curled up beside him and drew his arm around me. Within a minute, my head felt heavy and my mind swooned. I had the sensation of falling, which wasn't uncommon when dropping into sleep, and when I blinked my eyelids open, I was staring at Ethan's ceiling. I looked down at my own body lying in my arms. Ethan's arms.

My phone buzzed and tingled and I started awake, back in my own body. Wow—that had been weird. But, I couldn't deny it. I'd inhabited my brother's empty body. It was crazy, and completely impossible, but it had happened nonetheless.

I looked at my phone. It was a city number. I clicked the answer button and greeted whoever it was. It turned out to be the man from the hospital—the one with the lilac office who had suggested I put Ethan in either a hospice or a casket.

"Ms. Gold," he said. "Did you make arrangements to have your brother's body transferred out of our care last night?"

"Um," I said.

My mind whirled. If I said no, there would be an investigation and they'd surely find out Ethan was home with me. I shuddered to think of how the authorities would react to the idea I could possess my brother's braindead body. I wanted to keep Ethan as far from anyone official as possible. That meant there was only one answer I could give.

"Yes," I said.

"Oh," the man said, surprise evident in his voice. "We didn't anticipate you having him picked up so soon. It seems we've misplaced the paperwork for his release. I could have sworn he was registered for organ donation."

"My, uh, mortuary should have taken care of all that," I said. I was totally improvising now, focused only on getting Ethan's disappearance resolved to the point they wouldn't look for him.

"Which mortuary is this that you're using?"

"It's, er, I mean, hang on a second and let me go get their card."

I pressed the mute button and looked around. I had to come up with the name of a mortuary, and fast. Then, I realized I was a woman in mourning. It wasn't too much to claim I was too overwhelmed to remember right now, was it?

I cleared my throat and worked on a sob until I had it at its most pitiful and evocative. I clicked mute off.

"I'm sorry," I said. I sobbed for emphasis. "I'm not in my right mind at the moment. Can I get back to you when I find their contact information?"

He was silent for a moment. "Well, I guess that'd be all right."

I said goodbye and signed off. I looked down at my brother. I stared at him for a long time, but aside from his quiet breathing, he never moved.

— 3 —

Freefall

♂

Eight days later, I was inside Ethan's body, crouched on the roof's edge of a corner store a couple of blocks from our Decatur house. My breath was a spreading mass of smoky wisps in the chilly night. Ethan's maps indicated this was the entry point for one of his favorite Parkour routes into Midtown.

In the days since I had discovered I could possess my brother, the rain had seemed ceaseless. Now, though, the torrent had passed and remained only as a thin mist close to the ground.

As far as I could tell, my transition to Ethan and back reliably happened whenever I fell asleep. My consciousness didn't sleep now, except for a moment or two of dreaming in the half-awake twilight between slumber and switch. So far it didn't seem to be an issue, and I was getting used to being female during the day and male during the night.

Most differences seemed surprisingly small and inconsequential, like the fact that I loved frothy bitter beer as my brother and hated it horribly as myself. Or the fact that I held and kissed Fred as Ethan but could hardly stand to touch the snake as myself. I found it amusing that once I got used to additional inches in my pants, having a dick was profoundly anti-climactic—nowhere nearly as distinguishing as I would have thought.

The greatest difference was our size and strength. As a male, I could pull my two hundred pounds up on the chin-up bar, no problem. As a female, I couldn't get my one hundred and fifty pounds to budge. I still couldn't pick up a car, though, or bend a tire iron with my bare hands, and I had tried. Whatever supernatural power enabled me to possess my brother didn't seem to extend to any new abilities for him.

In spite of this, my brother's body was a hero's body, and now that I had it for a while, I wanted to use it to its fullest extent. I wanted to retrace his Parkour routes through the city, finally able to reach the handholds and jump the distances. Atlanta was uniquely home to a thick tree canopy of towering ancient sycamores, oaks, and magnolias that supported the most daring acrobatics in between buildings and bridged the most impossible gaps. Gaps, that is, such as the one I was currently contemplating.

I huffed out another swirling breath. What was the worst that could happen? I might break one of my brother's limbs. Oh well. He had broken an arm when he was younger and seemed none the worse for wear now.

A giant oak in front of me had shed enough foliage that I could make out Ethan's faded red scribble on the bar roof across the narrow parking lot. It was simple. Jump to the tree, springboard to that scribble. A break in the fog revealed the twinkling incandescence of downtown Decatur, lighting the cloudy sky in shades of orange and gold. Daredevil spirit swelled within me. I turned from the edge and retreated to the roof's center.

Deep breath.

I sprinted to the roof's edge, naturally dropping my center of gravity during the last step so I could launch myself into the night sky. My arms and legs were wide. I flew across the divide with my mind frozen.

Heartbeat.

I landed on a fat branch. It bent and groaned beneath my weight, a reluctant diving board. I leaped again immediately and flew toward the scribble, oddly attempting to increase my momentum by pumping my arms and legs in the diaphanous air.

Heartbeat.

My feet came down not far from Ethan's graffiti, but the rest of me didn't stop as abruptly as my feet. I toppled like a felled tree, face first.

"Shit!"

I horked up a speck of tar and spat it onto the roof. My face and hands stung and burned with scratches from the stucco. In my mind, I saw my brother leaping off a tall fence. He had constantly wanted to show off his skills for me, of course. The Ethan in my memory tucked and rolled in the soft grass at the base of the fence, then hopped to his feet with a big smile on his face.

The tucking and rolling. Obviously important. I facepalmed.

* * *

I took to the trees. It didn't take long to realize the advantages of these living passageways. Tangled, elastic masses gave welcome redundancy. If I missed my target branch, there was always another to catch. I learned quickly what circumference to aim for. Skinny ones couldn't hold my brother's weight; thick ones didn't bounce as well and were harder on my body. For Ethan's talent to work best, I had to put my conscious mind in a kind of suspended belief. His body knew where to go and what to aim for. As long as I didn't get in the way by constantly second-guessing myself, I made real progress.

Crack.

"Oops."

The branch I grabbed at broke, and I slid a couple of feet downward before several smaller branches came together to break my fall. I was way up in a giant oak. I hung, poised, for a moment to still my pounding heart. Then, onward. I had a rhythm developing.

Swoop.

Swing and grab, swing and grab.

Snap.

Forward.

Thwup, thwup.

My toe-shoed feet made hardly any sound on the roofs of intervening bungalows. They were closely spaced this near to the city and made a nice complement to the trees—as long as no one ran out with a shotgun and filled the night sky with burning lead at the sound of feet contacting their roof, that was. I sprinted and jumped across five roofs, then soared into the outskirts of a wooded park and headed up and up into a massive elm from where I could resume my rhythm.

Swoop.

Swing and grab, swing and grab.

Snap.

Forward. . .

Only there was no next tree. The mist and myopic overconfidence had me careening into bare space. The scrawny excuse for a tree beneath me was young, tiny, and many feet below.

"Oh, fu—"

Crack. "Ow!" *Crack.* "Ow!" *Crack.* "Shit!"

I clawed at the hapless tree on my way through. It slowed my descent, but I nearly decapitated the poor sapling. The earth, on the other hand, received me gracefully and yielded in the form of a hollowed-out mold that I stamped into the muddy grass.

Splat.

I was still for several moments, stunned and taking stock of my injuries. I rolled onto my back. Thankfully, I didn't seem to have broken anything. All of my limbs were intact. Sore and complaining, but whole nonetheless. I struggled to my feet, stumbled and stooped, then staggered to the nearest park bench and sat heavily with my head between my knees.

It was then I noticed an odd noise, crinkling paper. I raised my head.

There was an older gentleman in a ragged wool coat and scarf, sifting through the garbage can beside my bench. An oil-stained fedora sat askew above his heavily furrowed brow. Scruffy salt-and-pepper hair covered the lower part of his face. He glanced at me.

"Y'all okay now? That was some fall you took there."

I wondered how long I'd been in the man's view. I hadn't even noticed him before I heard him rifling through the garbage.

"Um. Yeah. I'm okay."

He found a Coke can and shoved it into one of several paper bags sitting around his feet. He sniffed loudly, rubbed his nose, and turned to contemplate me at length. His dark eyes shone in the streetlight. They had the shallowness of someone who's there but not really all there, yet their intensity was unexpectedly gripping.

"You got any change you can spare, brother?"

I blinked, the spell broken. My hand went to my waist pack. "Sorry, man. No cash."

He nodded slowly. Whatever brief connection we might have had dissolved as he shifted into one of his stock responses for dismissive passersby.

"God bless. Be careful now."

He turned and shuffled off into the surrounding mist. I frowned. I felt a vague hollowness at his departure, as if I'd failed in my hero quest before even beginning.

About three yards away, the man stopped. He turned, shuffled back to the bench, and sat down, mumbling quietly and incomprehensibly. I was about to ask him what was wrong when, through the fog, shadows caught my eye. There were men at the other end of the park, standing and talking. I couldn't distinguish if there were two or three of them. My heart pounded. If I went that way, I would have to pass them and endure their catcalls and...

Or maybe not. I wasn't an attractive female. I was a big male, six-two and two hundred pounds of muscle. Another man would be stupid to give me unwanted attention.

My companion said, "There's a church on Krog might have room for me. The others all filled up tonight."

"Okay."

He turned and looked directly at me. I realized part of the reason for his odd stare was that one of his eyes was lazy.

"You want me to show you where it is? Never know, you might need 'em someday."

I contemplated him. He was old and emaciated, no match for the shadows in the mist. I read immediately the subtext of his question—he wanted an escort to protect him. My heart went out to him. He wasn't a female, but he no doubt had to put up with just as much catcalling and intimidation.

"Sure," I said. "Why don't you show me. It's true, I might need them."

He smiled broadly. "All right, man. Follow me."

I offered to carry his bags, but he wouldn't let me touch them. He reacted as if they contained gold and jewels instead of recyclables and refuse. We moved toward the loiterers. As we got closer, I saw there were three of them. They looked young, probably late teens. All were smaller than me and skinnier. Almost unconsciously, I stood tall, puffing out my broad chest. I kept my face neutral but attentive.

The boys stepped off the path into the grass, giving us room to pass. One of them said something in a low voice, and they laughed. We were obviously the butt of whatever joke was offered. I clenched my fists. My companion ignored them, trudging on. I followed his lead, and we passed unaccosted. Once my back was toward the boys I was particularly tensed. Every muscle tightened in anticipation of an incautious breath or the rustle of clothing or anything else indicating someone was jumping us.

Nothing. The homeless man and I crossed the street and headed up Krog Avenue. The boys behind us were quickly swallowed by the mist.

I felt disappointed. How silly was that?

* * *

High in an oak overlooking Inman Park, I watched an elevated train pass, slowing in its approach to the station. The fact they were running meant it was after 5 a.m. already. The train screeched around a curve and stopped under the concrete awning.

Through the lit windows of the train, I could see a poster for a samurai movie—the sequel to the one we had a poster for in our living room. The warrior in the poster seemed to be following me around, like a tap on the shoulder by fate. Every time I saw his image, I felt an ache in my chest. How I wanted to be a samurai; how I wished I wielded a curved sword and struck down bad guys like brittle bamboo stalks. I sighed.

I hadn't been lying when I told the homeless guy I had no cash, which also meant no change for the subway. So I had to walk home. Or swing.

Or. . .

I dropped out of the tree, adrenaline surging. I raced the distance and scaled the fence surrounding the station, balancing myself between barbs on the wires on top of the fence. It wasn't far to the platform from here. I coiled deeply and leaped, landing with barely a sound on the concrete overhang. The train was already pulling out, and I ran alongside as it accelerated. Near the edge of the awning, I put on a burst of speed and leaped from the platform roof as the train's tail passed. I managed to land on the train, a couple of yards from the very end.

"Woo!"

My elation was cut short by a fast-approaching highway bridge. I dropped flat, throwing my arms over my head. The bridge whooshed by. My scalp crawled at its proximity. The train squealed, navigated a sharp bend, and nearly tossed me off the roof.

This train surfing stuff was harder than it looked.

At the next station, we started east toward Decatur but then slowed, stopped, and backed up. I looked down the side of the train car and saw green paint.

"Shit."

That meant I was on the green line instead of the blue line that continued to Decatur. I had to get off, now. We were speeding up but still fairly slow. I stood and looked around. Several rows of tracks stretched on one side of me. A fence followed the track on the other side but wasn't quite close enough to jump onto.

Then I caught sight of a huge, fast-approaching oak tree, its limbs spreading outward close to the tracks. I timed my approach, then leaped as far as I could. The oak was right at a bend in the track, and the train seemed to snap like a whip as it accelerated around the bend, adding to my momentum unexpectedly. I was hurled into the highest branches of the tree and broke right through them, scraping my hands and face as I struggled to grab something solid.

Whump.

I was knocked senseless. I didn't even know what hit me. A thick branch? A suspended electric cable? During my last conscious moment, I seemed to be floating, arcing through a slow loop away from the oak. Forward momentum ceased, and I slid from a great height, plummeting into oblivion.

— 4 —

Sidekick

♀

I bolted upright. My eyes flew open. I was back in my own bed, at home. I realized my brother's body was out there somewhere, mindless and abandoned. I jumped out of bed and struggled into the nearest clothes. I barreled into the living room and stopped short.

I shuddered at the prospect of heading east alone, into one of the worst districts of the city in the dark. Besides that, I couldn't imagine how I'd manage to retrieve Ethan without help. On TV, bodies got carried around all the time, but here in real life, he was two hundred pounds of dead weight I could hardly budge an inch. I knew he could carry me, easily in fact. But that's not how it was at the moment. I'd need help. And how could I get help? Ethan was legally dead, and I was guilty of stealing his body or, at the very least, failing to return it for organ donation. I realized I desperately needed what every hero needs—a reliable sidekick. Someone who would overlook the inevitable illegalities in being a superpowered crime fighter. There was really only one reasonable candidate.

* * *

It was hard not to speed recklessly on the way to Blaze's. I left my car on the curb near the back gate to Sal's Scrap and Salvage. Blaze and her mom, Saldene, lived in an aging mobile home at the rear of the junkyard. Between them and me stood the locked gate, about ten yards of scrap and junk, and a dog named Fury with a really bad attitude.

Blaze and I had met at juvie hall when we were fourteen. I had been temporarily jailed for intransigence, probably in a desperate attempt by my foster parents to scare me straight. Blaze was in for setting fire to her deadbeat dad's house. To this day, I didn't know her full name.

"Blaze," she had insisted. I retained a keen image of her at the moment we met: light from the wan wintry sun illuminating her long, fiery hair, her golden-brown eyes shining with disturbing brightness. "Just Blaze."

So Blaze was a pyromaniac with a dysfunctional family. And I was plagued by an overactive imagination and the stubborn idea I could be Batman. Frankly, I thought we were reasonably normal. With the world the way it was, how could a person not develop these little quirks?

"Psst! Blaze!"

I had made it through the yard to the shack and was rapping on Blaze's bedroom window. No sign of the evil fleabag of doom. . . yet.

"Blaze!" I rapped harder. "Damn it, girl. Wake up!"

A menacing growl behind me punctuated the staccato of my tapping. Fury, the evil burglar-chomping canine. I turned slowly to find him grimacing at me, drool dribbling down his chin. His teeth glistened in the yard lights. Adrenaline made me light-headed.

"Ni-ice doggie." My hands rose, palms out. "Good boy."

I might as well have been talking to a rock. A snarling, slavering rock. I sidled closer to the large crate next to me.

Fury lunged, I leaped. He smacked headfirst into the crate.

Thunk.

He recovered quickly, jumped up on his hind legs, scratched at the side of the crate, and barked furiously.

Blaze appeared, dangling a shotgun from one hand.

"Judith! It's you. Oh my God, I've been so worried."

Fury barked and barked, drowning out any halfhearted response I might have made. Blaze grunted a command, and he quieted down and heeled dutifully near her feet. I cowered on top of my crate and glared at him.

"Jeepers, Judith. How can you be so scared of a little Chihuahua?"

"He's a demonic hell-hound masquerading as a lap dog."

Blaze guffawed. She knelt, laid the shotgun on the ground, and admonished Fury tenderly, placating him with some kind of dog treat. He gave me one last snarl, then toddled off around the corner of the trailer. I sighed and stepped off my perch.

Blaze's freckled brow furrowed. "You don't look so good. You okay?"

"Yes." I sighed. "I mean, no. Well, not really."

Blaze's thin brows climbed up her forehead.

I fidgeted. "Um..." I still had no cover story. Then I noticed Blaze had a paperback sticking out of her pajama pants pocket. "Hey, were you reading? Did I wake you up?"

Blaze shrugged. "Nah. I was re-reading my favorite series."

Blaze's favorite series was the latest vampire craze among hard-core fan-girls. I knew her bedroom was covered with posters of impossibly handsome waxy men with airbrushed fangs, seductive smirks, and washboard abs.

Inspired, I abruptly came out with, "Ethan's come back as a vampire."

Blaze's eyes bugged out. "What?"

"Um... yeah." I bit my lip. "It freaked me out too. He just, like, showed up at home the day after he died. Now he sleeps all day and... I think he's developed an aversion to garlic."

"Really?" Blaze's eyebrows slid even farther up her wrinkled forehead.

"Um, yeah. Or something like that." I shook my head. "He got into some trouble near Candler Park, and I need your help to get him home before... um..." I looked up at the gloomy, subtly brightening sky. "I mean, before the sun rises and sets him on fire. Or, something."

Blaze followed my gaze skyward. "Wow."

I couldn't decide whether I was more disturbed or relieved that Blaze seemed to be taking me seriously.

"Poor Ethan," Blaze said. "I got to grab my boots, then we can go."

Only as Blaze said that did I notice that she was wearing large pink fluffy bunnies on her feet. I stared at them. What had I gotten myself into?

Blaze reemerged from the hovel a couple minutes later, having replaced the slippers with combat boots. They were comfortably appropriate to her flannel cartoon-covered pants, long-sleeved work shirt layered over an aging T-shirt, and army-green vest. She had her long azure hair in braids under a navy watch cap and a matching scarf around her neck. She flicked a flip-top lighter open and closed; the melodic jingle of stone scratching on steel was conspicuous in the junkyard's wasteland silence.

"I'm ready. Let's roll."

* * *

By the time we found the site, pale streaks of orange filtered through the dissipating mist in the east. Ethan's body lay at the bottom of a dumpster. Blaze scrambled over the side and extended a hand. I belly-flopped into the rubbish. I spit a random piece of plastic from my mouth.

"Damn it."

Blaze knelt beside Ethan. She gently pulled back his upper lip and checked his teeth. "Well, dang. His cuspids have definitely grown. He's a vampire now. That's freaking amazing. I knew they were real. I knew it!"

I stared at her. "Um, Blaze, we need to keep this very secret. He's supposed to be dead. If anyone finds out they'll, um... they'll kill him. I mean, kill him again, that is." I suppressed a snort.

Blaze nodded slowly. "Was he in a fight?" She caressed one of the scratches on Ethan's face.

I pointed upward. "Only with that tree."

Blaze glanced up at the broken branches that had only partially caught my earlier flight from the train.

"Poor Ethan. I wonder why he was up there. Do you have any idea?"

"You know, we really need to get—"

A metallic *clunk* sounded, and the bin lurched. I fell on my face.

Blaze looked over the side. "It's a garbage truck! It's picking us up!"

Groaning metal and grinding gears echoed off their surroundings. How had we missed the damn thing's approach? Blaze threw a piece of siding at the truck. It bounced off the cab.

"Dang it! I don't think he sees us."

How could he? The bin was blocking the windshield. We were slowly being raised into the sky, brushing tree branches as we went.

I slid around in the trash. "Shit! We have to stop him."

Blaze leaped from the bin. "Hang on, I'll make a distraction."

"What?"

The bin tilted sharply, and the flanges began to pull the dumpster over the cab. Its contents started to slide into the gaping compactor, and Ethan and I slid right along with them.

"Blaze! Do something!"

There was nothing for me to hold onto. I clutched Ethan's body and tried to use my legs against the bin floor to slow us down. The rubble behind us pushed forward. Soon everything would be upside down, and we'd be careening into the man-crushing, woman-eating garbage truck.

Suddenly, a bright flickering light shot out from behind the truck's cab. Blaze's scarf hung from the fuel tank, aflame.

I screamed.

The bin's forward movement halted, but mine didn't. I slipped out of the bin, barely catching the lip. Debris rained over me. Ethan's body and a chunk of concrete slid toward me. The garbage man jumped from the cab, pulled the scarf from the tank, and threw it on the ground. He stomped around on it, extinguishing the flames.

"Help!" I yelled.

At last, he saw me. "Jesus! Hang on, lady!" He ran back to the cab.

A moment later, the bin reversed direction, righted itself, and returned to the ground. I managed to pull myself up enough that I flopped awkwardly onto Ethan.

The man poked his head over the side. "What in the hell are you kids doing? Are you all right?"

I saw Ethan's legs sticking up above my head, silhouetted against the brightening sky. I could only hope I hadn't caused my brother even more irreversible brain damage.

The garbage man disappeared, then metal parts screeched against one another and the clunk of large slide locks opening echoed around them. The side of the bin swung open. Just like that. I burst into laughter. How convenient! I wished I knew about the easy way to access the dumpster before this whole stupid, stupid escapade.

The utterly confused garbage man didn't have much time to contemplate the blubbering, swearing, dust-covered crazy woman in the garbage bin. He made a strange gurgling sound and pitched forward, his eyes rolling back in his head. Blaze stood behind him with a thin pipe almost as long as her arm.

"Shit!" I yelled. "What'd you do that for?"

"He was attacking you, wasn't he?"

"No, actually he was helping me."

"Oh. Oops."

— 5 —

The Iron Menagerie

♂

The next night, in spite of Ethan's body's soreness and our awkward adventure, I was out again. I wound my way east, along Buford—a wide boulevard of melting cultures and capitalist extravagance. Among the sights was a billboard advertising a samurai movie. I was drawn to it, as if an unseen hand guided my path. I crouched on the shelf of the billboard. My breath condensed into shining clouds, reflecting light from the gargantuan image behind me. I was intent on that silver blade and the hero behind it. It wasn't Batman, but it stood for everything I wanted to become now that I had the world's greatest secret identity. After all, who would ever suspect that the person behind Ethan's Parkour prowess was a woman by day?

Aside from the billboard, there was a very interesting building in sight, across a side street, facing me from behind an overgrown ditch and a cracked parking lot. The shop resembled a small aircraft hangar, a semi-cylindrical structure of corrugated tin. But what really had my attention was the sword in the window. It was a real-life counterpart to the silver blade in the larger-than-life image behind me. As if that weren't enough, a small sign in the window proclaimed, *Heroes Made Herein.*

How did someone make a hero inside a grimy urban bunker? Was it a dojo? Some kind of military surplus store? A role-playing store for repressed emos who liked sharp, pointy weapons?

I had no idea what the shop sold and couldn't tell from its name, *The Iron Menagerie.* A subtitle of intricate sinographs accompanied the English, but I couldn't begin to read whatever language that was. I also couldn't find even the slightest bit of information about the place on the Internet, a suggestive oddity in and of itself.

I decided to get a closer look. I leaped from my perch and swung through the trees, then jumped across the street and onto the parking lot. I cautiously approached the bunker and peered in the window. Up close the sword looked expensive, lovingly and expertly fashioned from shining steel. Was that real gold on the scabbard?

A sign hanging in the front door clearly said *Closed*, but I tried pulling the handle anyway. To my surprise, the door swung open. A tiny jingle announced my presence as I ducked behind the nearest shelves.

On my left, a neon logo illuminated the cashier's counter. On my right, across the room, reddish light emanated from an open doorway, and I crept there to have a look. The retail part of the building only went halfway back; a metal shop with towering machines and a small foundry occupied the other half. The room was empty, even though the lights were on and the furnace glowed with ember-colored light. The heavy scent of molten metal hung in the air.

Back in the store, metal art and armaments of all sizes and shapes sprawled on the shelves. Prices were brutally expensive. Heavy shadows obscured the walls opposite the workshop, but I could make out what seemed like magazine stands and glass display boxes. I went to the glass boxes and looked inside. My eyes had to adjust to the dim light of a glowing exit sign before I could see the contents properly. Tiny dragons and warriors in intricately crafted metal sparred in a suspended dance to the death, flanked by oversized heroes and impossibly proportioned aliens. I recognized Batman and a couple of his more over-the-top adversaries.

Batman.

I craned my neck to look at the magazine racks beside me, still bent over the figurine display. The racks held comic books; I could see them clearly now in the gloom. Comic books. Of course. How else would you make wannabe heroes? Give them comics to read and fake swords to wield. It had worked for me.

"Ah, shit," I whispered, all hope dashed for the miraculous appearance of a worthy mentor. This wasn't a bunker or a dojo, or even a gun store; it was just a comic shop. A useless comic shop.

Suddenly, the hard barrel of a gun was pressed to my temple. Behind me, a deep voice boomed.

"Hands up, fuckball."

I raised my hands.

The anonymous gunman rummaged around in my waist pack, seemingly unimpressed with my smartphone, subway tickets, and small change. I had no weapons. As I was being patted down, it occurred to me I should probably carry something, like a knife or a gun. But if I was going to carry a gun, I'd better make sure I could shoot it properly—or at least make sure I wouldn't shoot my brother's nuts off with it.

I didn't move an inch, other than to raise my arms. The gun didn't move until the man was done with my waist pack. Then the barrel disappeared.

"You got no ID. Who the hell are you, and why the fuck did you break into my store?"

I started to turn around. He shoved the gun into the small of my back.

"I didn't say turn around. I asked you a question."

"I was just, uh, browsing."

"Browsing? You're shitting me. You don't break into someone's place of residence in the middle of the night so you can window-shop. You think I'm stupid, assclown?"

Assclown. I would have laughed out loud, but I couldn't be sure I wouldn't get my brother's head shot off in response.

"The door was open. I didn't think it'd be a big deal."

"What?!"

He walked away. I heard the bells tinkling and the door open.

"Goddamn it. I told that girl to lock up. Can't trust the fucking help these days."

I turned toward his voice but didn't see anything. I moved around the intervening shelves and stopped in the first aisle. My mouth dropped open. The man was maybe four feet tall, with a huge pile of dreadlocks that added another few inches to his height—or lack thereof.

I couldn't believe it. I had been rousted by a midget. And he didn't have a gun; it was a metal bar. Apparently, it felt like a gun barrel when pressed to a head; although, technically, I couldn't say I'd had an actual gun barrel pressed to my temple to compare it to. The man looked fighting mean with his dreads, black clothes, and stick weapon, except for the fact he barely came past my waist.

I broke out laughing.

"Yeah? What're you laughing at, shitwaffle? How 'bout I bust your kneecaps for you?"

He whacked the door, and the little bells shook off and fell on his head, immediately becoming entangled in his dreads. So now he jingled every time he moved, which was a lot as he flailed around like an injured animal trying to get the bells out of his matted hair.

"Goddammit! Motherfuck, so help me... "

I was paralyzed with laughter.

Finally the bells fell out. "Damn it. Now I gotta get the ladder and put those back. I need those bells. How am I gonna know if I got customers without the fucking bells?"

I strode over, scooped up the bells, and placed them neatly on the hook. It was an advantage of being over six feet tall as opposed to... well, much shorter. I turned to face the man. He whacked my kneecap with the pipe.

"Ow!" I pitched forward, almost toppling onto him. "Asshole!"

I hoisted him up by his hoodie and threw him clear up to the cashier's counter, into some white boxes resting on a table.

"Aw, fuck! Not these ones. These are special editions. Get me outta here! I can't get these messed up."

I took a deep breath and limped over to drag him from the comic boxes. They were indeed filled with special editions, including several I recognized. I picked up a copy of the Bane origin story.

"Hey, this is one of my favorites. I can't believe you have a first edition."

Rasta Midget eyed me through narrowed lids. "You wanna buy it? 'Cuz I ain't taking it out of the wrapper for no browsing shit. It's fifty bucks, and I don't take credit from no trespassing-ass crackers."

I gently re-filed it. "Maybe some other time."

We glared at each other for a moment. Then I remembered why I was there in the first place.

"What's that sign in the window about?"

He answered in some Asian language, or so I thought. I could probably tell an Eastern language from a Western one. Maybe.

"Come again?"

"You know any Mandarin, douchewad?"

"Mandarin. That's a fruit, right? Like a little orange that's really sweet and only gets imported around Christmastime?"

"Ha, ha. We got a stand-up comic here. That was so funny I almost laughed. No, bonehead, the language." He pointed to the sinographs painted on the window. "Anyway, I told you what they say."

"Not those signs." I retrieved the little cardboard sign and held it up. "This one."

"Oh. That's for the new Freedomman series. He's, like, starting a school for superheroes. I can hold copies for you if you want." He eyed my nearly empty waist pack. "But only with a cash down payment of course."

I replaced the sign. Some part of me had still been hoping for a martial arts or military hero. But this guy was simply a height-challenged, potty-mouthed, comic book store owner. My hopes must have been up excessively high because when they deflated, I felt a rush of anger.

Rasta Midget studied me under a heavy brow. "Or not." He shrugged. "What's your name, kid?"

"Huh?"

"Oh, c'mon." He waved his arm at me. "It's not a trick question. You don't have to give me your Social Security number. Just gimme a name so I can call you it when I throw your thieving redneck ass outta my store."

"Yeah? You might need your stick to do that. But you dropped it, didn't you? And I'm bigger and stronger than you, and I'll rip your head off if you try to go get it."

His face fell. "Well, you don't have to get all testy and shit. I was just making conversation."

"You're black, and you're a midget. If you were female, I'd call the affirmative action police to come arrest you for impersonating their mascot."

The man's face reddened. "Fuck you. Piece-of-shit redneck loser."

I snorted. I couldn't stop myself. It wasn't Rasta Midget's fault I was disappointed but still I found myself taking it out on him.

"Yeah, that was beneath me. Really." I held out my hand, level with his head. "Like maybe three whole feet beneath me."

That was too much for him. He threw himself at me, clawing and snarling. His surprising momentum knocked me down. He bit deeply into my leg.

"Ow! Sonofa—"

Great, I thought. Now I'd have to get disinfected. And, possibly, a rabies shot. I bashed him against the nearest shelves and kicked desperately. The little prick had a lump of flesh in his mouth and wasn't letting go. I grabbed his dreads and pulled. This would only get worse before it got better.

Blam!

The shotgun blast was so loud my ears would be ringing into the next day. Bits of plaster dislodged from the ceiling and fell on us. The metal-toting, leg-biting Rasta Midget finally let go. Blood covered my thigh and oozed down the midget's chin.

Silhouetted in the foundry doorway was a man of impressive stature, even without the monstrous shotgun smoking in his hands. Incandescent light from behind diffused around his sallow-skinned figure and hairless head, casting his face entirely in shadow. It worked for me—I was scared shitless.

"Go back to bed, hon," the midget crooned. "I got this."

"Wait, you're gay too?" I was nearly speechless—only nearly, though, as I never seem to be at a loss for caustic witticisms. "Holy crap. Can I be your agent?"

The midget and his looming boyfriend stared at me in astonishment.

"You know, you're practically a celebrity." The sight of my ravaged leg shut me up. Blood was everywhere.

The giant said something in a foreign language. My last sight was of the shotgun butt angling toward my chin.

— 6 —

Bungalow

♀

The sun had risen and washed out the city by the time Blaze and I made it to the comic shop. For the second time in two days, we were having to rescue Ethan's body. So far, I couldn't say my time as a superhero had been anything but ignominious. I did ponder the wisdom of bringing Blaze along, but my need for backup defeated my doubts. I made Blaze promise not to set anything on fire or club anyone over the head.

Blaze parked her aging pickup across two spots in the crumbling parking lot. Nothing had changed from the previous night, except the hangar looked even more forlorn and dingy in the penetrating sunlight. The front door was locked now. I left Blaze banging on the glass and peering through the grunge while I checked out the back. An addition was built off the rear of the hangar that looked promising. I stepped onto the cluttered porch and rapped on the door. When no one answered, I returned to the gravel driveway and looked up. There was a second-story window with a sash up.

"Hey! Hey, up there. You've got my brother. Open up!"

The sash was abruptly pulled down. My eyes narrowed. I picked up the nearest thing from the ground, intending to toss it gently against the glass like a serenading lover. Instead, what I picked up was a brick, and I winged it toward the window. Fortunately, it missed.

Thunk.

A noticeable dent appeared in the siding. The dreadlocked midget threw up the sash and popped his head out.

"Bitch! Quit it. You're going to break something."

I picked up a rock and hurled it, missing the window by less than a foot. Rasta Midget retreated, then poked his head out again after the rock ricocheted away.

"You crazy ho! Go away. I'm calling the cops."

Of course, the last thing I wanted was the cops involved. Thank God he didn't seem to have already called them. Come to think of it... why hadn't he called them? Wasn't that the first thing people did when someone broke into their home?

"Just give me back my brother, you little jerk," I yelled.

"Your bro—"

He looked carefully at me then, seeming to notice for the first time that I was a female version of the man who had invaded his shop. He withdrew. Then *clump, clump, clump* came heavy footsteps on stairs. Locks scratched and clicked open, and I was face-to... well, belly-to-face with the midget. I cuffed him.

"Give me back my brother, you little shit."

"Hey! Leave the locks alone, bitch. We don't know a damn thing about your brother."

"Don't call me bitch, asshole. You knocked him out here last night. What'd you do with him?" Again, I bopped him.

"Ow! Stupid cow."

Suddenly, I had a highly disturbing thought. "Oh, shit. You didn't, um, you didn't... take advantage of him or something, did you?"

"What? What the fuck you on about?"

I grimaced at the thought. Understanding dawned abruptly across his dark face. "Oh, fuck. You asking me if we stuck crap up his ass or something? 'Cuz I don't do that shit, especially with passed-out loser home invaders." His face fell. "Oh, shit. I wasn't supposed to say anything."

"Yeah, oh, shit is right, shorty-pants. Now step aside."

Blaze had come up behind me. The midget looked us over.

"Or what? You and little Miss White Trash here are going to flog me with your pantyhoses? Get lost, bitches."

He tried to close the door, but I reached over him and stopped it. I glowered at him, making it clear that we weren't going to leave.

At last, he rolled his eyes. "Oh, for fuck's sake. Fine. Follow me."

* * *

He led us across the alley behind the hangar. We passed through an intricate iron gate into a surprising garden paradise. A beautiful miniature Japanese maple tree stood in a bed of exotic greenery, its brilliant fall color stark against the kaleidoscope of greens. A stone walkway twisted through the growth, ending in front of a modestly sized bungalow that stretched below us. It was distinctly Asian with a balanced aesthetic. It had stucco walls, vermilion trim, and a golden lion knocker. We decided Blaze would wait outside.

"Don't try anything funny," Blaze said. "If Judith's not back in ten minutes I'll be coming back with the cops."

Rasta Midget scoffed. "Whatever."

Inside, I entered a hushed mudroom with white walls and shoji doors of blond wood and cream-colored paper.

"Take your damn shoes off, bitch-lips."

"Cute."

I complied, then followed Rasta-Midget through the doors into an expansive rectangular room with thick tatami mats almost completely covering a shiny wood floor. Imposing weaponry hung on the walls along with parchment watercolors depicting sinographs and Asian scenes.

I took a deep breath. "What is this? Where are we?"

"This is our dojo, stupid. Not that you need to know that."

My heart rate quickened at hearing that. Had I found my martial arts master after all? Was the huge man in the doorway with the shotgun last night some kind of sensei? I became nervous at the thought. I'd broken into his shop and attacked his boyfriend. It hadn't exactly been the best way to introduce myself to a potential mentor.

We crossed the dojo, and Rasta Midget murmured in Mandarin in front of a second set of shoji on the far wall. A curt response came from within. Shortly, the doors slid back. Spanning the entrance with his long arms was the shotgun holder from the previous night. He wore a black silk tunic embroidered in gold and orange that hung open, revealing a massive and very muscular torso. His dark pants were loose around well-toned legs. He was barefoot. His jet-black eyes burned darkly and settled directly on me. His eyebrows dropped to his lashes, and he stared at me intently. I was too intimidated to speak. Cold adrenaline descended through my spine. I was five-ten in heels, but the man towered over me by at least six inches. And he obviously worked out. *A lot.*

I stepped backward, nearly treading on the midget.

"Hey! Watch it, ho-monkey."

The giant barked a quick foreign word. Rasta Midget's gaze dropped to the floor.

"Sorry, Sh'fu. I couldn't keep them out. What was I supposed to do? Shoot a couple of ladies on our doorstep?"

I inhaled sharply. Shoot us? They hadn't called the police. Who doesn't call the police? Criminals, that's who. I shuddered.

"Of course not," the big man said. He smiled broadly, revealing straight white teeth between thick lips. "I'm grateful for our lovely visitor."

Lovely. The word struck terror as deep as my bones. I glanced behind me. The exit looked awfully far away. And I was not a sprinter.

"Please don't be afraid. We've had a misunderstanding."

My gut flip-flopped. "A misunderstanding?"

He lowered his arms to his sides. His entire posture drooped, as if he were trying to make himself smaller and less intimidating. He bowed toward me, dipping his shaved head low.

"Please, forgive me. I will retrieve your brother."

The giant gave me a respectful berth and moved toward the exit. I followed him.

"Where are you going?"

He paused. "Please, stay here. I will return with him."

"No," I said. "I want to see him. What did you do to him?" I glanced at Rasta Midget, who stared at the floor, saying nothing.

The big man also seemed to be studying the floor. He bowed again, bending in an arc toward me.

"Very well. This way, please."

* * *

The bungalow had a daylight basement with sliding glass doors leading to a large patio. The main room in the basement was a huge living space with a brown leather couch, two fat reclining chairs, and a massive marble coffee table. There was a long desk against the east wall underneath an array of nine large flat-panel monitors. Computer components, manuals, and tech magazines lay around the desk and living space.

I stepped closer to one of the monitors. It was divided into several windows, each of which depicted a scene from outside. I saw Blaze in one of the windows and realized the entire place was wired for video, and possibly sound. I saw everything from the comic shop entrance to the glass patio doors on the wall opposite me.

"Wow," I said.

The giant stood beside me with his hands folded into his sleeves. "Yes," he said simply.

Along the wall opposite the monitors were two closed doors. The one closest to the stairs was a plain wood one. He went to the door and opened it, then stood back so I could enter. It seemed to be a storage room. Wooden shelves held plastic boxes as well as neatly folded linens and supplies. The faint scent of fabric softener wafted through the room, and I thought it highly odd they were keeping my brother in their laundry room.

The washer and dryer made a sort of half-wall, and there was another area behind them, darkened and musty, with cinder-block walls and concrete floors. There were no windows to dispel the gloom. The giant flicked a light switch, and overhead light flooded us. As soon as I rounded the washer, I saw Ethan's body. It sat on a straight-backed chair in the corner, head bowed, in underwear, with a bandage on his thigh and his hands bound to the chair behind him.

I shrieked. I clapped a hand to my mouth. I whirled to face the two men, who stood between me and the only exit. I trembled. The big man spread his arms, palms out.

"Please don't be afraid. It's not—"

"Let him go!"

"Of course."

He said a quick word to Rasta Midget who toddled past, grumbling and wielding a utility knife. He slit Ethan's bindings, and my brother's body slumped forward in the chair. I stared at Ethan. Some kind of psychomagnetic pull arose, and I felt dangerously giddy. I thought for a moment I was in both bodies at once, staring at Ethan through my own eyes and at myself through Ethan's. My knees buckled. The giant sprang forward and caught me. I recovered and struggled; he released me at once.

"I'm sorry," he said, his voice deep and neutral. "We've frightened you."

I shrugged him off. "Don't you touch me. Don't you dare."

"My apologies."

Rasta Midget sniffed the air loudly.

I shuddered. "Wh-what are you doing?"

He turned to the big man. "Do you smell smoke?"

* * *

Outside, the beautiful Japanese maple amid the exotics was on fire. The giant ran over and beat at the flames with his tunic. Rasta Midget got a garden hose and sprayed water everywhere. I had seen a fire extinguisher in the storage room and ran back to get it. I was just about to go in the sliding doors when Blaze rounded the house.

"Judith! Come on. Let's get Ethan now while they're distracted."

"Did you start that fire? I told you, no fires."

Blaze smiled sheepishly. "Maybe."

I shook my head. "Never mind. Let's go."

We went inside, into the storage room, and struggled with Ethan's inanimate body. We loaded him up around our shoulders and managed to carry him with his feet dragging along the ground. It was slow going. By the time we made it out the sliding glass doors, the fire was out. The giant and midget stood before us. Rasta Midget was sopping wet. The big man was covered in ash and soot. He held his beautiful tunic, which was sopping and ruined. On his bare torso, I saw the edges of an elaborate tattoo—serpent tails wound around from his back to barely touch his ribcage.

Everyone froze and stared at each other.

Rasta Midget said something to the giant in Mandarin. The big man smiled briefly. To me, he said, "Would you like some help?"

I blushed. "That would be nice."

He dropped his tunic and picked up Ethan. He simply loaded the two-hundred-pound body onto his back as if Ethan were no more than a slightly inconvenient backpack. Jealousy filled me, until I realized I could do the same thing in my brother's body. Now all I had to do was stop getting him knocked out in random places and having to rescue him. Then maybe I could take advantage of the gift of muscle I had been unbelievably given.

Blaze walked alongside the giant, and I walked alongside Rasta Midget on our way back to the comic shop. From behind, the big man's tattoo looked like a two-bodied snake. It was hard to see underneath Ethan's dangling body, but looking at it made me feel prescient, like looking at the samurai of the billboard or the sword in the Iron Menagerie. I didn't know what it meant yet, but I knew I'd have to find out.

The poor little maple tree was a blackened, smoking, half-dead thing now. A wave of anger at Blaze washed over me.

"Sorry about your tree."

"Yeah. Stupid fire-starter fuckstick. Why didn't you warn us?"

I sighed. "So what's his story?"

"Huh?"

I waved at the giant, now ahead of us by several strides. "Him. What does he do?"

"Whatever he wants."

"Great. Is he Japanese? Chinese?"

"He's half Chinese."

"Half. Mom? Dad?"

"His dad's American, a soldier. In and out, so to speak. Jack's stepdad blamed him for everything and beat the shit out of him constantly. So he ended up alone on the streets of Beijing. You got any idea what that's like?"

"Not really. I barely know Beijing's in China."

Rasta Midget chortled. "Dummy."

"I know. Is that his name? Jack?"

"Yeah."

"And what's your name?"

He eyed me, saying nothing.

"I'm Judith. My brother is Ethan."

He sighed. "Fine. I'm Gumbah Sarbloh Singh."

I stopped. Jack and Blaze were almost at the pickup. Rasta Midget stopped just ahead of me. He looked back.

"What? Why'd you stop?"

"You got a nickname? Something that normal people can pronounce?"

He rolled his eyes and started walking again. "I'm not going to trample all over my heritage for some mentally challenged white chick."

"Fair enough." I fell into step beside him. "But I think I'll call you Goom, because that's all I could make out in that mess."

"Don't call me that. Useless flake."

Ahead of us, Blaze opened the truck cab, and Jack gently slid Ethan into the center seat and buckled him in.

"Are you going to be all right carrying him home?" Jack said to me.

I nodded. "Sure. We've done it before."

Rasta Midget eyed me. "Your brother gets himself into a lot of fucked-up scrapes, does he?"

I sighed. "Let's just say this isn't the first time."

He chortled. "Whatever. I wish I could say it's been fun, but it really fucking hasn't."

Jack nodded at us. "Be safe."

— 7 —

Chin's

♂

There's nothing like a suit of black leather to transform a man into an icon of vengeance. I was in my brother's body in our garage, staring at Ethan's superbike. In my arms I held a jet-black helmet; its visor reflected the streetlights and cityshine outside. Slowly, I pulled it over my head.

Ethan's body had done this a thousand times. It was as entrenched into his muscle memory as Parkour and breathing. But my heart beat wildly. This was how he died. This was how it all began, how I inherited his body in the first place. In my impressionable state, I fancied I wasn't born twenty years ago from our mother, but rather this fateful Halloween when Ethan left his body behind.

I straddled the bike and started it up. Of course it was far easier than the couple of times I'd tried it in my own body. My legs were longer. My limbs were more powerful. I revved the engine and burned out of the garage, nearly flying off the machine at its stunning acceleration.

I had to overcome any fear of riding that might be lingering in Ethan's unconsciousness. I wanted full speed and fury on the roads ringing the city. My brother had known them well, every dip and rise, every off-ramp and twisting thoroughfare, every alley and shortcut as evanescent as the mist swirling from manholes in the brisk November air. I put my conscious mind on hold and "remembered" routes, not interfering with any inclination to go right or left or up or over. Exhilaration swelled within me until I was in a state of perpetual thrill.

It was probably my lack of conscious direction that brought me at last to that particular dim street on the decaying, industrial side of Doraville.

It was around midnight when I found myself idling across from the comic shop, alternately contemplating the samurai of the billboard and the sword of the Iron Menagerie. The destination seemed inevitable: the billboard, the sword, the big man with the dimorphic snake tattooed on his back. I was certain my destiny somehow lied with Jack. Now I just had to convince him of that fact.

***

The rooftop of Jack's bungalow was greenery, fresh and fecund in spite of the season. Lush plants encircled a zen garden. I stood for a few minutes, contemplating its raked pebbles and carefully arranged rocks.

I realized the plants sheltering the northwest corner of the roof actually enveloped a large canvas tent. I crept over to it. The tent door was splayed, held open by rope sashes. Inside was a room large enough for a round table and two chairs, a small counter with a hot plate and half-size fridge, a sink, and an oversized military cot along the rear wall. The floor was stone, covered with a huge oriental rug that stretched from the table back to the cot. An archway beside the sink led to an adjacent nook that held an outdoor shower with cinder block walls and a trellis roof.

The main space was illuminated by a hanging lantern. Above the cot hung three gorgeous metal plates, each burned with sinographs. The first two had single symbols, the last had six symbols. I gently fingered the larger plate. It seemed a reverent way to treat a phrase, so I gathered the words held some meaning for whoever normally occupied this space. Was it Jack? Why would he sleep outside on the roof instead of inside?

Suddenly, a shrill yelling shattered the silence around me. I jumped and my heart smashed against my ribcage, but it was only my brother's smartphone. He had set it to a particularly obnoxious tune consisting of a siren, bells, and every known percussion instrument. I glimpsed the caller ID as I picked up the hollering phone and didn't recognize the number.

I accepted the call warily, saying nothing. If it was Julian, I didn't want him to hear Ethan's voice.

It was Goom. "Why the fuck you messing around on our roof, you useless fart-nut?"

I laughed. Ethan's low chuckle was an unfamiliar rumble in my ears. "I'm looking for you guys, in fact. Where are you? And how did you get this number?"

Silence. I heard muttered conversation in the background. After a moment, Goom returned. "You know where Chin's is?"

"Chin's. Sure. It's on your face. Below your lips, right?"

He snorted. "Dumbass. It's a restaurant. On Peachtree."

"Everything's on Peachtree in Atlanta, Goom-boy."

"Don't call me that. It's near the farmer's market, dipshit. Use the back door." He disconnected.

"Right," I said to the silence.

* * *

I found the restaurant ten minutes later, on a dedicated lot across from a strip mall, surrounded by cracked concrete and dense forest. I parked behind it, where a gravel road was cut into the woods. In the shelter of a large dumpster, the back door was open, illuminated under a buzzing streetlight. A sullen-looking Asian in a white cap and dirty apron was smoking a cigarette on the stoop. He looked at me through narrowed eyes.

"You lost, bro?"

"I don't think so. I'm looking for Jack."

He jerked his head toward the open door. I moved past him and stepped into the kitchen. Dirty dishes were piled in an industrial sink and encrusted pots stacked on steel counters. Other than that, the work surfaces seemed clear, organized, and relatively clean. I passed a plate of egg rolls and helped myself. Then I realized someone was sitting by the swinging doors at the end of the room, watching me intently. I chewed laboriously and swallowed the delicacy. It wasn't bad.

"Howdy," I said to the man, with one hand raised in greeting.

He was probably a septuagenarian, although he had the ageless appearance of all skinny people past fifty. He sported long, thinning, dark gray hair and a Fu Manchu mustache and beard. He wore gold pince-nez and a full Mandarin suit in black with a white collar and cuffs, topped off with an embroidered skullcap. He said nothing and sat motionlessly. For a moment I wondered if I'd confused some kind of life-sized wax statue for a real person. Then he blinked. I was taken aback.

"Um. . . right." I sidled around him and pushed through the doors.

The main dining room was carpeted in thick green shag covered with an intricate vine-like pattern. The walls were half wood and half dark velvet, generously arrayed with Asian watercolors that depicted happy grottos and smiling ladies in brilliant floral cheongsams. Aside from the traditional decor, the large room was filled with the detritus of a winding-down party. A handful of Asians milled about, picking at the remains of a vast buffet and sitting around talking. Several tables were vacant and uncleared. Near the front of the room was a long, boardroom-style table that could easily seat twenty. It was empty now, except for Jack and Goom.

I went over. Jack's chair was pulled back from the table, and he sat casually with his knees crossed and his hands folded in his lap. He wore a gorgeous shiny mandarin suit in pristine white silk, threaded throughout with subtle silver embroidery. Goom sat beside Jack and pecked at his laptop. The midget wore a brown-and-gold silk caftan and matching skullcap that pushed down on his ponytailed dreads.

I sat across from them, near the middle of the table. "Howdy, gents. What's the occasion? Wedding?"

"Funeral," Jack said.

I started. "Funeral? You wore white to a funeral?"

"White is traditional at a Chinese funeral. It is a sign of respect."

"Wow. Who died?"

Goom spoke up. "A man named Shun Yan Pii was shot to death."

I blinked several times. "I'm sorry to hear that."

Goom shrugged. Jack stared silently at me.

I said, "He wasn't related to the stereotype in the kitchen, was he?"

Goom sneered. "What?"

"There's some old guy in the kitchen who looks like he just walked out of a Charlie Chan movie."

"Oh, him." Goom rolled his eyes. "That's Guan Ho. He only wears that getup to impress the tourists."

A squat, handle-less cup of green tea appeared in front of me. I looked up to find the Wax Man from the kitchen staring down at me.

"Um. Thanks."

He smiled broadly. He had yellowed teeth and a huge gold crown on one of his premolars. "No pwohblem." He shuffled away, chuckling to himself, arms tucked into his broad sleeves.

"Okay, that's really freaky."

Goom snorted. "See? This is exactly why he does that. It's like brain candy for stupid white people."

"I'm sure it works on stupid people of other colors too."

Goom chuckled. "Maybe."

"Ethan, was it?" Jack said.

I nodded.

"Why are you here? What did you want with us?"

I blanched at the question. I didn't have a good answer for that. How could I tell the truth? That I wanted a mentor, someone to train me to fight? I licked my lips.

"Jack, are you a martial artist?"

He nodded. "I am."

"What's that got to do with anything?" Goom said.

I swallowed. "I want to take lessons."

They both stared at me. I fidgeted under their gazes.

After an awkward few moments, Jack said, "I don't give lessons."

I stared at the table. Damn. So much for the direct approach.

Goom said, "Yeah. He especially doesn't give lessons to rednecks who break into our shop."

"Sorry about that."

Jack frowned. "Why don't you tell us why you're really here?"

"What do you mean?"

Jack didn't answer, preferring to stare at me in silence. I squirmed under his penetrating look. I was completely out of ideas as to how to explain myself and what I wanted. *I have a superpower. I need your help to learn to use it to fight crime.* Would someone like Jack be able to help me, even if he wanted to? It was crazy.

I stood. "I'm sorry to have bothered you."

Neither of them said anything. I turned toward the back of the restaurant and took a couple of steps away, my face burning with defeat.

"Judith," Jack said suddenly.

I stopped in my tracks and turned around. Then I frowned. "Yes? What about her?"

"Is she all right?"

Of course he was only asking about my female self. It was silly to think, as I had for a split second, that Jack saw right through my brother's body into my squatting mind.

"Um, yeah. She's great."

"Please extend my greetings."

"Right."

— 8 —

The Blond Smoker

♀

The next evening was Saturday, and Blaze and I were waiting for Msti at the Blue Bulldog in downtown Decatur. Why we hung out in a cop bar, I couldn't say. I guessed it had at least two features we couldn't do without—location and notoriety. It was easy walking distance from my house and less than a mile from Blaze's mom's junkyard. Also, everyone knew us. I was the headstrong daughter of a detective gunned down unceremoniously after nearly twenty years on the force, and everyone still said "hi" to me, even new recruits I didn't know. Blaze was also constantly relating to cops in her own way, which usually involved questioning over some fire or another. Her deadbeat dad in particular seemed to own several properties, all of which were oddly likely to burst into flame on any given night.

Before Msti got there, we rehashed the previous morning's rescue.

"I guess it could have been worse," I said. "They could have been pulling our raped corpses out of the ditch right about now."

"I don't think gay vampires rape women. They probably would have just stuck us in the freezer for snacks or something."

I stared at Blaze. She blushed into her beer.

I cleared my throat. "Anyway, it's over and done. Ethan's fine. I'm fine. You're fine. Those two weirdos are fine. Everybody's fine."

Blaze laughed. "Did you get their names?"

"Well, the big one's Jack, and the little one is Goom. At least, I call him Goom because I can't pronounce his real name."

"Oh. It's probably in Vampyr."

"What?"

"His real name. It's probably a pet name given to him in Vampyr."

I blinked several times. Why did that make no sense to me?

Blaze shrugged. "You know, *Vampyr*, vampire language. When an alpha vampire takes a pet, they'll usually rename them."

"A. . . pet?"

"Didn't Ethan tell you about vampire hierarchies?"

"Apparently not."

"Well, vampires are above humans."

"Okay."

"So they like to take pets. We're like dogs to them. Or helper monkeys."

"I. . . see." It was all I could do not to burst out laughing.

"Jack's obviously a monarch. I bet he has lots of pets."

"You think Jack is some kind of king vampire?" An insistent guffaw piqued the edges of my mouth. I fought to keep it at bay. "Actually, I guess he'd be a queen vampire since he's gay."

Blaze's hand flew to her mouth. "Oh my God. Don't make fun of him like that. He'll find you and eat you."

"Sure he will."

"Vampires are very particular about their pets." Blaze chewed on her lower lip. "I wonder. . . "

I frowned. "What?"

"Do you think Ethan will take a pet? Maybe?"

I studied Blaze. Something in her voice made me think of her eternal crush on Ethan. Was she hoping Ethan would make her one of these "pets"? The idea was absurd.

"No. Definitely not."

"Aw. I'm sure I'd make a good pet."

"Blaze—"

"Oh, hey, there's Msti." Blaze waved to someone behind me at the other end of the bar.

"Okay, not a word about Ethan. He's cremated, in an urn, on my coffee table. And no vampires."

"Oh. Yeah. No problem."

"I mean it. No vampires!"

Msti's wail suffocated any response Blaze might have made. "Ooochh, Jude! My poorest little chickadee!"

I stood to greet Msti, who threw her arms around me and squeezed. After she'd nearly crushed my ribcage, she finally relented. She held me at arm's length and contemplated me closely. "I am devastated." She shook me. "Absolutely devastated for you."

"It's okay. I think I'm still in shock. I don't feel so bad."

"Yes." Msti's dark brow furrowed. "You look not bad for a woman broken with mourning."

We sat. Msti crossed her legs under her crimped full-length skirt.

Blaze said, "Oh my God, Msti, I love your boots."

Indeed, she was wearing crimson leather boots with pointy toes. They were studded throughout with diamond-like rhinestones. Msti lifted the edge of her skirt, and Blaze and I peeked at the boots beneath the table.

"Me too," I said.

Msti smiled. "Sale. Designer, from a friend. Very nice, no?"

"Oh, yes."

Msti raised a bangled arm high in the air and snapped her fingers, showing off half-inch blood-red fingernails to match her boots.

"Waiter! Wodka!"

Mstislava Fairholme, or Msti as she was known to us, was older than us by about twenty years and married to a retired police major. If Msti's stories were to be believed, the major brought her to America after they met online, rescuing her from a bloody war in her homeland. Ignorant of Eastern European etiquette, I once made the mistake of telling Msti I thought she looked like a beautiful gypsy. She cut me down ruthlessly. "I am nothing like the useless scourge. This is you calling me cheap, painted whore." Blaze had once carelessly alluded to circulating gossip about the "Russian mail-order bride." Msti had an equally enlightening response to that. "God above us, calling me Russian pussy is bigger lie than Jude thinking I am gypsy. I am *Abkhaz* mail-order bride."

At those times, everyone laughed. I wondered at how Msti had that effect. She could slap someone with one hand, but they were still prepared to kiss the other. She was impossibly magnetic in spite of her sharp tongue and dissolute ways.

Clunk.

The waiter plopped down a shot of vodka, snapping me from my reverie.

Msti blew out a lengthy, melodious sigh. "Och, what a day. I need booze." She knocked back her shot. "It started with three rape kits. Can you believe? Three. These shit-eating sons of donkeys will love hell. They will graze on the devil's ass hairs."

Msti worked in the city's main crime lab, culling criminal secrets from whatever they gave her: blood samples, bone fragments, burnt remains. I didn't know her exact title, but she must have been pretty high up because everything seemed to cross her station sooner or later.

"And now we have overtime because goat-turd drug dealer is setting meth lab on fire. Stupider than rat making sex on leg of cat. They are simply killing themselves. Soon there will be no need for police department."

There was silence as we contemplated the latest additions to Msti's colorful repertoire of insults.

Graze on the devil's ass hairs. Rat making sex on leg of cat.

We burst out laughing. Msti smiled widely, prominent white teeth gleaming between broad crimson lips. She rapped her shot glass on the table. The sound was sharp and unsettling, like gunfire.

"Waiter! Where is my wodka?"

* * *

Three hours later, Msti was blasted, and the three of us were playing pool in the back room with a random beat cop. Others milled around, amused by Msti's antics.

Blaze and I hovered at the fringe, awaiting our turn at the table. I had stopped myself after one glass of wine, realizing quickly where the evening was going. In spite of the cop's best effort and vast talent, Blaze and I were in the lead due to Msti's drunken incompetence. At the moment, she was leaning over the pool table, disturbing a cluster of balls with her dangling necklaces. She lined up her shot, licked her lips, and... completely missed.

She slammed the cue onto the table and shook her fist at the hapless white ball. "Donkey assh goat-foot little ball. I use you ash a toilet and dance on your shtupid grave."

Blaze almost fell off her stool laughing. I had been sipping Coke and ended up with soda in my nose. I sputtered and coughed with laughter. We gave Msti another chance. The cop covered her body with his and laid his hands on hers, intimately guiding their shot.

Blaze chewed on a fingernail. "Do you see that?"

"Yeah. We'd better pry Msti away from him before he does something his wife will regret."

We watched as the Msti-Officer creature sunk two more balls, then managed to follow up with the eight ball. So much for that.

I snorted. "How did that happen? We were ahead."

"Well, I'm drunk and can hardly see straight, for starters."

I looked at Blaze and noticed she was slightly swaying. Any response I might have made was cut off by a booming shriek from Msti, who fell and rolled around on the ground, legs in the air, jewelry jangling and skirt twisting everywhere. The cop tried to pull her to her feet, but she tripped him so he fell on her.

"Well, hello, shailor," she purred.

I winced. "Okay. Msti's definitely had enough. Let's drag her out to the Battle Buick and get her home."

* * *

I was intent on getting to my car, so I wasn't paying attention when I nearly stumbled over the man standing at the end of the alley. I stopped short, dropping my car keys at his feet. Acrid smoke intruded on my breath, and I realized he'd been standing there for some time, smoking. He was a bit taller than me, with a very broad chest and muscular physique. He had pale skin and close-cropped, dirty-blond hair. He had piercing, close-set light brown eyes, a long nose, and a pointed chin. His expression was wolf-like; I almost expected his lips to curl back into a snarl at my intrusion.

"Um, ex-excuse me." I stepped backward, heart pounding.

"No, excuse me."

His voice was deep, and I caught some kind of accent, similar to Msti's. The man smiled, a gesture that only served to highlight the coldness in his sienna eyes. He bent to scoop up my keys and handed them to me. In my mind, I dubbed him the Blond Smoker.

"Here you are."

"Thank—"

Behind me, Blaze yelled, "Msti!"

I whirled to find Blaze struggling with Msti's collapsing form. I stepped up to help. Msti was surprisingly heavy even though she was a slender five-four. Her swoon passed almost as quickly as it had come. She clutched at her chest and swayed, then waved us away.

"Is okay, is okay." She straightened up, noticeably sobered. Her normally olive complexion was ghostly sallow.

I still gripped her arm. "Jeez, Blaze. What happened?"

"She passed out for a sec. Must be those last couple of shots she downed. Who were you talking to?"

"Some smoker. Didn't you see him?"

I turned to see that the Blond Smoker had disappeared. Only malodorous smoke remained, wafting up from a smoldering butt.

"Nah, I didn't see anyone," Blaze said. "Was he cute?"

* * *

Msti was green and contrite all the way home. I was worried her silence boded puking all over the backseat.

Msti's house was a generously sized mansion after the Greek Revival style, in cream stucco and white trim. I eased the Battle Buick up the long drive and parked near the front steps, headlights washing out the area into a stark monochromatic landscape. White ionic columns guarded a shadowed staircase leading to an oversized entryway. Manicured topiaries flanked the stairs, jet-black in the car's lights. The building was otherwise completely dark.

I pushed the gearshift into park and idled. "Is the Major home?"

Msti stared up at the lifeless house. "No. He is in hospital."

"Oh. Sorry."

"It is routine testing for his heart. I think this business destroys it."

Blaze and I exchanged glances. I said, "What business?"

Msti frowned. "I didn't tell you. He has received death threat. I am sure it is because of my work."

Blaze said, "He was a cop. It's probably because of his work."

Msti waved her hand, gold bangles shining in the spillover from the bright headlights. "No. Is me, is me."

I said, "Do you want us to come in with you? Are you safe here?"

Msti opened her door. "I want I am alone."

Blaze said, "Is that really a good idea? What if—"

"No." Msti shook her head, arm, and whole body at us. "No. I wish to be alone."

Again, Blaze and I exchanged glances. Blaze said, "Okay. Sorry."

Msti got out and walked up to the front steps, her feet crunching along the gravel drive. At the top, she turned and waved to us. Then she opened the door and disappeared into the lonely darkness.

— 9 —

The Hawk

♂

At the southern end of Midtown, there was a mosque, a jail, and a venerable old gay bar known as the Hawk. I loved the juxtaposition of those establishments, mutually oppositional bastions of an open-minded America, pariahs alike, sitting practically atop one another in Midtown's eclectic fringe. Next to the Hawk was an old warehouse whose sunwashed brick exterior declared it the property of a now-defunct textile manufacturer. A large, unlit ghost billboard rose from the roof, giving me a perfect secret perch. Apparently, Monday was free pool night, so the club was well attended in spite of it being a weeknight. The mild clear weather meant there was also lots of activity out back for me to ponder.

Why was I watching gay guys come and go? The answer was complicated. Or, rather, it was simple but embarrassing. I was a woman in a male body. Naturally, I was curious. What else would I do with my new physique? Save the world and experience gay sex. Obviously.

The only problem was that, as far as I could tell, my brother's body was distinctly unwilling to cooperate with my gay sex ambition. Persistent nausea irritated my throat. I pulled the waistband of my pants open and glared inside.

"Stupid penis. Why can't you at least be bi-curious?"

I had known for a while there were aspects of my brother's body I didn't control. There was something of Ethan remaining, at least in his gut. It was a purely visceral presence and dictated his physical tastes, like beer and women. His body was heterosexual, and that was just tough shit for its new inhabitant.

While I considered whether this whole vigil was a good idea and argued with myself over what I actually controlled in his body, a beautiful youth broke away from the revelry and headed up the alley.

"Oh, hello," I whispered into the night air. "If he's twenty-one, I'm the pope." I would have put him at eighteen or nineteen.

I followed him away from the Hawk to the back lot of an apartment building in the next block. Soundlessly, I crept onto the darkened balcony above him and watched him fidget and wait. After a minute or two, another man stepped from the shadows. They were both dressed to the nines in club clothes. Between them, they probably had more hair products than most pharmacies. I ignored the bile rising in my uncooperative throat and watched them embrace.

Suddenly, two additional men leaped out from the shadows and jumped the anxious kid.

Shit.

I hesitated. There were three of them, and the boy would be no help. He was already down, and they were kicking him. Adrenaline poured out the base of my neck and washed through my blood, forcing my fingers into white-knuckled fists. The assailants were too intent on their prey to notice me standing above them.

The sane thing to do would be to call 911 and wait, hoping the boy wouldn't die in the meantime. Naturally, that course of inaction would have been hard to justify for a superhero.

* * *

"What the—"

I dropped right on top of one of the men, knocking him to the ground. The other two spun toward me, pausing their relentless assault. The one in club clothes had blood on his fists. I growled and threw myself at him, slamming into him shoulder-first and forcing him against the side of a dumpster with a deafening *slam!* I stepped back, wound up, and punched him in the head with all my brother's might. He dropped to the tarmac like the sack of shit he was.

The guy I'd jumped on recovered and came at me, slashing with a butterfly knife. Adrenaline and a lifetime of honed reflexes helped me twist and dodge, but still he caught me on the arm, making a nasty slash.

Thug Three, who had until then stood apart stupefied, threw himself into me, knocking me to the ground, exactly where I didn't want to be. Knife Boy came in close while Thug Three pummeled my face and torso. I kept my arms up and blocked most of the blows. I kicked desperately at the blade-wielding assailant, keeping him at bay as best I could while bucking and snaking my body around, trying to squirm out from under the asshole sitting on me. Finally I managed to jerk him forward off my waist so I could bring my legs up and wrap them around his neck. I yanked him backward, and his head bounced off the pavement with a satisfying *smack!*

Knife Boy came in fast. I rolled and squirmed, then jumped to my feet and took another slash on the arm. Blood soaked my hoodie. I bobbed and weaved, then managed to grab my attacker's outstretched arm. I whacked it against the corner of the dumpster once, twice—after three times he finally dropped the knife, and I kicked it away, underneath the dumpster. I elbowed Knife Boy in the face, feeling his nose give way. He screamed, almost drowning out the vicious cursing behind me. I threw Knife Boy to the ground and whirled.

Club Clothes had recovered. He was raging. He pointed a snub-nosed revolver directly at my chest. My blood chilled at his venomous voice.

"Time to die, you fucking fag lover."

Did I stand there and let him shoot me?

No. I dove to the ground, rolled and rolled. Two shots punched the pavement, one after the other, missing my head by fractional inches. I sprang up and zig-zagged toward a chain-link fence on the opposite side of the alley. I slammed into it, but knew I couldn't climb it before Club Clothes shot me. I turned toward him, expecting to die. I stopped short.

He was lying facedown with his pals, motionless on the pavement.

I frowned. How did that happen? I was sure he was still up and shooting at me when I ran for the fence.

Motion in my peripheral vision made my head snap upward in time to witness a dark figure leaping from balcony to roof. I blinked, and the figure was gone. The realization hit me that there was another Parkour expert floating around, and he must have knocked out Club Clothes to save me. Why? Who was he?

I ran back to the balconied building and scaled it. I was still flooded with adrenaline and hardly noticed the slashes on my arm. I pulled myself up from the top balcony the same way the figure in black had. When I made it over and stood up, the roof seemed empty. Where had he gone? The building was stand-alone, surrounded by trees. I was afraid he had leaped off and taken to the trees, but I hadn't heard anything. I walked across the roof and looked down into the street. Traffic passed unaware. Beyond, the cityshine lit the base of the clouds.

I wasn't sure what gave him away, but suddenly I felt the urge to turn around, and when I did, I saw him. He was no more than ten yards from me on the opposite side of the roof. He seemed huge, even a couple of inches taller than Ethan's six-two. There was something familiar about him. He was in a black suit with a full facemask. We stared at each other for several seconds—him in his face mask and me in my balaclava. Then, he turned and jumped from the building.

"Wait!"

The high-pitched wail of sirens approached. I hesitated for a moment, but decided to follow the stranger. By the time I leaped from his side of the roof into the nearest tree, the stranger was on the ground, running, and already halfway up the block. I planned my route and followed quickly, staying in the trees. He was fast, but my route was more efficient. I was gaining on him.

Then he jumped a fence and ducked into the parking lot of an apartment building. I miscalculated, leaping onward to the next tree, and it took me a second to turn and get down to the ground. By the time I was over the fence, he was nowhere to be seen. I ran through the lot, looking everywhere. Nothing. He wasn't scaling the building, nor was he in the street beyond. I'd lost him.

Or had I?

* * *

When I got to the tent on the roof of his bungalow, Jack's head was bent over his sink. The face mask was beside him on the table. He stood and wiped his face dry with a hand towel, and I saw he had a fat lip. He caught a glimpse of me in the mirror, standing at the door to the tent, and froze. Slowly, he lowered the hand towel and turned toward me.

"Ethan," he said.

This close, I saw Jack's suit had red piping. It was skintight and seemed to be made of some thick, armor-like material. I wondered if it was bulletproof. Years of watching action movies meant I knew a supersuit when I saw one. I pulled off my balaclava.

"Hello, Jack."

We faced each other. He was silent.

"I like your suit," I said.

He nodded, saying nothing. His dark eyes glittered in the lantern's dim light. I stepped forward into the tent. We stood nearly toe to toe next to his cot. I was gratified to see I came up well past his chin. I put him at six-four to my brother's six-two. We had similar builds, although Jack's suit looked substantial, like it probably blocked punches almost as well as bullets. And Jack had whatever training he had, whereas I had virtually none.

"You're a superhero."

His eyes narrowed. "No. Just an amateur."

"Why were you following me?"

"What were you doing at the Hawk?"

Now it was my turn to be silent.

Jack said, "Why did you fake your own death?"

I started. "How do you know about that?"

"We're getting nowhere."

I sighed. I turned my head and looked at the metal plates above his cot. "What do they say?"

Jack spoke in Mandarin. He said three phrases. I stared at him. Of course I had no idea what he said.

He smiled slightly and said, "The plaques contain the three truths."

He held out an arm and pointed to the largest plate. "Contain your arrogance." He spoke slowly and sonorously, enunciating each word carefully. His arm moved to the second plate. "Restraint." Finally, he pointed to the first plate and in the same captivating voice said, "Mercy." His gaze was particularly intent. I was sure a shadow crossed my future grave when he said it. He watched me then, saying nothing further.

I thought carefully. I wondered how much I could confide in Jack. Perhaps I could tell him enough to interest him, to get him to agree to train me. It was clear to me now that this was my chance, and I had happened on him not by accident, but by design.

"I didn't mean to fake my own death. It just happened."

"That needs explanation."

"They declared me brain-dead. But I walked out of there, and apparently no one saw me. Then I—I mean, my sister—told them she had me cremated."

"Why?"

"What?"

"Why would she do that?"

I stared at Jack's toe-shoed feet. "I'm not sure."

"Come on, Ethan. You two had to have some reason for doing something that out of the ordinary."

"You won't believe me."

"Try me."

"All right, fine." I lifted my gaze and looked into his bottomless brown eyes. "This is my secret identity."

His brows lowered and met above his nose. "Secret identity."

"I want to be a superhero. Like you. Train me, Jack."

His face went blank. He blinked several times and said nothing.

"Please?"

"Is that why you keep coming back here?"

"Yes."

"You want me to train you to be a superhero."

I felt my cheeks grow hot. It sounded really stupid when he put it like that. But it was true. "Basically, yes."

"What do I get out of it?"

"What?"

"I'm not running a charity for superheroes."

"Oh. Well, um, I guess I can pay you."

"I don't need money."

"Well, then what do you want?"

He cocked his head, and his eyes narrowed. "For training you to be a world-class fighter and a feared vigilante?"

"Exactly."

A fleeting smile crossed his face. He rubbed his chin. "All right, Ethan, I'll tell you. For all of that, and more. . . I want your sister."

— 10 —

Engagement

♀

"I'm here. So what did you want with me?" I faced the big man down, eyes blazing, hands on my hips.

He stood placidly, hands folded in front of him. He was in a silken dark suit with a Mandarin collar and butterfly buttons. He bowed low. "Please. Join me." He waved a long arm over our table.

We were outside the Blue Bulldog on the street-side patio, confronting each other under a bright blue sky. It was warm, in the seventies, and sunny. A cool breeze lifted the edge of the table linens, barely hinting at autumn. I glared at Jack for a couple more heartbeats, then sat. I folded my arms across my chest. He unbowed and sat across from me, resting his hands in his lap. The waitress came, and we ordered. Jack got a Tsingtao, and I ordered the drink special.

After the waitress left, Jack sat back and crossed his legs. He seemed content to simply sit and look at me. I frowned.

"Are you blackmailing me?" I said.

"I beg your pardon?"

I couldn't believe how polite he was with me. Everything about him, from words to body language, was deferential. In contrast, I remembered how he'd verged on sarcasm the previous night and how he seemed intent on making Ethan uncomfortable. It was ironic. In my female body, I wasn't remotely a threat to him, but he acted intimidated nonetheless. As a male, everything I did annoyed him.

"Who are you planning to tell about us?" I asked.

He was silent for a moment. Then he said, "You mean, am I threatening to turn you in to the authorities if you don't do as I ask?"

"Are you?"

"No."

"Even if I tell you to fuck off?"

"Even if you tell me to fuck off."

"Then why am I here? I can leave at anytime, right?"

"Of course."

"What do you want from me, anyway?"

He sat forward and folded his hands on the table. "What did your brother tell you?"

The waitress brought our drinks. I immediately sucked up a huge glob of my strawberry daiquiri.

After the waitress left, I said, "Basically, Ethan told me that you'll only train him if I agree to, um. . . sleep with you."

Jack's eyes narrowed. "He has misunderstood me. I don't want sex."

"Wait. You don't?"

"No."

"So you really are gay?"

He was silent.

I slurped up more of my drink. It was cold and sweet. "But then what do you want, if not that?"

"Marriage."

I almost choked on my daiquiri. "Marriage? You're shitting me."

"No."

"You. . . "

I looked around. No one appeared interested in our conversation. I lowered my voice anyway.

"You're telling me that you'll only help Ethan if I marry you?"

He sipped his beer. "Eventually, yes."

"Eventually?"

"I'm willing to provide a trial period of engagement."

"For how long?"

"Three months. Until the new year."

I figured he meant the Chinese new year. I drank my daiquiri right from the glass, not even bothering to use the straw. I was starting to feel lightheaded. The air surrounding us appeared steeped in sepia, as if it were a faded dream. Across the street, blazing trees waved toward the waning sun.

"What happens if I dump you in the new year?"

"Then you dump me."

"Ethan?"

"I will no longer be his mentor in that case."

"That's it?"

"Yes."

"And no sex?"

"No."

"Do I need to move in with you?"

"Only if you wish to."

I closed my eyes. It was crazy. Or. . . was it? When I opened my eyes again, he was staring intently at me, resting his chin in one hand, long fingers running up the side of his chiseled face.

"What are you getting out of this, Jack? Why on earth would you want a fiancee, or a wife, that you're not sleeping with? You don't need a beard in this day and age."

He frowned. "A beard?"

"You know. Cover for being gay."

"That's not what I want."

"Well, then what do you want? Why would you want to marry someone you're not into?"

"I didn't say I'm not into you. I said you don't have to be into me."

"Fine. Let's pretend I'm not. What do you get?"

"A wife."

I shook my daiquiri-fogged head. "We're going in circles. Why do you want a wife so badly?"

"It is not a wife I desire, per se. It is you."

"Me?" My voice squeaked.

"Yes." His gaze dropped to the table between us. He said softly, "Let's just say that for me, this is love at first sight."

My mouth dropped open. "How is that possible? You don't even know me. What if I'm a homicidal superbitch?"

"Then I'll regret it, I suppose."

"This is crazy. You really don't fuck around, do you?"

"I see no reason to fuck around, no."

"How old are you?"

"Forty-two."

"Who are you? What do you do?"

"At the moment, I am a security consultant."

"What's that?"

"I provide guards and logistics for sensitive events or persons."

"Oh, so you're a bodyguard?"

"Something like that."

I swallowed the last of my fruity drink. "Goom told me you were born in China and you were in the army."

He sipped his beer. "Yes. I joined the United States Army at seventeen."

"Because your father was American."

"Yes."

"Then what happened?"

"After basic training, I was fortunate to be admitted to West Point."

"Oh, so you're a smartie."

"Enough of one, anyway. After West Point, I trained with Army Special Forces at Fort Bragg and the Ranger Regiment at Fort Benning. In ninety-five, I deployed overseas to Torii Station."

"Where's that?"

"Japan."

"Oh."

He took a deep swallow of his amber beer. "I left active duty six years ago and started a security company here. Two years ago I returned to active duty as National Guard training and Army recruitment coordinator for the Atlanta metropolitan area."

"Wow."

He shrugged. "I delegate."

"So you get to hang around and do what? What are your hobbies?"

"Martial arts."

"Naturally."

"Cooking."

"Really?"

"Really."

"What are you?"

"Pardon me?"

"I mean, like, are you a general or something?"

"No, not even close. I hold the rank of lieutenant colonel."

"And you're a sensei?"

"I am world ranked in several martial arts."

"Like Bruce Lee?"

"Mr. Lee was much more accomplished."

"Right. So you're modest too."

"Not particularly. I know my limitations. I have not founded my own school or formally set down my own style, limiting further advancement."

"Okay, well, that's an impressive list of stuff."

"Yes."

"I guess a girl would be stupid to refuse you."

"It happens."

I sat back and contemplated Jack. A faint smile was on his lips. Looking at his square jaw and brilliant jet-black eyes, I realized he was quite an attractive man. Especially with the gentle autumnal sun caressing his shaved head. And how I loved that hint of a smile.

"Do I at least get a ring?"

* * *

Half an hour later we were at a jewelry store in a mini-mall off Buford. An obsequious Asian-American woman spoke with Jack in Mandarin. Then he turned to me.

"Pick anything you want."

"Anything?"

His phone rang, buzzing in his shirt pocket. He pulled it out and stepped away from the shopkeeper and me, speaking in a low voice.

I looked at the saleswoman. She had long black hair and was in a navy shift dress with a string of pearls around her neck. She wore a fixed smile that made her clear skin stretch into small wrinkles around the corners of her mouth.

"Okay, what's expensive?"

The woman smiled and silently led me to a case of rings with diamonds as big as pebbles. I wondered if I'd get to keep the ring in the new year if I refused Jack or if I'd have to give it back. I had the saleswoman take one out with a nearly 15k price tag and slid it onto my finger. It was too large.

"We can certainly fit it to you."

I held out my hand. The ring was actually far too showy for my tastes, but I was wondering what Jack would do if I pawned it to pay for the bills piling up now that my brother wasn't working anymore. It might get me through several months, depending on how much I got for it. And I doubted Jack would break my long legs over it.

"Do you have any bigger—"

Jack was at my side. "I regret I must leave you. Ms. Wong will see to it you get what you desire." He handed Ms. Wong a platinum American Express card.

"What's my limit?"

"Limit?"

"I mean, how much can you afford?"

His eyebrows rose slightly. "If you like it I can afford it."

"Even that one?" I pointed to one for almost 33k in the case.

"Beautiful." He nodded at Ms. Wong and left the store.

"Did he just give me carte blanche?"

Ms. Wong smiled.

* * *

An electronic doorbell sounded, and two men entered the store. Something about the men made the hairs on the back of my neck tingle. Both of them were stocky and muscular. One had light red hair in a brush cut and was wearing a brown suit and yellow tie. The other had light brown hair and was in a navy suit with a powder blue shirt open at the neck and no tie. The men split up to browse. One neared me, and I could smell his aftershave, a subtle spicy musk that reminded me of my father.

Ms. Wong left me with a couple of rings and went to help No Tie look at tie pins. Yellow Tie came even closer to me so he was standing within my personal space. I looked up at him. Wide-set brown eyes looked back and he smiled.

"Hello. I'd like to talk to you."

"Um."

The man was at my elbow now and directed me toward the door. He was so smooth, I hardly realized what was happening until we were at the entrance and he was holding the door and pushing me outside. I balked.

"Wait. My friend will be right back."

"Oh, I'm sure he will. This will just take a moment, madam."

Then he gripped my arm. His fingers closed around my bicep as if they were a steel clamp. I dug in my heels but found myself being led away anyway. He dragged me toward a navy sedan parked in a handicapped space. It was only then that I realized what was happening. I struggled.

"Stop! Let me go."

I looked around. It was broad daylight and there were other people there, but none was looking in my direction. The closest person was on the sidewalk of the minimall, a thin man walking next to a Hallmark store. Would he hear me if I screamed at him? My moment of indecision was all it took for Yellow Tie to push me into the backseat of the car. I stumbled and fell into the footwell; impossibly strong arms lifted me up and righted me on the seat, then closed around my wrists so I couldn't reach for the door on the other side. No Tie slid into the driver's seat, and I realized the car had been left running. Whoever these men were, they were outrageously bold. Cold sweat trickled down the sides of my face. In a flash, they pulled forward, out of the parking space, out of the lot, and into the road.

I said nothing. I could barely breathe. My chest seemed weighed down, and I could only get short gasps of air into my lungs. Everything I'd ever heard about women's self-defense had warned me about getting into the car, and here I was in the car. It had happened so fast I didn't have time for anything—no kicking in the nuts, no stopping passersby, nothing. I was now completely at the mercy of two strangers. Bile rose in my throat, and I swallowed it down. I cleared my mind of images of what they might do to me. Now I had to keep my head. I had to force myself to be calm and look for any opening.

We drove for only a few minutes, during which no one spoke. My light-headed panic was replaced by a feeling of grim inevitability. Oddly, I started to feel normal, as if I were riding with a couple of friends, one of whom happened to have me in a constricting embrace.

We came to a motel on the edge of Decatur. We rounded the long building and drove to a secluded corner that abutted a chain-link fence.

"Here we go," No Tie said, being oddly ordinary.

I was flooded with panic. My armpits were wet, my thin sweater had been soaked through. No Tie parked in front of the last room, cut the engine, and came around to open the back door. He took over from Yellow Tie and hauled me from the car. I was nearly passed out from panic and stumbled. I opened my mouth when I tripped and got out the edge of a scream before Yellow Tie clamped a hand over my mouth. No Tie was suddenly on my other side, and together the men half-carried me into room 169. It was a small room with a double bed, a table beside the window, and a console along the wall. The men tossed me onto the bed.

"Now, will you be good, or do we have to tie you up?" No Tie said.

My heart was pounding so hard I thought it might break through my ribcage and take flight. I couldn't find my voice. I struggled to get my balance on the bed and backed up until I was sitting against the headboard. I drew my legs up to my chest and circled them with my arms as if to protect myself. I knew it was useless. The men would now do whatever they wanted to me, and I wouldn't be able to stop them. The only question was whether I'd survive. I stared at them. No Tie had his hands on his hips, and I could see the strap of a holster under the left side of his jacket. I had an intense moment of hope where I thought they might be cops. But why would cops kidnap me and stick me on a bed? They wouldn't. And if they did, it would mean they were criminals anyway.

Yellow Tie said something foreign to No Tie, and both men laughed. It sounded Slavic. I recalled the Blond Smoker from the Blue Bulldog. Was it a coincidence I was suddenly surrounded by angry Russians? Neither of these men was the one I'd seen at the bar.

I took a deep breath and closed my eyes. They didn't seem to be coming closer to me at the moment, and I wondered if I'd have a chance to try to switch to my brother. My nerves were fraught, my breath shallow, and I wondered how on earth I could possibly get myself to sleep. But I had to.

The bed rocked. My eyes flew open. No Tie was sitting on the far edge with his back to me. In his hand was the remote control for the TV, and he switched it on and started channel surfing. Yellow Tie sat down at the table under the window and picked up a newspaper. He eyed me, and I dropped my gaze from him. He backed his chair up so it was propped against the exit, unfolded the paper, and started to read. I realized that my trial hadn't even begun yet. They were obviously waiting for someone else, someone who would be the one to come and rip me apart. How long did I have? Minutes? Hours? It didn't matter. I had to get myself to calm down, to sleep. I had to switch to my brother and come save myself. I closed my eyes. If only I could sleep, everything would be all right.

— 11 —

Liberation

♂

I parked the Battle Buick at a Burger King two blocks from the motel. I walked through the woods between the shops and the back of the motel and scaled the chain-link fence between me and room 169 at the corner of the lot. I flattened myself against the brick wall on the non-window side and hesitated. There were two Russians, and they no doubt both had guns. I had no way of contacting Jack for backup. How would I even get the men to open the door and let me in? I realized that if they were waiting for someone, a knock might be all it took. Before I could lose my nerve, I knocked on the pale door. Within three seconds, Yellow Tie opened it.

I slammed into the door, catching him completely by surprise. The door whacked into his face, and I reached around and grabbed his head while he was dazed. I slammed him into the door a couple more times until he slid from me into a heap on the floor. But where was No Tie? I reached into Yellow Tie's jacket and pulled out his gun. I went to the sleeping female form on the bed and loaded her onto my broad shoulders. Just then, No Tie exploded from the bathroom.

"Nyet!" he yelled. He had his gun out but didn't shoot. I dropped my body behind the bed and leveled No Tie's partner's gun at him.

"Stop! Put your gun down," I yelled.

No Tie didn't hesitate this time and fired at me, then retreated into the bathroom. I ducked behind the bed, and only as I returned fire did I realize the shot had hit me. Blood poured from the side of my belly. The wound burned, and I felt light-headed staring at it.

No Tie peeked around the bathroom wall, and I shot in that direction, missing him but hitting the mirror above the sink in the alcove. A thick crack opened, splitting the mirror into jagged shards. I felt sick. My side ached, and red liquid oozed from it. I wondered how long I had before I passed out from blood loss. I became aware of sirens in the distance, nearing with my every breath.

"Shit," I whispered.

No Tie jumped out from the bathroom and shot continuously. I shot back. He made it around the bed and almost to my side before I managed to hit him. He jerked backward as a bullet cut through his chest. I shot again and hit him right between the eyes, a lucky shot. His head snapped back, and he dropped to the floor, dead. I was bleeding all over myself and my female body that lay underneath me. I put my hand to my side, and it came away drenched with blood. The sight made me dizzy. The sirens neared. Looking at the unconscious body under me, I felt a psychic magnetism rise as a fog that muddled my senses. It didn't take much to pull me out of my brother's body, since I was already on my way out.

— 12 —

Hospital

♀

Inside the comic shop, Goom was behind the counter, sitting on a high stool and engrossed in a comic book. He didn't seem to have heard the bells. I made sure the door was closed behind me and shoved the deadbolt into place. He did hear the *thunk* of the bolt, and his head snapped up.

"Hey!"

When he recognized me, he rolled his eyes. "Oh, it's just you. What's up, sugarlips? Your bro's not here."

"Okay, first of all, you need to not call me sugarlips. Secondly, I need your help."

It was only then he seemed to notice my deathly paleness and trembling limbs. That and the blood splashed all over my face and clothes might have been a clue.

"Shit."

He jumped off the stool and fumbled with his smartphone. "Lahngxian, we got a situation here." There was no answer, and he raised his voice. "Lahngxian!"

I felt tears welling in my eyes. I bit my lip and willed myself not to cry. It would be just like a woman to cry.

We heard Jack come through the workshop door before Goom could yell again. The big man came directly to the counter. His brow furrowed at the sight of me, but otherwise, his composure never wavered.

"Where were you? I got kidnapped."

Jack frowned. "I was called away. I'm so sorry. Who was it?"

In spite of myself, I felt tears run down my cheeks. "I have no idea. It was horrible."

Jack reached for me. "I can't tell you how sorry I am, honey. Let's get you out of those clothes."

I jumped backward. "Don't you touch me, you bastard."

He dropped his arms and folded his hands in front of him. "You're covered in blood. We need to clean you up."

I was sure I blushed from head to toe. "Sorry," I mumbled. "That, um... that just slipped out."

Goom piped up. "You know, you're awfully ornery for someone who's come begging for our help."

* * *

An hour later, I stood staring at Jack's firepit. A hearty fire burned, and smoke blew away from me in great puffs, its acrid scent filling my nostrils even as the wind took it from me. We burned my clothes, shoes, and anything else I touched that Jack and Goom felt they couldn't bleach sufficiently. The three of us stood around the fire, watching it leap and dance.

"I hope it's enough," Goom said. "Nowadays CSI can find a fucking molecule of blood on a thread the size of a dust mite."

I felt numb. I wondered if the entire ordeal had really happened. It felt far away, as if it had happened to someone else.

"How does the car look?" Jack asked Goom.

The little man shrugged. "I did the best I could. We should dump it."

"No!"

They both stared at me. I cleared my throat. "I love my car. I can't afford a new one."

Goom sneered. "It's not like you parked in a loading zone or jaywalked, you know. You guys fucking killed someone. You need to—"

He stopped short. My eyes watered, and my shoulders shook. Goom's complexion dipped a couple of shades toward gray.

"Oh, for fuck's sake, don't cry again. I can't stand that shit."

I gritted my teeth and wiped my eyes. "I'm not crying. It's the smoke from the fire."

"Uh-huh. Sure it is."

Jack shifted from foot to foot. "Judith, can you tell us more about what happened?"

I hadn't been able to bring myself to speak much. I felt stunned, as if I'd been hit over the head with a blunt object.

"Well, the two of them grabbed me from the jewelry store."

Jack's lips pressed into a thin line.

"My brother found me at a motel."

Goom said, "A motel? There's a motel? Is that where you shot the guy?"

I turned to the midget. Anger coursed through my veins. "I didn't shoot anyone. Ethan did. But they shot him first."

Goom's dark eyes widened. "The redneck got shot? Where is he?"

My head dropped, and I stared at the hot pit near my feet. "I left him at the motel. But I'm sure the cops are all over it by now."

Goom shook his head. "We're boned. You're boned, sugarbeet."

Jack said, "Gumbah Sarbloh, please go listen to the scanners."

"Scanners?" I asked.

Goom shrugged and left us, headed for the basement.

"We can listen to the police frequencies," Jack said. "We'll see what they know about Ethan and whatever motel you mean."

The fire seemed to burn ever hotter. I had to take a step backward it was so hot. The flames crackled and snapped, and I wished briefly that I could step inside so the fire would consume my guilt and clean my spirit. And Ethan? I had abandoned his body yet again. Was it even still alive? I closed my eyes, and I could see him, lying in his own blood on the dark motel carpet. The paramedics must have had him by now. But would they be able to save him? And then what? Prison for life for shooting the kidnapper? I opened my eyes and watched the big man next to me.

"Jack," I said. "Help us. Somehow."

He turned to me, a look of pure sympathy on his ashen face. I knew he was seeing nothing but despair in my watery blue eyes. He frowned. When he spoke, it was with a confidence I knew he couldn't possibly feel.

"I will."

* * *

At sunset, Goom pulled into a sparsely populated parking lot next to University Hospital. His car was a dark brown, old-school Mustang with the tricked-out engine sticking out of the hood and extra chrome pipes hanging off the back. I had taken one look at his rearview mirror and said, "I like the purple fuzzy dice you got hanging there. It says, 'I may be gay, but I like my muscle cars.' Classy."

Goom's response had been typical. "Bite me, chick-whack."

I also wondered how a midget could even drive. How would he reach the pedals? It turned out he used leg extensions. It was unnerving, like being driven around by an oversized toddler wearing stilts.

The three of us sat, and contemplated the hospital. It was a five-story structure of white-washed stone, steel, and glass. It looked calmly innocuous in the dregs of evening light, with long shadows dappling its pristine facade and glowing lights streaming from its windows. Goom and Jack were in the front seat, I was in the back.

"So," I asked, "what's the plan?"

Jack opened the passenger's side door. "I'll go see what Ethan's status is." He nodded at Goom. "You stay with Judith."

"Great." Goom eyed me in the rearview mirror. "You ain't gonna bust out crying again, are you, cupcake?"

"I might. Especially if you keep calling me stupid names."

He snorted. His fingers drummed the steering wheel. I sat back and watched the twilight give way to darkness.

Goom craned his neck around. "Shit!" He looked positively frantic.

"What?" I slid forward. "What?!"

"It's that white tra—uh, I mean, that friend of yours."

I twisted so I could see out the back window. Blaze was making her way through the parking lot toward us. "Yeah, I called her."

"You called her?" Goom facepalmed. "Does she know your brother's the walking dead?"

"Yeah."

Blaze opened the passenger door, pushed the seat forward, and climbed in next to me. "Hey, guys. I'm glad I found y'all. I parked a block away so no one would see the truck."

Goom faced forward and busied himself with inspecting his fingernails.

Blaze gave me a hug. "You okay, Jude? You look awful. I saw the monarch go in. Is he looking for Ethan?"

Goom's head snapped up. "Monarch? What the hell do you—"

I cleared my throat loudly. "Blaze knows about our underground vampire cell, dork-boy. I told her all about how you and the king vampire, Jack, resurrected Ethan and initiated him into the cell."

Goom stared at us, open mouthed, for several seconds. "Our... cell? I don't even... for fuck's sake." He covered his face with his hands and muttered something to himself. It seemed to regard crazy people making up vampire stories. To his credit, he recovered quickly. "Remind me what our super-secret, uh, cell does again, sugarface?"

I glared at him. "We fly around at night and eat bad guys."

Blaze grinned toothily.

"We fly around and—" Goom smacked himself in the head. More muttering to himself, under his breath so we couldn't hear. Then his phone beeped. He answered it. After a few seconds, he signed off, wordlessly. He turned to us.

"That was Jack. They won't talk to anyone but family."

* * *

It turned out Ethan was in post-op. The four of us settled into the waiting room. It was highly modernized and tastefully appointed in thundercloud gray, shining white, and steel. I felt closer to the future simply sitting there. In fact, it felt like tomorrow. But then I realized from the clock on the wall that it was tomorrow. I'd fallen asleep, exhausted and anxious, and it was nearly one o'clock in the morning.

Wait. I had fallen asleep. But I hadn't switched to my brother. I startled.

Jack was in a chair next to me and straightened up. He folded his hands in front of him and eyed me benignly. I looked around. Goom was stretched out in an impossibly shaped easy chair. The little guy fit pretty well and could almost lie down. His legs were propped up on one arm, and the rest of him let loose a baritone snore every few seconds. We were the only three in the waiting room.

I asked Jack, "Where's Blaze?"

He shrugged.

"Great. She's probably setting something on fire."

Goom opened one eye, rolled it at me, turned over in his chair, and resumed snoring.

I didn't have time to worry further because at that moment a doctor walked in. He was a stout, bearded man with sandy brown hair and thick glasses.

"Susan?"

I had given a fake name. It took me a second to recognize that the doctor meant me. "Yes-s?"

He eyed me carefully. I had claimed to have no ID, but it must have been clear nonetheless from my face that I was related to the gunshot victim. "Your brother will be fine. He'll make a full recovery."

"Oh, thank God." Relief flooded me. "Can I see him?"

The doctor frowned and adjusted his glasses higher on his nose. "I don't think he should have any visitors tonight. He's recovering and still under sedation."

Sedation. Perhaps that was why the switch hadn't happened.

"Where is he?"

"He's in 301c. You should be able to see him in the morning. If you wait here a moment, the nurse at admitting would like to speak with you." He turned and left.

Goom had roused himself and stood next to Jack. I faced them. "I'd really like to *not* be here to speak with the admitting nurse."

They exchanged glances.

* * *

Intensive care was a long hallway, indistinguishable from any other except for signs declaring it intensive care. The swing doors that led to patient rooms were guarded by a nurse's station occupied by a bleary-eyed aging Latina. Conveniently, she left her post as we approached. I took the opportunity to sneak through the double doors into the ward. I almost ran into a uniformed police officer standing outside the room nearest the entrance. His eyes narrowed, and his hand automatically hovered over the gun strapped to his waist.

"Oops. Excuse me, officer." I gave him my brightest, most helpless and ditsy smile. "Wrong way, sorry." I fled back through the doors, almost knocking over Goom and Jack. "Not that way," I said and herded them to the nearest alcove.

Goom shook his arm from my grip. "What? What did you see?"

"There's a cop guarding the door." My mind raced, but nothing helpful zoomed out of it.

"A cop?" Goom snorted. "Fuck."

Blaze came up behind us. "Hey guys."

I jumped. "Jee-eezus, Blaze! Where were you?"

"I was starving and got some food. They've got some really fantastic eggrolls here. Want some?" She held up a paper bag.

Jack shook his head. Goom said, "No way."

I was about to say no when the delectable scent of fried dough wafted up to me from the bag. I couldn't remember when I'd last eaten. "Um, sure. I'll take those." I unrolled the bag and stuffed one into my mouth. It was indeed delicious.

"So, what're y'all up to?" Blaze looked at me hopefully. "You hear anything about Ethan?"

My mouth was full of eggroll, so I couldn't immediately answer. Goom picked up the slack. "The idiot will be okay. But there's a cop on his door we need to get rid of."

Blaze nodded. "Okay, I'm on it. When the cop leaves, go get Ethan."

That scared me. "Mgmph," I began, then swallowed the last of the eggroll. "I mean, hold on, Blaze. What are you thinking? No fires."

"Well, that kinda ties my hands."

"No fires."

Goom sneered at Blaze. "Yeah, no fires, bitch."

Blaze flushed darkly, obviously offended by Goom's careless profanity. I growled at him. "Shut your mouth, you pipsqueak. I don't hear you coming up with anything."

"You neither, fatty."

"Fatty? Fatty?!" I was five-ten in heels and weighed one-fifty on a bad day. Only in Hollywood would I be considered a fatty. "I'm not fat. I'm curvy. Guys love that shit."

"Well then, why don't you go get that cop to notice your curviness and get him the fuck away from the door, fat ass?"

"Like hell. He'd probably arrest me."

"So what? At least he'd be distracted."

"That's the stupidest plan I've ever heard. Think of something better, or I'll whack you with my purse."

"Ooh, I'm scared." Goom stuck his tongue out at me.

I gave him a whack and almost knocked him off his feet.

"Ow! What the hell you got in there? Bricks?"

"Don't make me whack you again." I raised the purse menacingly.

"Wait." He held up his hands. "Where'd Jack and Blaze go?"

I looked around. They were nowhere to be seen. At that precise moment, the fire alarm went off, and the sprinkler system kicked in, drizzling cold liquid on us from above.

The Latina nurse was back. She hurried over to us. "We'll need to get everyone to the east wing. Can you help direct traffic?" The area was rapidly filling with nurses, doctors, and orderlies.

"Um, s-sure," I said. I grabbed Goom by the scruff of his T-shirt. "C'mon. Let's go direct some traffic."

We held the double doors of Ethan's ward open for a tall male nurse pushing a gurney. As we stepped through the doorway in his wake, I was preoccupied with eyeballing the gurney's occupant and not watching where I was going. I ran smack into a doctor coming out of Ethan's room.

"Oop—"

I gasped. It was the Blond Smoker from the alley behind the Blue Bulldog. I didn't know why I recognized him so quickly. Perhaps it was his ferocious wolf-like face or the cold sienna eyes. Or maybe I was particularly sensitive to Russians after my kidnapping ordeal. The man wore a long white coat and had a stethoscope hanging from his neck. I froze, locked in an open-mouthed stare.

The man's eyes narrowed, but he hesitated only briefly. "Excuse me," he said smoothly, and disappeared through a door across the hall.

Goom smacked me. "Come on, hurry up. Why are you just standing there? What's wrong with you?"

I was shaking. Water dripped from my chin. "I know that man."

"What? Who? The doctor? What about him?"

I shook my head. "Never mind. Let's just get Ethan."

Goom slammed the wet lever down on Ethan's door. We burst through the doorway and skidded to a stop. The cop I had seen outside was lying face down on the floor at our feet. He was awfully still for someone I hoped was only napping. In the room's only bed lay a horrific corpse, its arms and legs contorted wildly. Its pale face was contorted into a frozen rictus. Yellowed, blood-encrusted teeth were clenched amid the gaping mouth. I was speechless. Goom was less so.

"For motherfucking fuck's sake. Holy fuck."

I could hardly believe it, but I recognized the body on the bed. It was Major Fairholme, Msti's husband.

I said, "I can't believe it. It's—" A wave of nausea shut me up. I willed myself not to retch.

"It's who? You know that hideous corpse? How is that possible?"

"That's police Major Fairholme. He's my friend's husband. Or was. He's supposed to be here for routine tests."

Goom's face contorted into a display somewhere between disbelief and disgust. "Doesn't look fucking routine to me. Someone poisoned the bastard."

I immediately thought of the Blond Smoker. "It must have been—"

The door rattled as someone worked the lever from the hallway. Both of us turned to the door. It seemed to be stuck because whoever was opening it hesitated, then the door bucked against its jamb. Goom didn't accept our predicament with the calmest of comportment. He hurtled around in a circle, ripping at his dreads.

"We can't be seen! There's two dead cops in here. Two. I mean, it's life for one, but two? We'll be fried like fucking hush puppies."

"Shut up." I considered slapping him, but the door was opening. I ran over to intercept the intruder. "We got this one. . . "

I looked carefully at the big orderly with the shaved head coming through the door. Although he was wearing a mask covering half his face, I recognized him at once.

"Jack!" I almost hugged him.

He nodded. "Judith." He opened the door farther to reveal a gurney. "We've got to get him out now."

I shook my head and stepped aside. He came into the room and saw the two corpses, including the only patient in evidence—who was clearly not Ethan.

"Wrong room."

"Wrong room?" Goom's eyes bugged out, and he waved his arms. "There's two fucking murdered cops in here, and that's all you can say?"

I studied the ceiling. "On a positive note, the sprinklers cut out."

Goom's face crumpled, and his lower lip quivered.

I scoffed. "Jeez, you dork, crying's not going to help. Let's get the hell out of here."

We fled the room, running smack into the Latina nurse in the hallway. She was accompanied by one of the rent-a-cops working hospital security. "Where's the Major? He's not checked off in the east wing yet."

Everyone looked at me, as if I had any freaking clue what was going on. "Um, we just sent him down the hall with that other guy."

"Well then, make sure the other rooms are emptied and get to the east wing and wait there for further instructions." This was directed at Jack the "orderly," who nodded.

The nurse and security guard turned around and left.

Goom said quietly. "You shouldn't have lied. Now when they find him they'll wonder why you lied, dummy."

I blushed. "Shut up, geek-boy. At least I'm not blubbering like a baby."

He made an odd gurgling sound, as if he was being strangled.

I huffed. "Oh, jeez, what now?"

"Didn't that doctor say Ethan was in 301c?"

"What?"

"You stupid bitch!" Goom whacked himself in the face.

"You did not just call me that."

"That's 301*e*, you twit." He jerked his arm wildly at the room with the dead cops. I contemplated the plates above the doors more carefully. Goom was correct. The murdered policemen were in 301e. Room 301c was right next door.

"Oops."

"Oops? Oops?! We're going to fucking burn for those cop corpses, and all you can say is oops? So help me, motherf—"

Jack was already pushing through the door to 301c. "Nevermind."

My soaked brother was peacefully resting on a wet bed in 301c. We loaded him onto the gurney and then returned to the hall.

"That was easy," I said.

Goom looked like he was about to hit me. "Easy? You stupid—"

Jack interjected. "Gumbah Sarbloh. Blaze will have the Mustang ready near the south emergency entrance. Please, go find her."

Goom's eyes bugged out. "What? You gave that crazy ho my car keys? Are you totally nuts?"

Jack's eyes narrowed to thin slits.

Goom gulped. "I mean... great idea, Sh'fu." He stalked off, through the same door to the stairs that the Blond Smoker had gone through.

"What's sh'fu?" I asked.

"I beg your pardon?"

"Why does he call you sh'fu?"

"It means sensei in Mandarin."

"Oh. Cool."

Jack sighed. "Let's head for the elevators."

We started down the hall. A growing whistling disturbed the air. Before I could ask what it was, Jack pushed the gurney away from us and jumped on me to cover me with his body.

He yelled, "Incoming!"

I didn't know if the explosion was truly muffled or if my ears were simply overwhelmed. Behind us, the wall exploded outward into the hallway with a violent *whuff!* Both 301c and 301e seemed to crumple until they blocked the entire area behind us, including the stairwell Goom had recently entered.

I struggled to look out from underneath Jack. "Ethan!"

The gurney had rolled away from the blast. My brother's body was crooked and almost falling off. Jack pulled me to my feet and shoved me toward the exit signs at the far end of the hall, away from the blast zone. In the distance, I heard screaming, and the fire alarms and sprinklers had started up again.

"Go!" Jack yelled.

"No! I can't leave Ethan!"

"I'll bring him. You run ahead, now!"

A second ominous whistling joined the din around us. There was a highly disturbing flash of dismay on Jack's face before he threw us to the floor again.

Phoomm!

My ears popped. Heat blasted over us. I screamed. Jack jumped up, yanked me to my feet, and hustled me down the hall. "Go! South exit! Go now, I'll be right behind you." He returned to the gurney and loaded Ethan onto his back. "Go!"

My muscles seemed blubbery and sluggish. Tears and sweat comingled on my blood-drained face. I hesitated for another second, then turned and ran for my life with Jack laboring behind me.

* * *

I got lost. The sprinklers flooded the air with a fine, cold mist. I was in a daze, sucked along by a panicked crowd, unable to find any "south exit," and separated from Jack. At a large junction, the crowd merged with several more groups, and our progress became less orderly and polite. I was elbowed and pushed, lost my footing on the slick flooring, and fell. People didn't stop. I couldn't seem to get my balance. Someone stepped on my hand, then my leg. I curled up into fetal position, fearing I'd be trampled to death.

Strong hands gripped me and hauled me to my feet. Someone immovable stood over me so the throngs had to go around. I was awash in gratitude, until my vision cleared and I recognized him. The Blond Smoker. He was still in his doctor's disguise and soaking wet. His eyes were as cold as the drizzling rain from the ceiling. My knees buckled. He gripped me tightly, dragging me to the nearest door. I was flooded with an extreme sense of deja vu.

"No!" I struggled. "Help!"

In all the chaos, no one paid attention to the doctor and his reluctant companion. He shoved me through a door into a stairwell and pulled me down a flight of stairs. At the bottom, we stumbled out into a dim basement hallway. The alarms and intercoms were muted here, overshadowed by thumping utilities.

"Let me go!" I pulled away with all my might. I had learned from last time, and this time I wasn't getting in the damn car or going wherever he wanted to take me.

He backhanded me. "Bitch!"

I spun around at his strike and almost toppled over. Adrenaline and a rush of anger propelled me—I whirled back to him and thrust a pointy-toed shoe into his kneecap. He doubled over, and I clocked him with my purse.

He cursed in his guttural foreign language and sagged against the wall. I sprinted away from him down the hall. A miracle appeared in the form of two cops stepping out of a T-junction. I put on a burst of speed.

"Help! He's chasing me!"

In front of me, the two cops drew their weapons. Behind me, the blond man shouted at someone in an incomprehensible language.

Thwup! Thwup!

I dropped to the floor and threw my arms over my head. My momentum slid me forward over the slick linoleum until I was almost at the cops' feet. They were going through a jerky, slow-motion fall. I couldn't comprehend the red liquid squirting from them. Hadn't they fired those shots? Once they crumpled to the floor, I saw a figure in a jet-black suit standing behind them about three yards away. It was a woman wearing a supersuit much like Jack's only with gold piping instead of red. She had a full face mask and a handgun with a silencer in her hand. I gasped. The blond man was on me by then, dragging me to my feet.

I went nuts. I bit one of the Russian's hands and flailed around with my fists until I felt a soft area yield to my punches. His hold on me faltered. Through my struggle, the woman in the black suit simply stood there, waiting. I broke away from the Blond Smoker and took off down the hall with him close on my heels.

Mere inches from his outstretched hands, I stopped short and swung myself around on a door handle. The Russian couldn't stop and slid right by on the wet floor. I wrenched the door open, threw myself inside whatever room it was, and bolted the door hastily behind me. I backed away from the enraged banging and swearing on the other side.

I had gotten free for the moment. Now what? Who was the woman in the superhero suit? For that matter, who was the blond man, and why did he seem to want me so badly?

Apparently, I'd chosen a laundry room. Industrial-sized washers and dryers dominated, interspersed with counters and shelves. Rolling linen baskets, both full and empty, stood around the room. Unfortunately the only exit was the one the Blond Smoker was thumping at. There was a row of narrow clerestory windows along the outside wall, but all were locked and reinforced with chicken wire. I cowered behind one of the rows of machines, noting that the banging had stopped for the moment. That didn't strike me as a good omen. I fumbled through my purse for something, anything, that might help. My grasping hand happened on an object of hope—my cell phone.

No reception. Maybe over by the windows?

* * *

The blond Russian was searching the room. I caught a glimpse of him as I peeked out from my hiding place. He brandished a gun and crooned at me, his sing-songy lilt belying his murderous intent. "Come out, come out, wherever you are. . . "

I was ensconced on top of a row of washing machines and hardly dared to breathe. Stacked towels squeezed me from both sides, obscuring me completely and, unfortunately, also obscuring most of my view. Through a narrow gap, I could make out shifting reflections in the large convex mirror near the entrance.

"Are you in. . . here?"

The Russian reached into a rolling bin and tossed the laundry from it. When he didn't find me, he shot into the bin. Blasts echoed off the concrete floor and naked ceiling. I winced. I was glad I hadn't hidden there.

"You know," he said slowly, "the longer it takes me to find you, the more I'll make you pay."

Suddenly, a bizarre and melodious interruption sounded in the form of a lonely whistled song. The door opened, and someone came into the room. From the sound, they were wheeling a rolling cart with squeaky wheels. I couldn't distinguish the new arrival from the other shapeless blobs at the mirror's edge.

"La-la-la," a disturbingly familiar voice sang. "Doin' laundry, la-la-la."

It was Blaze. She lapsed into whistling again, her oblivious tune floating over me and settling on the Russian, who had pressed himself to the machines on the other side of the row. Panic surged within me, tinged with insane hope. Blaze stopped near the end of the aisle of washers, opened one up, and started casually loading sheets into it, singing and whistling her tune all the while.

I couldn't see him, but I assumed the blond Russian had stepped out near the exit. He said, "It's not a lucky day for you, nurse."

At the same time as I pushed a stack of towels onto the man's head, I heard Goom's yell.

"Eat lead, fuckball!"

Blaze hit the floor while Goom jumped out of the laundry cart, firing away. I screamed and twisted wildly, covering my ears with my arms. Shots exploded throughout the room. The Russian dove through the doorway with Goom's shots echoing after him. Goom missed entirely, but fortunately the Russian did as well.

It fell quiet. Blaze and Goom looked up at me. Goom held up his smartphone.

"Hey, sugarcheeks. I got your message. You wanna come the fuck down anytime soon so we can get the hell out of here?"

* * *

Ten minutes later, we pulled up to a nondescript row of two-story brick buildings off of Buford. The ground floor held several businesses; the second story looked like apartments. The place was wedged between a wooded field and a large, hyper-modern mini-mall with various stand-alone superstores. The dingy aging brick storefronts before us looked oddly antique in the shadow of the neon-lit shopping mall behind us. We stopped at the endmost shop, next to some dumpsters and a wild tangle of bushes. A sign in the front window promised tai chi and qi gong as well as a host of traditional Chinese remedies.

I frowned. "Where are we?"

"It's a guan," Goom said.

"A what?"

"You know. A dojo."

"Oh. Right."

Blaze nodded. "We gonna hire some ninjas to help us?"

Goom rolled his eyes. "Of course we are. What else would we be doing, you fuckstick."

I cuffed him.

We slid from the truck and sprinted through the rain to a narrow entryway. We crowded into a tiny foyer, then ascended a dimly lit stairwell to a small landing. Goom knocked softly on the door. Presently, it opened. A short, wizened Asian with long gray-streaked hair and a Fu Manchu mustache and beard stood inside. He was barefoot, wearing blue jeans and a white T-shirt with a colorful mixed martial arts logo.

I gasped. "Wax Man!" Everyone looked at me. I shrugged. "I mean, Guan Ho. You look really different without the suit and hat."

Guan Ho chuckled. "Wax Man, I like that." He stared intently at me. "Lahngxian was right. You are the spitting image of your brother. That's freaky, man." There was no trace of his roots in his voice.

"Your accent's gone."

"I was born in San Francisco. Lived in America all my life." He stepped aside and waved them in. "Come, come. Welcome."

The apartment was tidy, compact, and generously decorated with Asian artifacts and tapestries. We entered into a large open room that served as dining room, kitchen, and living room. As my eyes adjusted to the dim lighting, I realized the plush, heavily patterned couch held a familiar man.

"Jack! Where's Ethan?"

He lounged with one arm across the back of the sofa. "He's fine. He's in the bedroom."

Wax Man led me down a short hall, through a colorful beaded curtain into a bedroom where Ethan rested on a gigantic bed between golden sheets. I hustled over and felt for a pulse. A strong beat reassured me.

"Thank God."

Wax Man was beside me. "You mean, thank Jack. He nearly got himself barbecued getting your brother out of the hospital." He lifted the sheet covering Ethan's abdomen. A medicinal stench wafted up from a gooey poultice underneath.

I grimaced. "Ew. That smells horrible."

Wax Man shook a finger at me. "Doan mawk aaancien' Chine med'cin!" He tucked his lower lip under his teeth, giving the impression of an unfortunate overbite. At once I saw the inscrutable wax statue from Chin's reemerge. "Youah brothah be gud as new tuhmorrah!"

I laughed heartily.

— 13 —

Protection

♂

In the limbo between asleep and awake, I walked through a thick forest. Warm sunlight and chilly darkness alternately crossed my oddly unfamiliar face. I walked and walked, and the wood was endless until at last there was a clearing, a brilliantly sunny meadow of golden green grass. My eyes opened. Stark afternoon sunlight filtered through thin silk curtains, and gilded sheets covered me. The world came into focus slowly, and I realized I was at Guan Ho's. And, holy crap, did I ever have to pee.

I struggled to sit up and swung my legs off the bed. I slid out from between the sheets and nearly fell on my face. I staggered from the nightstand to the dresser, determined to make it across the hall to the toilet. When I got there, I peed sitting down since my legs were shaking so badly.

I must have passed out for a moment because I missed Guan Ho's approach entirely. I opened my eyes, and he was standing over me, holding me up against the toilet tank and inspecting my wound.

"You shouldn't be up."

"I really, really had to pee."

He laughed. "Okay, back to bed, and I'll get you cleaned up."

Jack arrived as Guan Ho was re-dressing my wound, pulling tape and gauze from a big leather medic's bag that looked severely battered by age.

"Wax Man, are you a doctor?"

He smiled. "Navy. Long time ago."

Jack stood by the bedroom door silently.

I asked him, "Jack, what's on your mind?"

He came closer and studied my face. "What do you remember?"

"Just some big-ass Russian shooting me in the gut. That's about it."

"And before that?"

"What do you mean?"

Jack folded his hands behind his back. "How did you know?"

"What?"

"I presume the Russians didn't let your sister make a phone call. How did you know where to find her?"

Guan Ho glanced at Jack, then finished taping the bandage to my side. He interrupted, "Good as new."

I smiled at Guan Ho. I didn't know what to say to Jack. How could I possibly explain?

Jack stood motionless, saying nothing.

I decided to change the subject. "The Blond Smoker. Who is he?"

Jack cocked his head. "I'm not sure."

"What about the woman in the black and gold suit?"

Jack's brow furrowed. He said nothing.

"And Major Fairholme? I assume he's very dead due to the bomb."

"Indeed." A look of confusion crossed Jack's face.

"What? What's wrong?" I asked.

"How do you know about them?"

"What?"

"The woman in black and gold. And the death of Major Fairholme. Has your sister been here this morning talking to you?"

I stared at Guan Ho, who was studying the floor. Of course I couldn't lie and say I'd been here. Unless I wanted to claim my female self had climbed in the window to avoid Guan Ho. I swallowed, remaining silent.

Jack shifted from foot to foot. "You're telepaths, aren't you?"

My eyes widened. It was as good an explanation as any. "What if I say yes? Will you believe me?"

Jack said nothing. Guan Ho said something in Mandarin, and Jack replied. They talked briefly and quietly in their native tongue. I understood none of it. I laid back against the pillow and closed my eyes.

"There is a myth," Jack said at last, then stopped.

I opened my eyes and stared at him. "What myth?"

"A myth of powers like yours. I never thought I'd see it in real life."

"But you believe."

Jack nodded. It was a slight movement of his head, down and back.

I sighed. "Now that you know, what are you going to do?"

"I'll do what I would do anyway. Protect you and your sister."

"From who?"

"Ethan, they kidnapped Judith once and tried again at the hospital. If the Blond Smoker is who I think he is, he is very dangerous. Help me convince your sister to stay with me until he's gone."

The harrowing kidnapping was fresher in my female memory than my male one, and I knew that in my own body I would be entirely freaked out by Jack's statements.

"I won't have to work hard at that," I said.

— 14 —

Suspect

♀

Jack waited outside the house by his shiny black Jeep Wrangler while I gathered the essentials for my stay at his place. In the bathroom, I paused to look in the mirror. Haggard eyes stared at me, and I noticed my long hair needed washing. It hung in limp waves around my shoulders. My smooth, unshadowed face was very pale and, vaguely, I wondered if I was losing weight. My gentle curves seemed more angular and defined underneath my tank top; my collarbones seemed to protrude more than I remembered.

When I came outside, Jack took my duffel bag and guided me into the Jeep. "If it's all right," he said, "I'd like to make a stop on the way home."

"Uh, sure, I guess. Where?"

He slid into the driver's seat and started the car. We pulled away from the curb, and I realized I had forgotten to get my mail. Oh well, I thought. I was only missing bills that I couldn't pay and junk mail I didn't care about. If I remembered when I became my brother again, I'd go get it.

Jack's mirrored sunglasses reflected the brightness of the afternoon sun and the deep colors of the tree canopy around us. He said, "Do you recall the name Shun Yan Pii?"

I frowned. It did sound familiar, but I couldn't place it. "I don't think so. Who is he?"

"Your brother came to Chin's on the night of his wake."

I recalled, then, the aftermath of the party at the restaurant and Jack's gorgeous white suit. "Oh. Right. I remember now."

Jack glanced at me. His expression was as opaque as his sunglasses. "He was murdered."

"Yes, you said. Shot, right?"

"Yes. There was a witness."

"A witness? Wow."

"We're going to see her."

"Oh. Okay." I thought about that. Why would Jack be questioning the witness to a murder? He wasn't law enforcement as far as I knew. "Why are you investigating? You said you're in security. Are you a private eye?"

Jack rubbed his shadowy whiskered chin. "Something like that."

* * *

Our destination was five miles north of the comic shop in a sporadically occupied industrial neighborhood where the sun glared on stained brick warehouses, boarded-up shops, and the occasional biker bar. Jack pulled into an alley and parked behind a tiny store that promised overnight dry cleaning and shirts pressed in an hour. Two slender Asians in dark suits stood outside the back door, smoking. Both wore dark sunglasses, so I couldn't see their eyes.

Jack cut the engine, and we stepped from the Jeep. I followed him inside, past the anonymous Asians. The store was narrow and long, and rows of anemic florescent lights didn't suffice to illuminate the cavernous space. I could hardly make out the sales counter near the front, nestled in the gloom beyond vast clothing racks.

"Who are those guys?" I asked. "They don't look like they work here."

"Those are bodyguards."

"Bodyguards? Why? Is your witness a celebrity?"

"In a manner of speaking, she is now."

"What does that mean?"

We spoke in hushed tones that seemed appropriate to the dim interior.

"It means she witnessed a murder. The perpetrator is still at large."

It took me a second to realize what that meant. "Oh, jeez, you think he's after her? Who is he?"

"He or she is very likely to be after Li Jong."

At that moment a pretty Chinese woman came out from a side room and greeted us. She'd been in a large alcove that contained a stand-alone sewing machine and was littered with tailoring paraphernalia. She had very long hair, past her waist, and could have been anywhere between thirty and sixty, given that I was a terrible judge of age, especially where Asians were concerned. The woman had on a pantsuit made of fuchsia silk and matching nail polish. She kissed Jack on both cheeks and greeted him in that foreign language that I felt everyone except me must speak.

"Judith, this is Li Jong."

We shook hands.

The woman nodded. She said, "My boss was killed. I saw it."

I frowned. "Sorry. He was your boss?"

Jack said, "Shun Yan owned a line of cleaners that runs across the Sun Belt, including this one."

"Oh. Cool."

Li Jong looked at Jack. "You said you wished to ask me some questions?"

"Tell us how it happened. Don't leave anything out."

Li Jong fidgeted with her long fingernails. "It was Tuesday."

I remembered I'd seen Jack and Goom at Chin's on Thursday. Two days seemed about right for the time of the wake.

Li Jong hesitated before continuing. "I see him Tuesday afternoons."

Jack asked, "When, exactly?"

"It was almost four o'clock, I think, when the woman came."

"A woman came at four o'clock?"

"You know I bring Shun Yan his laundry every Tuesday afternoon. He wants fresh clothes always."

I noticed the woman was particularly eager to tell us that. I thought there might be a different reason Li Jong had been at her boss's house to visit him, but who was I to judge?

"Fresh clothes," Jack said. "So you brought some to him."

"Yes. And then the woman came. She was very, very angry with him when she saw me." A red hue crossed Li Jong's smooth, oval face. She scratched one of her cheeks and licked her lips. "I am sure she was a jealous girlfriend."

So the murdered man was a womanizer, I thought. At least that probably gave a ton of suspects.

Jack said, "Did you recognize the angry woman?"

"No. I have never seen her before. That was the first time."

"Please describe her."

"She had Russian accent."

I started. More Russians?

Jack rubbed his chin. "Go on."

"She had very dark hair, but brown. Not black like mine. And shorter. She wasn't as tall as me. She came up to my nose."

I thought Li Jong was about the same height as me, which, considering I was in flats, would have put her about five-eight. That probably meant the woman Li Jong saw was five-four-ish.

Jack nodded. "Anything else?"

"She had lots of jewelry. On her wrists, especially. Oh—and she had very beautiful boots. On top of white pants. They were red with sparkles."

"She had red boots with sparkles?"

"Yes. Very nice. Suede, I think. I appreciated her boots very much."

I frowned. My mind churned. Why did that spark a memory? Where had I seen red boots on a woman recently?

"Then what happened?" Jack said.

"Well, the woman was extremely angry. Violently angry. She pushed me away, and I had to leave then. When I was outside, I heard the shot."

Jack frowned. "You didn't actually see her shoot Shun Yan?"

Li Jong shook her head. "No. But I know it was her."

"Did you tell the cops about her?" I asked.

"I do not speak to cops. They are fat and rude and will lock me in jail."

"Well, some of them are thin and rude, surely," I said.

Li Jong stared at me. I figured my sarcasm had been lost in translation.

Jack chuckled. "Li Jong, is there anything else you can tell us?"

The woman stared at her fingernails without speaking for several moments. "I do not think so. That is all I remember."

Jack nodded. "All right." He moved toward the door. "We'll be in touch."

* * *

Jack had the windows down on our way to his place, and an unseasonably warm wind whipped around us as I studied my companion's stark profile. The late-afternoon sun reflected off his sunglasses in burnished hues.

I faced forward. I was trying to remember where I'd seen red boots before. Li Jong's statements rattled around my brain, and suddenly I had a vision of the Blue Bulldog and our dark table with Msti's legs underneath.

"Oh. Shit!"

Jack glanced toward me. "Are you all right?"

I rubbed my forehead. "I can't believe it."

"What's wrong?" Jack glanced over his shoulder before changing lanes. He eyed the rearview mirror and looked all around us for an unseen enemy.

"It seems incredible, but I might know a woman like Li Jong described."

Jack was silent. He stared forward, a deep frown on his face.

"But the woman I know isn't Russian; she's Abkhaz."

"Abkhaz?"

"Yes. It's some Eastern European country. I don't know where it is."

Jack said, "It's a breakaway region of Georgia."

"Georgia?"

"The country, not our state."

"Oh. Duh. Why does all that sound familiar?"

"Abkhazia and Georgia have been at war since the late nineties. The phrase 'ethnic cleansing' applies."

I recalled the phrase from news reports about atrocities in the region. I shuddered. "That's terrible."

"Tell me more about your friend."

"Her name's Msti—as in Mstislava—Fairholme. She has red boots with rhinestones and very dark brown hair. She's also about five-four and wears a ton of jewelry."

"Fairholme? Is she any relation to Major Fairholme?"

"She's his wife."

Jack inhaled sharply. "This means the Major's murder may be tied to the murder of Shun Yan. Amazing."

"How does any of that relate to the fact some angry Russians seem out to get me?"

Jack was silent.

"Do you think maybe the ones trying to kidnap me are Abkhaz then?"

"The Russians are intimately involved in Abkhazia. I think your friend's past has come back to haunt us."

"Us? You mean you think they're after me because I'm Msti's friend?"

"It fits. She may be the link between everything that's happening. Can you contact her?"

"She hasn't been answering my texts or my calls."

Jack sighed. "In this case, we're out of luck. We'll have to lie low and see what happens next."

— 15 —

Missiles

♂

The sun had set, and I was yawning ferociously. My side ached where the bullet wound was still healing. At least it had stopped bleeding profusely and needed nothing more serious than a bandage at the moment. I contemplated Fred's habitat. I felt antsy and eager to return to Parkour.

Fred slithered out from her hidey-hole and bumped her nose gently on the top of the cage. I opened the box and let her out. She slid up my outstretched arm and settled closely over my shoulders. I kissed the top of her snout. Fred's tongue flicked out and briefly touched my lip. I marveled for a moment at how smooth and cool Fred's skin was. I could see why this snake had been so important to my brother. If I felt like this in my own body, I would have been hooked too instead of repulsed.

Clink! Thud!

I jumped. That had come from our living room. With Fred across my shoulders, I ran from Ethan's bedroom in time to see smoke pouring into the living room from something that had fallen behind the sofa. Whatever it was had clearly been thrown through the front window—the blinds were crooked, and there was glass on the floor.

"Wha—"

Smash!

Someone punched through one of the frosted panes on our front door. An arm reached through the hole, feeling around for the lock. Outside, a blurry figure stood with the outline of a nasty assault weapon in his hands.

I bolted. I sprinted through the kitchen and yanked open the door to the back porch. I stopped short. In front of me stood a big man with dark face paint. I surprised him slightly more than he surprised me, and in that split-second hesitation, I stepped in and head-butted him. He went down, blood gushing from his nose. I leaped over him onto the porch. Another man in black face paint with a brush cut rounded the corner of my house.

"Wait!" he yelled.

Wait? He couldn't be serious. I took off, jumping down the steps and crossing the backyard at top speed. I used one of our garbage cans as a springboard and launched myself over our back fence into the alley. Fred distracted me, and I came down hard on both feet, unbalanced and flailing, then finally slammed down on one knee to catch myself.

"Ow! Shit."

I struggled to stand and saw Brush Cut leap over the fence in pursuit. I galloped down the alley as fast as I could, limping and favoring my injured knee. Brush Cut was almost on top of me when I zagged sideways and burst through a hedge into an adjacent yard. A querulous growl greeted me from my neighbor's Doberman. I popped his gate open as I ran by.

"Slow that guy down for me, will ya, Toby?"

I didn't stop to see what happened, but behind me I heard barking and swearing. I smiled, tearing across the front lawn and circling a hedge into the street. I skidded to a halt, unable at first to comprehend what I was seeing. A big black sedan was parked crookedly in the street. All of its doors were open with men crouched behind them firing automatic weapons. One of the men was loading some kind of particularly long rifle. As I gaped, he aimed and fired at my house.

Phoom!

I felt the blast from where I was, halfway down the block. The entire front of my house rose up in flames, and parts of the roof rained into the front yard.

"Holy shit from hell."

As if that weren't enough, one of the men noticed me standing under the streetlight and shouted to his comrades. He sounded Russian. Another man turned in my direction, then yelled similarly.

"Oh... that's not good."

One of the men leveled his weapon at me but, incredibly, shots from the side of my lot sent all of them scrambling for cover. I couldn't believe it—who on earth was firing from my house? Finally, the gunfire broke me out of my stupor, and I took off, retreating back through Toby's yard. I burst through the rear hedge and returned to the alley. Toby had Brush Cut cornered against the opposite fence. I ran by.

"Coming through!"

Brush Cut jumped out and almost grabbed me, then pursued me closely, ignoring the dog chomping at his heels. The three of us plus Fred barreled down the alley and emerged onto Ponce De Leon. Brush Cut almost had me in his grasp when I zigged into traffic.

"Hey! Watch it, asshole," a man yelled as he slammed on his brakes.

Horns honked and brakes screeched, injecting the scent of burning rubber into the air. From the corner of my eye, I saw a car jerk to a halt mere inches from poor Toby. Brush Cut was still right on top of me. I put on a burst of speed, jumped the median, and ripped open the door of a taxi stopped at the light. I dove into the backseat.

I yelled at the open-mouthed driver, "Go! Go, go, go!"

Hands blocked me from closing the door. Brush Cut grabbed at me. I smacked his hands away and kicked him square in the gut, slamming the door closed in his wake.

"Go! Or he'll kill us."

The taxi driver shook all over. "Don't hurt me! Take the cab!" He wrenched his door open, coincidentally knocking down Brush Cut, who had recovered and was trying to get inside. The driver leaped from the car and took off across the median.

"Oh, for crying out loud."

I threw myself into the front seat, pulled the door shut, slammed the car into reverse, and made room for us to maneuver into the left turning lane. I cut several people off, nearly ran over Brush Cut, and floored it. I careened through the turn and left the whole mess behind me.

* * *

It was almost eight p.m. when I pulled up to the comic store. The shop was dark, illuminated poorly by a weak pole light in the parking lot. I parked across several spaces, jumped out of the cab, and flung the back door of the taxi open to look for Fred, who had disappeared under the seat during the reckless drive over. I stopped short. My mouth dropped open.

Sitting calmly, watching me with Fred sitting on her lap, was a little old Asian lady. I had driven the whole way to the shop without noticing her. The woman's aged face was incredibly wrinkled, and other than glittering dark eyes, it was stony and expressionless. She wore a colorful bandanna hooded over her dark gray hair and a thick red wool coat. She said something that sounded like it might be Mandarin.

"Um. Someone will be right with you."

I stood and swung the door shut. I slowly shook my head. Before I had a chance to decide what to do, a huge black Humvee screeched into the lot. Brush Cut jumped from the passenger's seat.

"Shit!"

I took off toward Jack's bungalow, racing past the comic shop and leaping over the fence. I crashed through Jack's beautiful undergrowth, missing the path completely, but emerging beside the house. "Open up! They're right behind me!" I stumbled down the slope, rounded the side of the house, and banged on the basement door. "Open up! Let me in!"

Jack had barely pulled back the sliding door when I exploded into the basement. I spun, fists out, ready to fight. A stocky man all in black with a brush cut stepped through the doorway.

I pointed. "That's him. Get him!"

Instead of knocking my pursuer on his ass, Jack stood calmly at ease, hands folded in front of him. Brush Cut clicked his heels together, stood straight, and stared forward, not at anything in particular.

"Colonel," he said.

"Captain," Jack said. "Problems with your charge?"

I frowned. "What the hell's going on?"

Before anyone could answer, Goom called from the bottom of the stairs. "What the fuck is all the ruckus now?" He came into the room rubbing his eyes. We all stared at him.

"Oh. It's just you." He glared at me. "And... your grandmother?" He gaped toward the porch.

I looked up. On the patio behind Brush Cut stood the old lady from the taxi. She said something loudly in Mandarin.

"Oh, yeah." I sighed. "That's the lady from the taxi."

Jack brought a hand up to his forehead and hid his face behind it. The lady repeated her question. It might have been a command.

"What'd she say?" I asked Goom quietly.

A silly smile was plastered across Goom's face. He muttered through clenched teeth, "She says she's supposed to be at her nephew's, you dumb shit. Why did you kidnap a hundred-year-old gramma and bring her here?"

"It's not my fault. She was in the taxi."

Goom's smile wavered. I could tell he wanted to burst out screaming and cursing at me.

Jack was slowly rubbing his forehead, as if these shenanigans had given him a killer headache. "All right. Everyone back to the cars."

* * *

Jack's eyes followed Goom as the midget climbed into the driver's seat of the taxi. Captain Brush Cut, who was actually called Captain Pike, climbed in next to him. The ancient Chinese lady waited patiently in the backseat.

They were going to drop her off where she needed to be and then "dispose" of the taxi, whatever that meant.

"You have no idea who the men at your house were?" Jack asked me.

"They seemed Russian. But none of them were the ones that kidnapped my sister. And they blew up my house. What am I going to do now?"

"We are fortunate you made it out alive."

"Yeah. I guess you were right. I should have stayed at Guan Ho's."

Before Jack could respond, Goom exploded from the taxi.

"Ahh-h! Help! Save me!" He stumbled and lurched toward us, still wearing his driving stilts. The stilts gave out, and he tumbled over and over, ending up in a heap at Jack's feet. Jack helped him up. Goom was shaking all over.

"Motherfucking fuck, there's a snake in the taxi!"

"Oh, right." I cleared my throat. "I forgot about her."

Pike emerged from the passenger's side and slammed the door shut. His face was pasty white in the streetlight. He peered through the window at something on the front seat.

I called loudly to him, "No need to worry. That's just Fred."

"Fred?" Goom snorted. "Who or what the fuck is a Fred?"

I sighed. "She's a pewter corn snake. She's quite rare, actually."

Goom, Jack, and Pike stared at me.

"Um. She's my pet."

Goom's eyes bugged out. "Your pet? Who in the hell has a snake for a pet? And why'd you name a chick snake Fred? You dumb shit-for—"

"Oh, pipe down, you pint-sized pussy," I shot back. "She's harmless."

I stalked over and opened the door. Fred was coiled in the middle of the front seat, contemplating me amid a puddle of reflected streetlight.

I scoffed at Goom. "She's just sitting there. Completely minding her own business. It's so chilly she can probably barely move."

"She's a vicious, wild reptile." Goom waved his arms around. "She kills things for a living."

I reached in and gently extracted the serpent, wrapping her over my shoulders. I cocked my head and bent to kiss the top of Fred's shiny nose. Fred's tongue flicked out and brushed my lip.

Goom shuddered. "That's fucking crazy. The redneck kissed a snake."

Jack sighed. He nodded at Pike, who got into the driver's seat.

Goom shook his head. "I ain't getting back in there. Thing's got snake cooties all over it now."

Jack quietly said a few words in Mandarin.

Goom rolled his eyes. "For fuck's sake. This guy is a freak." He toddled over to the passenger's side, muttering to himself.

Jack slapped me on the back as Goom and Pike drove off. "Come on," he said. "Let's go find Fred a new home."

* * *

We found an old glass display case in Goom's shop, lined it with newspapers, and added an iron turtle shell to serve as shelter. To top off the makeshift home, Jack poked several small holes in a thick piece of cardboard, which we weighed down with a couple of two-by-fours. He set the box on top of a gorgeous mahogany chest of drawers that lined the west wall of his worship room.

I studied the room. I'd seen it once before, but only briefly through the sliding doors the first night when I faced down Jack in my female body. The room was on the opposite side of the dojo from the front entrance. It was about ten feet square and lit by an elaborate, multi-tiered Chinese lantern with red tassels. Jack's altar traversed the wall opposite the room door, built directly into the elegant mahogany paneling covering the bottom half of the walls. Amid an array of religious icons, it held two burning oil lamps, three ornate incense holders, and exactly seven bowls of dried fruit.

Jack removed three sticks of incense, lit them, and held them in his right hand as he knelt before the altar, quietly chanting Mandarin with his head bowed low. It sounded like he might be apologizing for intruding on his gods' domain with a corn snake. As he prayed, I marveled at the statue front and center on his altar. It was an intricate depiction of two deities wrought in dark metal. The figures were half-human and half-snake; one was male and the other female. They stood back-to-back in a heavily arched pose with their tails intertwined, their arms out, and their human heads joined at the skull. I remembered the huge tattoo on Jack's back and thought it was probably something similar, a serpent with two bodies.

The roots of my hair stood on end. No wonder Jack was so understanding of my special talent—his worship predisposed him toward twins with a single mind if the icon in front of me was any indication.

Jack had risen again and carefully inserted the incense into the holders.

I nodded toward the statue. "Who are they?"

He faced me, his jet-black eyes deeply overshadowed by the lantern's downward glow. "That is the goddess Nuwa and her twin brother, Fuxi."

"They're joined at the head."

"Yes. They are telepathic, like you and your sister."

My gaze returned to the statue. I couldn't believe Jack worshiped a myth that so succinctly captured my newfound superpower. I was coming to the conclusion I should no longer believe in coincidences. Such a confluence of personalities must have a deeper meaning.

I smiled. "Good-looking pair," I said.

— 16 —

Spirits

♀

An elongated slice of sunlight descended against my cheek. It felt like afternoon sun. Had I really spent so long tossing and turning, not sleeping but refusing to be awake?

It had been three days since the bombing of my Decatur house. We didn't seem to be making progress on either murder or on finding the Russians who were after me.

I blinked my eyes open. Indeed, the light streaming through the crack at the edge of Jack's blinds had the burnished nostalgic quality of oncoming dusk. Somewhere a window must have been open as a cool current of air carried the scent of decaying leaves. I turned over, tucking my head back under Jack's covers.

"Ugh."

My body wouldn't sleep, but my mind was exhausted. I was sick to death of the farce my life had become. My home and most of my belongings were gone. My brother was gone. I was a murderer and engaged to a scary soldier I barely knew. As if that weren't enough, some Russian paramilitaries were trying to kill me, for no reason that I could fathom.

Perhaps I should turn myself in to the authorities. Every day I ran from the horrors I'd inflicted in the motel room was probably another year or two in Ethan's life sentence for killing my kidnapper. Maybe I could even turn myself in directly to Julian. Possibly he could get me committed for a couple of years instead of imprisoned. After all, I imagined I was possessing my brother's brain-dead body. With that, it shouldn't be hard to convince a jury I was certifiably nutso.

I threw the covers off my head and frowned at the ceiling. "Ah, fuck it."

* * *

After a shower, I was refreshed enough to contemplate emerging from Jack's suite. I stared at myself in the bathroom mirror. I wore a clingy camo shirt and black leggings. Ethan's pendant was around my neck.

Soft creaking and the occasional muted thud sounded in Jack's dojo. I slid the bathroom door open about an inch and peeped out. It was Jack, wearing only loose black pants and wielding a very long, very sharp-looking sword. He was obviously practicing an advanced routine. It was like the sword was an extension of his arm, no more cumbersome than another fingernail. He moved through blocks, strikes, and even jumps, his strapping, well-defined muscles glistening with a fine covering of sweat. I felt hot as I watched and realized I was blushing.

At last, he ceased movement, coming to a stop in a deep crouch with the sword held stiffly in front of him, pointing skyward. He waited for several moments, still as a statue.

I stepped from the bathroom. "Um. Nihao."

"Nihao," he returned easily with a smile.

I frowned. "I pronounced it wrong, didn't I?"

"No," he said, but I knew he lied. "It sounded fine."

He straightened up and tossed the sword into the air. It turned full circle, and he caught it handily by its hilt before slipping it into the scabbard at his waist. I knew if I tried that—in either body—I'd decapitate myself.

"Wow."

"Would you like to give it a try?" He detached the sword-in-scabbard and held it toward me, hilt first.

I ran my fingers through my hair. It was still wet, and I was sure it was sticking up in the wrong places. It usually did. "Um, sort of. But I'd probably manage to cut something important off of one of us."

He grinned. "I'll assist."

Moments later, Jack was spooned to me, his arm against mine, his hands on mine holding the sword. He guided my motion in a smooth, firm swoop of the weapon downward. "That's the basic cut." From behind me, his other hand let go of a piece of tissue paper. It fluttered down in front of us. We made the basic cut—*swoop*—and cleanly divided the paper in two.

I gasped. "Amazing."

I heard him inhale next to my ear and felt the accompanying exhale on my neck. I was rooted to the spot, acutely aware of every point of contact between our bodies. Abruptly, he pulled away. I almost toppled over.

"Now you try it," he said quietly.

He dropped another piece of tissue paper from a great height, and it lazily floated toward the floor. I waved the sword in front of me to no effect.

"Damn it."

I whipped the sword back the other way, missing completely but making the paper float higher. I tried twice more, utterly in vain. My wispy nemesis finally settled on the ground, and I smacked it, slicing the mat and embedding the sword in the floor. I lost my balance and stumbled forward, leaving the sword behind. I snapped to standing, smoothing my tee and clearing my throat. The sword remained embedded in the mat, reverberating slowly and sonorously, like a discarded musical instrument.

Jack had one arm across his chest. The other rested perpendicularly in it, his hand covering his mouth. Laughter he couldn't quite stifle ripped through his naked chest.

"Um. Sorry about the floor," I said.

"That's all right." Jack recovered his poker face. He extracted the sword cleanly, slipped it back into the scabbard, and closed the gash in the mat with his foot. For the first time, I realized the mat had several repaired gashes. They were obvious now that I knew what to look for. "I'll sew that up later," he said.

* * *

Crisp vegetables hitting the surface of a five-hundred degree wok hissed violently, filling the kitchen with palpable sound and fragrance. In seconds, the dish was done, and Jack eased it expertly onto warmed plates. I followed him out to the porch table. He set the steaming dishes at our places and lit several candles in glass cups on the table. Afterward he sat opposite me, folding his napkin neatly into his lap.

"Enjoy," he said.

"Manman chi," I replied. Goom had told me the phrase. It was supposed to mean *bon appetit,* as long as I didn't horribly mispronounce it, in which case I worried it might be a vile insult against a person's ancestors.

Jack smiled. "Mahnmahn chi."

I had no desire to break the silence for the next few minutes, being too occupied with inhaling the food. I couldn't believe such a simple dish tasted so incredibly yummy. I realized every other bite of Chinese food I'd ever had was Americanized crap.

After we finished, Jack sat back and sipped his Tsingtao, his gaze particularly dark and unfathomable in the fringe luminescence of candlelight. He wore a loose-fitting black silk suit with a Mandarin collar and butterfly buttons that had a gorgeous intricate dragon pattern subtly embroidered in dark gray thread. I had never seen it before. I fingered the unadorned edges of my T-shirt self-consciously. My gaze wandered over our surroundings. At the edge of Jack's pond, a torch burned. Cold, reflected moonlight bled from the pond's placid surface to encircle the flame's incandescence. I thought I saw large, pale flowers resting on the picnic table, their color eroded by the full moon.

Jack spoke in a quiet voice. "A man called today, looking for you."

I started. "One of the Russians?"

"An FBI agent."

"Oh. Julian?"

"Yes. Julian Bead."

"Wow. How'd he know where to find me?"

Jack studied the tabletop for several seconds before responding. Finally, his eyes returned to me, but he didn't answer my question. "Special Agent Bead is your legal guardian?"

"No, only until I was eighteen."

Jack rubbed his chin. "He still considers you his responsibility."

"Maybe. But I'm my own person."

"Nevertheless, I would not like to negatively impact your relationship with family."

"You know we're not related, right?"

"Right."

"What did he say to you?"

Jack frowned. "He indicated he would prefer it if you stayed with him." He sipped his beer, eyeing me, seeming in no great rush to continue the conversation. But then, I couldn't ever remember seeing him in a hurry. Intent, yes; hurried, no.

I fidgeted with my place mat, wondering exactly how Julian had "indicated" his desire. Did he yell and scream? Threaten Jack with all kinds of prison time? Or did he gently insist in his role as the closest thing I had to a living father? I blurted out, "Julian doesn't know about Ethan. He thinks he's dead and cremated. He can't know the truth."

Instead of asking the obvious question—*Why not?*—Jack finished his beer and reclined in his chair, casually crossing his legs, saying nothing.

Disconsolation settled heavily on my shoulders. I found my gaze again drawn to the pale flowers below us on the picnic table. Silence reigned for several minutes, broken only by the gray noise of the urban night.

"Would you like me to make you a drink, Judith?"

I started. "Um. What do you have?"

He held up his empty Tsingtao bottle. "You've said you don't like beer. How about a Hong Ying?"

He could have offered me flaming shit for all I knew. "What's that?"

He smiled, his fingers moving along his chin absent-mindedly. "Red Hawk. It's a Jack special."

"S-sure. Why not?"

* * *

My drink required some preparation. I waited at the pond's edge, fingering a beautiful paper flower in my hands. It was made of translucent blues, in at least three shades. After a few minutes, Jack approached from the house with a tray carrying another Tsingtao and a squat, multicolored glass. I glanced at the picnic table where the other crafted flower rested, equally delicate and convoluted, in shades of gold instead of blue.

"Did you make these, Jack? They're amazing."

"Yes." He set the tray on the table beside the golden lotus.

"Wow. Origami?"

"Yes."

"I thought that was Japanese."

"I was stationed in Okinawa for many years." After a moment he added, "I made these for Zhongqiu Jie."

My brow furrowed. "What's that?"

"I think you'd translate it as something like Mid-Autumn Festival."

"Oh. Cool. What's the significance?"

Jack held an arm outward. "Spirits surround us."

I didn't get the feeling he meant that metaphorically. I looked around at the moonlit exotica of Jack's garden and beyond, to where the city haze swallowed the horizon.

"On Zhongqiu Jie we float lanterns on the water to light the way so the spirits of our pasts can find their way back to us, joining us once again, at least for an evening."

I watched him. His expression was as opaque as ever. I sighed. "I'm not so sure I want the spirits of my past to find me."

He said quietly, "They're never gone. They are only closer or farther."

I placed the blue flower on the table and picked up my drink. There were some flesh-colored balls floating in it. "What are those little thingys?"

"Lychees."

"Eyeballs?"

He smiled. "Fruit."

I sipped the concoction. It was delicious and surprising. "It's warm."

"Better for your digestion." He arced his head in a slight bow toward me. From a pocket he took a lighter and used it to start two tealights, which he then carefully lowered into the lotuses he'd created.

He lifted the golden lantern from the table and held it before him. I marveled at the pattern of light and shadow on his face, rising flamelight shifting amid falling moonlight, emphasizing his angular brow and full lips. He held the light for some time, mouthing a silent prayer. It might have been my own guilt reflected at me, but I couldn't shake the feeling he was asking for forgiveness. I was halfway through my drink by the time he finally approached the placid water and released his lantern with the barest of shoves. An unseen current buoyed the offering, slowly reeling it toward the pond's center. Jack stared after the lantern. His face was impenetrable as sheet marble.

"Are you all right?" I hiccuped. My hand flew to my mouth. "Jeez. How much alcohol did you put in here?"

He half-smiled toward his receding lantern. "Two fingers."

I hiccuped again. I flushed deep red, although the color was lost to the monochromatic night.

He glanced sideways at me. “I have big fingers.”

* * *

We lounged in the grass, watching our lanterns circle the pool. Our shadows commingled on the earth, elongated dark doppelgangers disappearing into the water’s edge. Silent tears ran down my cheeks. Jack was motionless, a pale statue in the moonlight, the bamboo torch having burned itself out a while ago.

“Jack,” I said softly.

“Yes?”

“You killed people before, right?”

“Yes.” He said it flatly, with neither satisfaction nor regret, and waited.

I sat up and turned toward him, folding my legs underneath me. “How do you deal with it?”

The furrows on his forehead deepened. He said nothing.

“Doesn’t it bother you?”

“To be honest, not really.” He sat up as well, duplicating my pose.

“None of them?” My shoulders drooped. “How many are there?”

“Dozens. At least.”

I gasped.

“Many were long-range. I’m not certain exactly how many are directly attributable to my actions.”

My voice rose an octave. “None of them bothers you? Not even the close-up ones?”

He steepled his hands before his mouth. “Perhaps one.”

I wiped my cheeks.

Jack sighed heavily. "It was in the early days of the war, during our advance from Mazar-i-Sharif to Khandahar." His jaw muscles clenched and unclenched as he spoke, although his intonation gave no sign of distress.

"Afghanistan?"

"Of course."

Pause. I pulled Ethan's pendant out from my T-shirt and caressed it.

Jack frowned. "We set up an outpost near a river, about five miles from the nearest village. I was at the perimeter when a group of women approached. You know they make them wear the burqa." He waved his hand in front of his face, denoting the cover they wore.

I nodded.

"There were three of them. Coming back from the river. I could barely distinguish their eyes." He squinted into the darkness. "There was something not quite right. A furtiveness." He let out a long, slow exhalation. "Perhaps a lucky guess."

After a while, he continued. "The middle one, she was very small. Probably little more than a child. She held herself. . . awkwardly. And she wasn't carrying any water." His eyes found mine. "You don't walk five miles in that hellhole and come home empty-handed."

I bit my lip.

"I shot her. Right here." He brought his index finger up to his face and tapped himself between the eyes.

"Oh, jeez."

"The others scattered. But they didn't get far before the bombs taped to her went off. We were pulling body parts out of the brush for days." His hands returned to his lap, and he sat, unmoving.

"I can see why that bothered you. Shooting a little girl."

"It wasn't that."

I frowned. "What then?"

"She made her choice. But. . . I could have been wrong."

"You weren't, Jack. You had to shoot her."

"And if Ethan hadn't shot that Russian, he would have killed both you and your brother. The two of you had no choice."

— 17 —

White Room

♂

Sunday afternoon I knelt with Jack in the dojo, bent at the waist, nose to the floor. Behind me, the sun saturated the mats, rendering the tatami in shades of gold. We were bowing to pay homage to the pictures above Jack's worship room doors at the north end of the dojo. They depicted the men in his martial arts lineage, back to one of the earliest samurai.

After a moment, Jack sat up. I sat up after him since he'd told me as my superior he needed to move first. I pivoted around so I was facing him and we bowed again, to each other.

"Onegaishimasu," Jack said. "Say it, Ethan."

"Own-a-geish-ee-mass."

"Close enough."

"What does it mean?"

"It is a Japanese greeting of respect. The traditional way to start working out with someone."

"Japanese? Not Chinese?"

"As I said, I lived in Okinawa for many years. The Japanese is a habit."

"Okay."

He jumped to standing. "Rise."

I stood.

"We will work on blocks first."

"Blocks? Blocks of what?"

Jack punched me, hard. I went down for a moment, then sprang back up, wiping my bloodied mouth with the back of my hand.

"Shit, that hurt. What the hell was that for?"

He punched me again, this time in the gut. I doubled over.

"Sonofa—"

"Shhh," he warned.

I coughed and choked.

"The second strike was because there is no swearing in my dojo. It is disrespectful."

"That's fu—"

Jack raised a fist.

"I mean. . . fiddlesticks."

"And both of those should answer your question about blocks."

I straightened up. "Right."

Jack drew back his arm and punched me again, but in slow motion. I watched his fist come for my face.

"Don't stand there. Move."

I stepped backward. He leaned forward and tapped me on the chin.

"Shit."

Another strike to the gut and I was down on the floor, face to the mats.

"F-fu-fudge," I said.

Goom toddled in from outside, carrying his ever-present laptop.

"Yo."

He looked at me squirming on the floor clutching my belly.

"I take it the lesson's in progress. Can I watch?"

I said, "No, get lost."

Simultaneously Jack said, "Yes."

Goom sat just off the mats with his back against the wall and set the laptop beside him. "Okay. Carry the fuck on."

I struggled to my feet. "Why does he get to swear in the dojo?"

"He's not in the dojo. You are."

I stared at Jack.

"The dojo is a state of mind."

"Great. So I'll know I'm in it if you deck me every time I swear?"

Jack's closed expression was unaffected.

"Don't step backward when a strike comes. Move off the line of attack."

He punched me in slow motion again. This time I stepped to the side so his fist passed next to my head.

"All right. Good. Now, arms up."

He raised his bent arms, palms outward. I raised mine likewise.

"Not so high. You need your arms close to your center at all times."

He punched again, slowly, and I slid to the side and put my arms up so I was neatly blocking his arm.

"Very good. This is ikkyo-uke."

"Um. What?"

"Say it. Ikkyo-uke."

"Icky-yo oo-kay."

He sighed. "It means 'first block,' but you need to learn the Japanese. And you need to learn to pronounce it so that you don't sound like an ignorant Westerner."

Goom piped up. "We wouldn't want that, right, shitnugget?"

* * *

Two hours later we'd made it through blocks one, two, three, and four, and finally moved to five, or "osai-uke," whatever that was. Sweat dripped from me. Jack seemed fresh and placid. Goom futzed continually with his laptop as Jack punched, kicked, slapped, and choked me.

"You know," I said, "this is fun and all, but what do I do when the bad guys come running at me with automatic weapons? How do I block that?"

Goom said, "You don't. You die."

I scoffed. "That's great." I looked at Jack. "With all due respect, Sensei, I was hoping for something a tad more useful than that."

Goom said slowly, "Jack... do you think we should show him now?"

"Show me what?"

Jack frowned.

Goom sighed. He said, "Our relic."

"Relic?"

Goom hopped to his feet. "See that door over there?" He pointed to a narrow door next to the entryway. It was bathed in the last grasp of sunlight and seemed to glow with preternatural energy.

"Pretty," I said.

"Yeah, well, wait 'til you see what's inside. It's not pretty."

"What's in there?"

"Our secret, dingus." The little guy sounded practically reverent. "The source of our power."

I stared at him. "What is it?"

"It's ancient. Jack's grandfather passed it to his mother, and she left it for him. Before that it was a hundred generations of power, passed down in a line, all to us."

"You're kidding."

He shrugged. "Believe me or not, but go take a look. It'll answer your questions. Just looking at it, you'll understand."

I stared at the narrow door, gilded as it was in the shadowed light. I remembered the statue of the snake twins that Jack worshiped and how neatly it dovetailed with my newfound superpower. Was it possible there really was magic in the world? I walked to the door. It seemed ordinary enough, blond wood and white panels. I set my hand on the handle. It was warm, which I wasn't expecting.

"Careful," Goom said.

I looked back at them. Both watched me with intent, opaque faces.

Goom turned to Jack. "Should we really let him see it?"

Jack's lips pursed. He said nothing.

I swallowed. Slowly, I turned the handle. There was a click. I pulled the door open carefully.

A mop fell out and bopped me on the head.

"Ow. Shit."

Goom was in an uproar. He laughed so hard he couldn't stand straight. Jack smiled. My face burned.

"That's it. Come here, you little ass."

I ran at Goom.

"Oh fuck, now he's mad." Goom took off into the mudroom, heading for the stairs. I ran after him.

"Jack! Help! Save me!"

I caught up with Goom in the basement at the bottom of the stairs. I tripped him, and he faceplanted on the carpet.

"Ahhh! Jack! He's killing me!"

I sat on him.

"Christ! You weigh like three hundred pounds. Get off me, fatass."

I rubbed my knuckles vigorously in his dreads, messing up Goom's hair and scraping his scalp.

"No. No! Don't do that. Not the hair! Anything but the hair!"

Goom squirmed and groaned. "Nooo! Ow!"

After a couple minutes, I got up. Goom shook on the ground for a while then staggered to his feet.

"Asshole."

I stuck my tongue out at him. Jack was standing nearby, arms folded over his chest. Amusement subtly lit up his features.

"How could you let him do that? Thanks a lot, Jack." Goom swore to himself for several moments.

I turned to Jack. "That was fun and all, but it didn't answer my question. How do I use your martial arts against a gun?"

"You don't," Jack said. "At least, not usually effectively."

"That's not the answer I was hoping for."

Goom said, "Fine. We'll show you the real relics."

He walked over to the second door on the east wall. It was made of walnut and ornate, with four black sinographs burned into the dark wood. I followed Goom and ran my hand along the brands.

"What do they say?"

Goom said, " 'Swift as the wind, quiet as the forest, energetic as the fire, and steady as the mountain.' That's Sun Tzu."

"The *Art of War* guy?"

"Hey, you know about him. Maybe you're not as stupid as I thought."

"No, I am. But I read a lot. So what kind of relics are in here? More mops and brooms? Maybe some toilet brushes?"

Jack lifted the cover of a keypad next to the door. He entered a long sequence of numbers, then pressed his thumb to the pad. The lock released with a solid click. He said, "This room. . . "

He swung the heavy door wide and flicked a switch on the inside wall.

". . . houses our more-modern relics."

I gaped. "Holy shit."

It was a personal armory. The walls held guns galore, both handguns and rifles. Crates of ammunition and more guns were stacked against one of the white walls. A couple of boxes near the center of the room held more exotic weapons, if the illustrations on their sides were anything to go by. One wall held knives and flak jackets, as well as what looked like several pairs of night vision and infrared goggles.

"Wow!"

Jack's eyes gleamed in the overhead light. "This is the White Room."

Goom moved beside me, caressing a silver handgun on one of the lower shelves. "Yeah, we got you covered, shit-monkey."

I reached over him and picked up a large 9mm. I thumbed the release, and the empty cartridge shot out, smacking Goom square in the forehead, leaving behind an angry red welt.

"Ow! Fuck!"

"Oops."

"You did that on purpose!"

"No, I didn't." Of course I had.

"Stupid cock-munch."

He whacked my knee with the butt of the silver gun. Flaming pain shot through the front of my leg, and I almost toppled over. I punched him. It was only a jab, really, but it got the point across. His head snapped back, and his eyes glazed. He recovered quickly and launched himself at my legs full force, knocking me down. We struggled, wrestling on the floor. He head-butted me on the chin and then punched the kneecap he'd whacked.

"Ahhh! Shit! You little pecker."

I tried to get my arms around his neck, but he fought me every inch of the way. I knew I'd win eventually, being so much bigger and stronger.

"Yee-agh-h!"

Wow, ice was cold. Especially if it was paired with frigid water and thrown on me when I was unprepared. Jack had left the room and come back with a big bucket full.

"Now," he said as Goom and I sputtered and rolled around, the fight frozen out of us, "who's up for the shooting range?"

— 18 —

Line Up

♀

The next morning I came downstairs and found Goom at his desk. I watched the array of computer monitors above him for several minutes, sipping my coffee. I was particularly drawn to the monitor divided into surveillance windows that depicted scenes from outside.

"You guys sure have the house and shop wired up."

Goom snorted. "Yeah, so when fucktards like your brother come to break in, we can get advance warning."

"What are those?" I indicated a small pile of computer chips on the desk next to Goom's keyboard.

"Trackers."

I frowned. "Trackers?"

"Yeah. And that reminds me. Bring me your brother's phone."

"His phone?"

He waved his arm in the air. "Come on."

I went back upstairs. Ethan's new room was opposite the master bedroom, across the dojo. It was Jack's media room. My brother lay slumbering on a plush brown leather couch surrounded by stacked DVDs and Blu-Ray discs. I retrieved his phone from his waist pack and brought it downstairs to Goom.

Goom took it and popped the case off. A very thin, stamp-sized wafer fell out. It was the same as the chips in the pile of trackers.

I gasped. "You had a tracer on my brother. That's how Jack followed him to the Hawk."

Goom shrugged. "Standard operating procedure when we want to know what the hell someone's up to. Don't take it personally."

"I won't." I picked up one of the trackers. It was vanishingly light and only as big as my thumbprint. "These are amazing. How do they work?"

"Well, each one has wireless and a GPS." He waved his hand at his array of monitors. "I can see where it is on my computer, or on a smartphone."

"Wow. It's so tiny."

Goom rolled his eyes. "Welcome to the modern age, bubble-butt."

"Did you just call me bubble-butt?"

Goom crimsoned. "Maybe."

Jack appeared from the bottom of the stairs. "Good morning."

I smiled broadly at him. "Hi, Jack."

He folded his hands before him and bowed toward me. "Hello, Judith."

As usual, Jack's quiet deference impressed me. In spite of knowing about my "telepathy," he still treated my female and male bodies completely differently. Ethan's body was sore and bruised from working out with Jack the previous day, but I couldn't imagine Jack punching me in my own body. I wondered how he would train me, then, if I asked him. If he wouldn't brutalize me, would I get the same valuable education?

I chuckled to myself. "Jack, I can't believe you guys put a tracker on—"

Goom's computer shrieked an alarm. I almost spilled my coffee, it was so sudden and obnoxious.

Jack was immediately at Goom's side, bending over the feeds from their surveillance cameras. I elbowed him aside so I could see too. It took me a minute before I found movement in the sizable array of images from the house, shop, and garden. At last, I saw it. A man was casually making his way down Jack's garden path in broad daylight, bright reflections around him confusing our perspective. He was in jeans, a button-down shirt, and a tan suede jacket. His long black hair was pulled into a tight ponytail. I couldn't make out his eyes, but I knew their watchful intelligence well.

It was Julian.

* * *

The door chimes were audible outdoors as Julian held the bell for a second time. Jack and I rounded the house and came up behind him before he could ring a third time. Julian stepped off the stoop with his hand extended. "Julian Bead. We talked on the phone."

Jack looked at Julian's proffered hand, then folded his own hands in front of him, pointedly not shaking it. I noticed Jack towered over Julian by five or six inches.

I stepped out from behind Jack. "H-hi, Julian."

"Well, Judith." A broad grin crossed Julian's face. "Hi, beautiful."

He shouldered past Jack, and before I knew it, I was in Julian's arms. He kissed me square on the lips. I was so surprised, I didn't kiss back. Over Julian's shoulder, I caught a glimpse of Jack. In a rare moment of openness, the big man's eyes burned with a naked savageness. He shot a look of unadulterated fury at Julian's back.

I gasped.

"Hey, you okay?" Julian caressed my arm.

"Uh, yeah. Fantastic." A goofy smile plastered itself to my face.

When I looked again, Jack's expression had closed up, resuming its usual relaxed indifference. He gazed at the stones near our feet.

Julian said, "Well? Aren't you going to invite me in?"

* * *

Jack set us up at the porch table, then went to make tea. Once the doors slid shut and he had disappeared into the kitchen, Julian leaned in close. "Judith, do you have any idea who this man is?"

I started. "What?"

"God, Judith. He's a stone-cold killer. He's a mercenary."

I bit my lip. "So?"

Julian's jaw dropped open. I couldn't remember when I'd ever seen him so astonished. "Judith, this is insane. Are you sleeping with this man?"

"None of your damn business."

Julian's voice remained quiet, but raged no less. "None of my business? How can you say that? I arrive in Atlanta, and the first thing I find is you shacked up with a Chinese thug in the middle of a mob war. This is very serious. This man will get you killed."

My face burned.

"Is this how you deal with your brother's death? I wish I could have gotten here sooner to save you from yourself."

I tsked loudly. "What is it with you and Jack? You're both behaving like a couple of schoolchildren. Get a grip."

He returned my glare, and his eyes flashed the all-too-familiar insolent possessiveness I knew well from my teens. I threw my napkin on the table and jumped out of my chair; its metal feet screamed along the wood of the porch floor beneath us. I winced. Nails on a chalkboard.

I huffed. "I'm going inside to help Jack." I shook my finger at Julian. "When I get back, you'd better be nice."

* * *

When I returned with tea service, Julian was putting away his smartphone. I set cups out and filled them with steaming green tea, then sat stiffly.

Julian lifted his cup to his lips. He cleared his throat and spoke over the rim of the teacup. "I'm sorry about my outburst before, Judith. I know

I have to get used to the fact you're an adult and more than capable of making decisions for yourself."

I nodded.

"It's also a very difficult time for you. Have you thought more about a memorial service for Ethan?"

Before I could answer, Jack stepped onto the porch with platters of fruit and sweets. He set them down, then took his place at the table and settled his napkin in his lap. He turned to me. "Mahnmahn chi."

I smiled. "Mahnmahn chi."

Julian said in a languid, stuttering lilt, *"A li he li s di."*

We stared at him. After he finished, I said, "Wow, what's that mean?"

He smirked. "Same as what you two said. But in Cherokee."

"Cool."

A buzzing sounded, as if an angry insect had burrowed itself somewhere in Jack. He pulled his smartphone from his pants pocket and frowned at it. "Excuse me." He stood and moved across the porch. I heard him answer in Mandarin, then he descended the porch steps and rounded the house so he was out of sight and hearing.

I looked at Julian. He was nibbling a pear slice and wearing a bland expression. He looked so unconcerned I immediately suspected him.

Shortly, Jack returned. "Judith," he said on his way past the table. "May I speak with you, please?"

I jumped up and followed him into the kitchen. He slid the door closed and stood just inside with his back to it. He said in a low voice, "I'm afraid I must leave. There's a situation elsewhere requiring my attention."

"What? You're leaving me alone with him? Can't it wait?"

He looked at me silently. I glanced through the glass doors at Julian, who was sipping his tea nonchalantly.

"What do I do with him?"

Jack sighed. "Keep him on the porch. Don't let him goad you." His brow furrowed. "You could always claim a headache and send Special Agent Bead away."

* * *

"Julian. I'm not feeling so—"

"Judith. I'm glad you're back. I was hoping you could look at some pictures of people for me. It's possible some of them might be involved in the incident at your home."

"Uh. Incident?"

"You know, the shoot-out and firebombing that you didn't tell me about and didn't call the police for?"

"Oh. That incident."

His sarcastic tone made me wonder how much interference he'd been running for me with the local authorities. It also made me realize his request was on the required side. Besides, I'd rather talk about the firebombing than Ethan. I wondered how I could manage to avoid the topic of my poor brother entirely from here on out.

I frowned and sat as Julian indicated. He handed me his tablet computer. I scrolled dutifully, considering each image in turn. They were mostly generic-looking Caucasians, with the occasional African- or Asian-American thrown in. All were men, many were mug shots. Some looked as if they came out of surveillance cameras. I tried to take the same amount of time on each picture. I also tried to keep my face acutely neutral.

Several minutes of scrolling passed. I started to get bored, and it was progressively harder to stick with my plan of poker-faced browsing. My eyelids were drooping by the time the Blond Smoker showed up. I started and gasped. So much for poker-faced.

Julian had been watching me closely. "You recognize him?"

I paused, then said, "I saw him at the Blue Bulldog."

His eyebrows shot up. "You saw him in the cop bar in Decatur?"

"Well, just outside. He was in the alley smoking."

"Was anyone else there or just you?"

"I was with Blaze and Msti."

"Did they see him too?"

"Blaze didn't. She was lagging behind with Msti. As for Msti. . . " I remembered her scream. It had taken my attention from the man long enough for him to disappear. "She was blasted out of her gourd. I have no idea if she saw him."

Julian considered that for several moments. "Have you ever seen him around Msti before?"

"No."

He frowned. "Have you ever seen this man again at any point since?"

I bit my lip. "No."

His eyes narrowed. "Are you certain?"

I thought hard. Later I would remember this as a choice point, a quantum of time where, if I'd chosen a different response, an entirely different sequence of events would have unfolded. Like a butterfly flapping its wings in Texas—flap them *this* way and set off a hurricane over Hawaii; flap them *that* way and set off a typhoon over the Indian Ocean. If, at that moment, I had broken down and told Julian all I knew about the Blond Smoker and Msti, and Jack and Shun Yan Pii, if I'd confessed my part, would all of the bloodshed to come have been avoided? Or was the trail of death inevitable and my part in it simply a minor facilitation?

Julian waited for my reverie to pass, his gold-flecked eyes intent on every nuance in my face.

I sighed. "No, I didn't see him again. Who is he? Is he the one who destroyed my house?"

Julian was silent.

"You know, it isn't fair if this is one-sided. I'm not going to tell you things if you don't tell me anything."

He stared at me. I sat back in my chair, ignoring Julian's tablet and his gaze. Instead, I watched Jack's beautiful pond, stretched out beneath us, sparkling with reflected sunlight. I thought I saw shadows moving beneath its variegated surface.

After several moments, Julian picked up the tablet and tapped on its surface. He eyed me over the pad. "He was born Viktor Petrovich Rogov."

He didn't continue. I rolled my arm in the air.

Julian cleared his throat. "Born in Moscow. Joined the Russian army at nineteen and distinguished himself in small arms and munitions. Rose to senior sergeant by twenty-one. Went to college and joined Special Ops, where he earned. . . " Julian scrolled through whatever he was looking at. ". . . various honors. Left official service last year due to complaints filed with the ICC over—"

"ICC?"

"International Criminal Court."

"Wow. What were the complaints about?"

"His role in the 2008 South Ossetia war."

That sounded familiar, but I couldn't place it. "Where's Ossetia?"

"Eastern Europe. Every heard of Abkhazia?"

Ice descended my spine. "Abkhazia? Msti's from there."

He nodded.

"Shit. Do you think it means anything?"

"Maybe. Are you sure she didn't recognize him at the Blue Bulldog?"

I frowned. "Unfortunately my back was to her. She got sick suddenly."

"Suddenly? You mean like when she saw him?"

"I don't know. I suppose it's possible."

"Where is she now?"

"You don't know?"

"She doesn't appear to be at home and hasn't gone to work in days."

Msti had also continued to avoid answering my calls or texts. Now, I was distinctly worried about my friend.

"Shit. Do you think that Russian got her?" I asked.

"Do you think that?"

I pressed my lips into a thin line and said nothing.

"If she contacts you, I want you to get in touch with me immediately."

I nodded. I pointed at his tablet. "So what did Rogov, or whatever, do after he got thrown out of the army for being an asshole to the Abkhaz?"

Julian coughed. "Well, among other things, he changed his name."

"To what?"

"To Volkov. Viktor Petrovich Volkov. I guess he thought it went with his new profession."

"What's that?"

Julian smiled. "In Russian, 'volkov' means wolf. He's a hit man for the Russian mob."

— 19 —

The Prodigal Daughter

♂

When Julian was gone, I couldn't find Goom. I called him.

"Yo."

"Hey, Goom-boy. Where you guys at?"

"Chin's, dipshit. Where else would I be?"

"Okay. Well, how am I supposed to get there? Both my vehicles are in the burned-out husk of my house in Decatur."

"Take the bike. Keys are in the shop, under the forge, southeast corner."

"We have a bike? Where is it?"

"In the shed."

"We have a shed?"

* * *

Shortly, I rolled up the door to the shed.

"Oh . . . wow."

When Goom had said "bike," I had envisioned pedals and a D-lock. Instead, the keys I held in my hand were to a vintage Kawasaki 900. I couldn't believe it. The thing was custom-painted jet-black and purred like a panther. I burned out of the parking lot and took myself the long way to Chin's. As usual, a sullen Asian in a white cap and apron stood smoking at the back entrance. I parked, hung up my helmet, and went over.

"Howdy," I said to him.

He nodded curtly, and I passed him and went into the kitchen. Another similarly surly Asian was chopping vegetables. When he saw me, he pulled a 9mm from the drawer beside him. I froze, arms out.

Behind me, the smoker barked a quick word in Mandarin. The vegetable preparer dropped the gun back into the drawer and returned to his work, ignoring me. Cautiously, I passed the gun-toting, carrot-chopping employee and pushed through the swing doors into the main room. Goom was one of a handful of patrons in the large dining room. He sat at a four-seater near the kitchen, in a corner. I sat down catercorner from him.

"So do all the kitchen staff pull guns on people here?"

"If they're ass-ugly as you, sure. Where's your sister?"

"Sleeping."

"Sleeping? It's not even noon."

"Yeah. Filling Agent Bead in on all your secrets really wiped her out."

His upper lip curled toward his nose. "Asshole."

A shadow appeared at my side—Guan Ho in full Wax Man getup.

He said, "Help you, my son?"

I laughed. I looked to Goom. "What're we having?"

"Special, jerky. Always the special."

I folded my hands on the table before me. "Special, please."

Wax-Man nodded and slid back to the kitchen.

"Interesting place you got here. If this is the lunch rush, how does this place stay in business?"

"It's a front for the *sanerhui,* you clueless wonder."

"The what now?"

"*Sanerhui.* The Chinese mob, numbnuts."

I looked around. A table of seemingly ordinary Asian businessmen was enjoying a raucous meal. Near the front, a couple of skinny Asians in suits were reading newspapers.

I lowered my voice. “Those guys are all mobsters?”

“Everyone in here is, you dumb shit.”

“Should I be scared?”

“Not unless you’re planning on waving a gun around.”

“I guess I won’t then.”

* * *

The special was a single plate of delectable food with green tea on the side. I devoured it.

Goom watched me eat for a couple of minutes. “So what’d Bead have to say for himself?”

“The Blond Smoker I—I mean, my sister—saw.”

“What about him?”

“He’s a Russian. His name is Viktor Volkov. They call him the Wolf.”

Goom hid his face behind a hand. “Shit. He’s bad news.”

“You know him?”

He grunted. “We know of him. But how’d you find out? What’d your sister do? Polish Bead’s knob under the table?”

“No, asshole, he just told her. People do that.”

Goom lowered his head and stared at me from under a heavy brow. “You’re telling me an FBI agent told your sister information on an active case. What else can she get him to tell her?”

“It’s just a name, Goom-boy. Julian’s not on the take or anything.”

“Of course not. I’m sure he’s completely and totally legit.”

"So what's the deal between you and Jack?"

"What?"

"Well, you're gay, but I never see you guys kiss or hug or whatnot."

He sneered. "We're not real overt about that crap, shit-monkey."

"Right. So it doesn't bother you he's engaged to a woman?"

Goom scoffed.

"What does that mean? You guys have one of those mythical open relationships? Or, you're an old married couple whose dicks withered to dust?"

He groped himself. "Wither this, prick."

I sighed. "Simmer down, little buddy. I'm just curious."

"Do not call me that. Call me that again and I'll shoot you."

"Why do you guys stay together?"

"What?"

"You and Jack. He kind of treats you like crap, you know."

"No, he doesn't."

"He orders you around. That'd make sense if you're bottom to his top."

"Shut it with the gay stuff, dickmonger."

"How do you know Jack?"

"We've known each other since we were kids, jackass. Our relationship is not up for discussion with the likes of you. We've saved each other's lives countless times. Not that you'd understand."

"Don't be so defensive, little buddy."

"I told you to stop calling me that, you pussyfart."

"Why, you like mini-dork better? How about half-pint or toe-nibbler?"

"Shut the hell up, bitch."

"Ankle-biter knee-high shrimp-nuts—"

"Sounds like you two are really hitting it off today." It was Jack. And with him was the most beautiful woman I had ever seen in my life. She had bright blue eyes shaped like narrow teardrops and jet-black hair. She wore a black leather coat and blue jeans, her svelte figure apparent beneath the material. Her delicate features had settled into a slight frown, which served to highlight the plumpness of her lips.

I had never seen blue eyes on an Asian before. The effect was stunning to me. A giddiness rose in my gut, and I realized my brother's body was thoroughly attracted to the woman on sight. I had no idea that the feeling could be that strong. I managed to shut my flapping mouth and stand up, knocking my chair over behind me. I extended my hand.

"Hello, there. I'm Ethan."

The woman looked at my hand, didn't shake it, and instead sat down stiffly and glared at the tabletop. I picked up my chair, and we all sat. Wax Man came over and dropped off a fresh pot of tea.

"So," I said to Jack. "Where'd you go?"

He frowned. "I was bailing Paige out of jail."

"Oh." I looked at Paige. "Sorry."

She nodded slightly, eyes on her teacup. A crimson hue spread across her high cheeks.

"What were you in for?"

She shot me a furious glance. "Trespassing."

Goom said, "Yeah, she's a cat burglar. Dresses up in a black-and-gold suit and steals shit from rich people. Only she doesn't give it to the poor or anything. She just keeps it."

"You shut your mouth," Paige told him.

A black-and-gold suit? I wondered if Paige had anything to do with the hospital murder of the two cops. "You're a cat burglar? And a murderer?"

"You shut up too," she hissed.

"Oh. Um. Sorry."

Jack said something to Paige in Mandarin. She blushed deeper. She picked up her teacup and then smacked it down hard on the table, making all of us jump. She stood, spoke an angry few words to Jack in Mandarin, then stalked off toward the front exit. I watched her head up the aisle and push through the glass door. Something about the sashay of the woman's hips had me tingling. I shook my head. Apparently, Ethan's body was determined to lust for women, in spite of its new owner.

Goom scoffed. "Paige is really grateful you bailed her out, huh?"

Jack said nothing.

I said, "Who is she?"

Goom raised his eyebrows. "She's the spitting image of her dad, you moronic sack-of-piss."

"Her dad? Do I know him?"

Goom laughed.

Jack said quietly, "He's at this table."

I stared at Jack. "Oh, fuck me. You have a daughter? You're gay."

He frowned but remained silent.

Goom chortled heartily. "You are so dumb it hurts."

My eyes narrowed. "You two aren't actually gay, are you?"

Jack looked at Goom, who rolled his eyes. "No, fucknugget, we're not. You're the one who came up with that. We just let you believe it."

My brow furrowed. "You called him 'hon' when I first met you."

"What? I did not."

"I'm sure you did."

"Maybe I said 'hong'?"

"What's that mean?"

"Red."

"Why would you call Jack red?"

Goom sighed. "It's a long story. Forget about it, dipshit."

"Sure thing, little buddy."

"Do not call me that. Ever again."

"No problem, little buddy."

Goom's eyes narrowed. "I can hack your bank accounts."

"I'm dead, Goom-boy. How are you going to hack what I don't have?"

Jack said, "He's got you there, Gumbah Sarbloh."

I stuck my tongue out at Goom.

He opened his mouth, no doubt to start a tirade at me, but Jack cut him off. "Paige was arrested trespassing at one of Shun Yan's warehouses. She was caught on surveillance camera a week ago but only arrested today." He looked at me. "Presumably at a word from your friend, Bead."

"You think Julian had your daughter arrested? Why?"

"To get me away from your sister. What did they talk about?"

I told Jack about the photo lineup and that I'd gotten the name "Viktor Volkov" from Julian.

Jack frowned deeply. "If the Wolf is here, more death will follow."

"Great. So what do we do now? Are we going to go check out that warehouse? Goom asked.

"Yes. Before that, however, I need to speak with someone."

I sipped my tea. "Who?"

"Shun Yan's uncle. The warehouse is ultimately his. I want to find out how much he knows about all of this."

— 20 —

Dragon

♀

Jack couldn't get an appointment with Shun Yan's uncle until the following day. Brilliant sun reflected off the shiny Jeep Wrangler Jack had borrowed from Captain Pike again. I was in a silky, sleeveless shift dress in purple. The clunky chain hanging at my neck didn't go with my simple outfit or delicate collarbones, but I had been wearing Ethan's pendant constantly since I'd found it, and now I found it disturbing if I didn't have the weight of its reassuring presence.

My eyes widened as we pulled up to the ornate wrought-iron front gate of a nauseatingly large estate on the eastern edge of Buckhead. Jack said a quick word to the camera in the call box. I didn't hear a response, but presently the gate started to roll back.

"Wow. Shun Yan's uncle must be loaded."

Jack gave no response, his expression opaque under his mirrored sunglasses. I got the impression he wasn't looking forward to our meeting.

The long drive circled around an excessively large fountain, and we were met at the top by a couple of somber-faced Asians in dark suits. The two men were obviously bodyguards. I caught a glimpse of two more looking down at us from the second-floor balconies. One had an assault weapon in full view. I cringed. Jack took my hand and led me into the mansion.

Inside, the floor of the cathedral-ceilinged entryway was polished marble, and a wide staircase swept upward to a railinged, open landing. I was worried I might get a nosebleed from the cavernous foyer alone. I could hardly wait to see the rest of the house. Another Asian in a dark suit with a tasteful green tie came to greet us. He bowed deeply to Jack, who lowered his head in return. I was relieved to see no machine gun in evidence, but I figured Green Tie probably had something tucked into his suit.

I smiled at Green Tie. "We come in peace."

He returned my smile with an inflectionless, "Yes. But I'm afraid I must ensure you are unarmed."

This last he said to Jack, who raised his arms. The two goons who had met us patted Jack down. They glanced at me but showed no sign of touching me. I thought their inspection of Jack was pointless machismo. His hands were at least as lethal as any firearm, but I didn't suppose they'd cut those off. As far as that went, I could have hidden a lot under my dress.

Green Tie said, "One moment, please. I will inform Pii Jiang Li you're here." He moved away from us and took out his smartphone.

"Who's Piyan Lee," I asked Jack quietly.

He inhaled sharply. "Please, do not attempt his name like that."

I covered my mouth with a hand. "What did I say?"

"You called him Asshole Li."

"Oh, shit. Sorry."

Green Tie had finished talking on his smartphone and moved toward us again. Before he could speak, he was interrupted by a loud, lilting voice issuing from the staircase.

"Well, well, well. Look who's come to kiss Li's ass. Got your latest conquest with you too, I see."

The five of us stared stupidly at the queen-like woman descending the stairs. She was tall, very leggy, and blond. She wore a slinky, shimmering dress that barely came past her ass. Her hair was teased into a stylish bouffant, and she sported jewelry that, if it was real, would probably be worth more than my house. As she neared, it became clear she was older than her posture and poise promised, but she was still exceptionally sexy. I found myself blushing at the woman's tone.

When the woman got to us, she held her arm straight out, limp wristed. I thought it was for kissing, but Jack didn't take it. Instead, he bowed his head low and said, "Good afternoon, Sara."

She looked me up and down, then turned to Jack with a seductive smile that barely touched her cold blue eyes. "Your taste in women doesn't seem to have improved with time."

My mouth dropped open. The woman's demeanor became even more spiteful and sarcastic as she snarled a command in Mandarin to Green Tie. He bowed low and swept his hand toward the entrance behind them.

"Useless imbecile." She stalked out the door. Before it closed, I caught the Maserati convertible she was headed toward.

I shook with chagrin. I whispered to Jack, "Who was that?"

His eyes were ablaze with restrained hatred. "My ex-wife."

* * *

Green Tie led us through an archway at the far end of the entrance hall into a large, high-ceilinged living room. Sumptuous leather sofas and chairs opposed a gigantic lit fireplace, and one wall of the room was entirely covered with French doors, most of which stood open to admit the afternoon breeze. We crossed the room and exited onto a wide, stone-floored terrace. Beyond us, an expansive lawn and glistening swimming pool were flanked by manicured hedges. Late-blooming flowers and colorful trees grew everywhere, and the air was heavy with the musty scent of earthen bounty. Down a short snaking path we came to a six-car garage that abutted a wide driveway winding back around the main house.

I was still reeling from Jack's pronouncement and felt vaguely as if the landscape were a dream.

I whispered between gritted teeth, "Why didn't you tell me you had an ex-wife? And a daughter, for that matter?"

Jack was silent, his expression one of dismay.

We climbed a staircase on the narrow side of the garage, and Green Tie held open a plain wooden door at the top. After we entered, it took my eyes a few moments to adjust to the darkness after the brilliance outside. It was a simple apartment. Thin walls delineated a living space, kitchen, and bathroom. All was clean but spartan. I peeked through a partially open door and saw a single bed made up in plain white linen.

At the other end of the hall, a door stood open, and I heard scraping noises. We entered a large, well-appointed workshop. A shirtless Asian wearing plastic goggles was carefully running a device over a block of wood, shaving thin slices as he went that curled and dropped to the floor. He was small in stature, perhaps five-five at the most, and slender. Although his scalp was covered in stubble that was entirely gray and his skin hung somewhat limply, he had an agelessness about him and could have been anywhere between fifty and eighty. When he saw us, he lifted the goggles to his well-wrinkled forehead and gave Jack a wide smile. His yellowed and blackened teeth had mostly succumbed to the ravages of time.

"Enforcer," he said. "What a very great pleasure. And, at last, I get to meet your beautiful fiancee."

I felt myself crimson as the man took my hand and brought it to his lips. Afterward, Jack bowed deeply, and the man returned the bow in kind. I bowed my head as well, as it seemed like an appropriate response.

The woodworker eyed me keenly. He had the same black irises as Jack, and his eyes were equally inscrutable. He nodded. "Judith Gold," he said in a heavily accented lilt. I figured Jack must have told the woodworker about me, since I couldn't remember my name being mentioned to anyone.

"Hello, um. . . " I had no clue what to call the man. Jack had clearly warned me off using my pronunciation of his name.

"Why don't you refer to Xiansheng Pii as 'Dragon,' " Jack said.

I bowed briefly. "Hello, Dragon."

Dragon returned my bow with a smile. Then he turned to Jack. "To what is owed the distinct honor of your company this fine day?"

Jack lapsed into Mandarin and spoke some quiet phrases. Of course I couldn't understand a word.

Dragon chuckled at me.

"Your future husband wishes to know where my stepdaughter has been this last week."

"Your stepdaughter?" I asked.

"Paige," Jack said.

Dragon clucked his tongue. "I can only say that as her former father, he must be very aware of the problems of keeping track of the young lady."

It took me several moments to unwind that. Jack's ex-wife must have been married to Dragon now, so that Paige was Dragon's stepdaughter.

Jack bowed his head. "I'm afraid I must ask your forgiveness, Dragon."

The man waved his hand. "Yes, yes. Say what you have come to say. There are no secrets among us."

Jack took a deep breath. "Was Major Fairholme assassinated?"

My mouth dropped open. I studied our bare-chested, easygoing host. I couldn't see him as a mob boss, but what else would explain Jack's question and his deep deference? Or, a title as esteemed as *Dragon*?

Dragon moved to Jack and placed a hand lightly on his arm. "Walk with me, Enforcer. Let us discuss this on a stroll through my gardens. They are exceptionally beautiful in the fall."

I moved to follow but Green Tie, who had been practically invisible until then, interceded.

Dragon turned back to me. "Young lady, perhaps you will do my faithful deputy, Suhn Yihxian, the honor of accepting tea with him."

Green Tie bowed low. "Please. Call me Sam."

* * *

Some time later, Jack and I were back in the Jeep. My tea with Sam had been less than eventful; he was as much an indecipherable mute as Jack. As we cruised away from Buckhead's manicured estates and white-washed mansions, I asked, "Did you get anything from Dragon?"

Jack glanced at me. The mirrored sunglasses were back, as was his perennial poker face. "If Paige was at the hospital last week it was not at Dragon's behest."

"So Paige didn't kill those cops?"

"I find it highly unlikely she did."

"That means there are two women in black-and-gold super suits?"

"It would seem that way."

"I bet if I'd heard her speak, she would have had a Russian accent."

"That would be a good bet to place."

"So where does that leave us?"

We went under a bridge and a brief shadow crossed Jack's pale face. "Next we'll check out Shun Yan's warehouse."

"The one Paige was caught trespassing at?"

"Yes. Your friend Agent Bead must have known Dragon would not be pressing charges, but the fact he had the surveillance video in the first place means the warehouse is a place of interest for the FBI."

"Meaning it is also a place of interest for us."

"Exactly."

— 21 —

Warehouse

♂

That night Jack and I were in the White Room gearing up for our incursion into Shun Yan's warehouse. While I loaded the 9mm Jack gave me, he went to the far wall, reached up, and pressed an invisible panel. Part of the wall gave way to reveal a sectioned door, neatly disguised by shelf supports on both sides. He pulled it just far enough for us to get through, then flicked a switch, illuminating a narrow passageway nestled in the house frame above open earth.

"Come with me, Ethan."

"Where does it go?"

"You'll see."

He beckoned, and we moved to the end of the hall where we stepped through an archway into a hushed, darkened room. I realized with a start that we must be in the ground, completely covered by the rising earth alongside the house. Jack moved to the center of the room and pulled a cord hanging from the ceiling. Light flooded us.

"Holy shit."

Jack bowed slightly. Around us, steel shelving held crates and boxes of ammunition and assault gear. That, in itself, was impressive, but what really got my eye were the two suits arrayed on life-sized mannequins in front of them. One was jet-black; the other was black with red piping.

"This is the *Black* Room."

Jack went to one of the shelves and removed a box. Inside was a nasty looking .45.

I gently traced the red piping on the second suit with my fingertips.

"This one has red trim. What does it mean? Why is it different?"

Jack was loading his gun. He took a deep breath.

"It is interesting you have come to me now, at this point in my life, when I am. . . remaking myself."

"Remaking yourself? From what into what?"

"Into Hong Ying."

"What's that?"

"Red Hawk."

"Okay. From what?"

He frowned. "From something distinctly more sinister."

More sinister. That was hard for me to imagine.

"Our friend, Dragon, calls me Enforcer, you know."

I stared at him. He was obviously trying to tell me something, but I wasn't getting it. He was Batman going through a midlife crisis? I said, "Well, Red Hawk definitely makes you sound cuddlier than Enforcer."

He was silent.

I looked around at the military-grade equipment arrayed before us.

"This is damn impressive."

"We own every piece in the White Room legally. These," he indicated the wares stacked in shadow around us, "not so much."

* * *

The moon was an angry orange disk, partially eclipsed by gathering clouds, when we rendezvoused with Jack's man Davis three blocks from Shun Yan's warehouse in a small gravel parking lot. Jack wore his red-and-black supersuit, and I wore the all-black one. It fit my brother's body well, and Jack assured me it would stop most bullets, or at least slow them down a good bit. Both of us had large waist packs to carry our weapons and other gear.

Davis was a big black guy with a bandage over his nose. I recognized him as the man I had head-butted on the porch in Decatur when I was fleeing the Russians.

"Um. Sorry about the nose," I told Davis.

He nodded. "S'alright. You didn't know, man."

Jack cleared his throat. "Report."

Davis stood ramrod straight. "Been some activity. Sedan filled with white guys unloaded four Russians. They took out the guard house and the surveillance equipment."

"That was convenient."

Davis nodded. "Close on their heels, a van filled with Asians unloaded three, plus the girl in the suit. FBI's watching everything over yonder." He jerked his head south.

"The FBI?" It seemed my voice rose an octave. "They can't see me."

They both ignored me. Davis said, "You be needing backup, sir?"

"Perimeter. Report further incomings channel four."

Davis nodded and disappeared into the underbrush.

I gulped. "You sure you want to bring me, Sensei? I'm, uh, not real versed in this kind of thing."

Jack must have seen my fidgeting fingers and pale face. He frowned. "You have to learn sometime, Ethan."

* * *

We sprinted across a dark alley and made our way through tangled underbrush to the warehouse. We watched the back door for several minutes. No one entered or left. The yard contained several rows of truck trailers and seemed equally devoid of movement. We moved quickly around the trailers and positioned ourselves on either side of the door, Jack on the opening side and me on the hinge side. At his signal, I reached over and turned the door handle. It gave readily.

Jack slid through the opening, gun first. I shadowed him, making sure the door made no sound when it closed. We entered a cavernous, dimly lit storage space. It was two stories high and dozens of feet wide. Massive steel shelving held countless wooden pallets that held what appeared to be shrink-wrapped, folded apparel in shades of gray, blue, and green. On the shelf next to us some of the plastic had torn and I fingered the cloth inside.

"What are these?" I whispered.

Jack's masked face contemplated mine. "Military."

"Uniforms?"

He nodded.

"Is that significant?"

"Shun Yan Pii ran a supply network for military apparel. It would be more significant if it were prom dresses."

I snorted. Jack put a finger to his mask where his lips were.

A droning whine intruded on our conversation. A forklift? We ducked behind the shelves. The sound was so distant I thought it must be outside, but as I listened, I realized it was actually inside, near the front of the warehouse. The sound was almost swallowed by the vast amount of fabric in the intervening space.

Jack signaled: him right, me left. As I turned, hugging the shelves beside me, my foot hit something squishy. I looked down. I gasped.

Jack spun at my sharp intake of breath and quickly returned. There was an ankle, attached to a brown shoe, sticking out from a tarp on the floor. Jack knelt and gingerly lifted the crinkly material. Between furtive glances at our surroundings, I looked at the two dead men underneath. Even a neophyte could tell they had been shot multiple times.

I felt the blood drain from my face. "Shit."

Jack put his finger to his lips and resettled the tarp without a sound.

My heart beat wildly against my ribcage. Climbing buildings, fist fighting, and swinging through trees were one thing; facing an unknown number of murderous gunmen was something entirely different. Last time I'd done that I'd managed to get myself shot and it was very unpleasant.

Jack motioned again for us to split up and reconnoiter, but I went the same direction, hugging his back. He stopped and faced me. He jerked his arm out, clearly indicating I should go the opposite direction.

My voice was a hoarse whisper. "No, I'm not splitting up."

He stared at me for a moment. I thought he was probably wondering why, again, did he bring this useless ninny with him instead of one of Captain Pike's mercs. Then he nodded slightly and headed up the aisle closest to us.

We passed a cross aisle halfway up the space, and the forklift drone drew nearer. We turned and walked down the cross aisle. When we were almost to the east wall, we caught sight of the forklift and ducked into the nearest aisle. Jack poked his head out to look, and I got down on my knees and peeked around under him. The forklift sped by the end of the aisle, barely screeching to a stop before the outside wall, then it spun around and raced back the other way. The operator whooped loudly, oblivious.

After the forklift disappeared, Jack and I raced to the front of the aisle and peeked around. Two Asian youths in baggy jeans and colorful T-shirts stood near a hall leading to a staircase. One was fiddling with a smartphone. The other was pacing and smoking a cigarette. Phone Boy had a nasty-looking rifle slung over his shoulder. Cigarette Boy had a large, protruding handgun tucked into the waistband of his jeans.

As Jack and I watched, the forklift came speeding up to the young men, nearly spearing Cigarette Boy, who yelled and made a rude gesture to its occupant, also a young Asian man. I only caught a glimpse of the driver. He laughed at his companions, spun wildly, and took off for the far side of the front area again.

"Who is that?" I whispered.

Jack inclined his head slightly toward the forklift occupant. "That's Dragon's nephew."

"Shun Yan? I thought he died."

"His other nephew, Jun Lo."

"Ah."

Jack pulled me to standing. I had my gun out and at the ready, but he put his hand over it, pushing it down. "No guns."

"No guns?" I tucked it away. "Well then, what do we do now?"

Jack faced me. I couldn't see his gaze beneath the mask, but I squirmed under its implicit intensity. Suddenly, he gripped my shoulders.

"Why don't you go say 'hi'?"

Before I could react, he shoved me—hard—and I was suddenly in the direct line of sight of the two idling Asians.

"Hey!" I said loudly.

When I spun back around, Jack had disappeared.

The two youths had turned and were yelling at me by that time in Mandarin. Slowly, I raised my hands and backed away down the aisle. They followed. There was a silly smile underneath my mask—all the more silly because, of course, they couldn't see it. My heart pounded and sweat wet the back of my neck.

"Uhh. . . howdy gents." I expected to be riddled with bullets any second.

Cigarette Boy smirked, showing off yellowed teeth. "Harrow," he said, also showing off a thick accent. "You stay. Stay dere." He walked toward me, drawing his handgun for emphasis.

In Cigarette Boy's wake, Phone Boy followed, fumbling with the strap of his rifle. He still had his phone in the other hand.

Suddenly, Jack dropped on them from the shelves, knocking Cigarette Boy down with a solid kick to the head. Phone Boy was unwilling to let go of his phone to get a proper grip on his rifle. Jack smacked the phone from his hand, and the boy spun around to see where it went. Jack folded him in a clean sleeve-lock, making him pass out almost immediately. As Phone Boy hit the floor, the forklift neared, racing toward us. I ran back to the cross aisle and dove behind the end of the shelves. Before I was out of sight, I glimpsed Jack ascending rapidly toward the roof.

The forklift stopped and idled. Someone yelled over it, barking short unintelligible syllables that could have been names. After several moments of silence, the voice called again, distinctly nearer.

"Guys? Where the fuck are you—"

I heard the man swearing, then nothing but the forklift's engine. After a brief pause, Jack's voice came to me.

"Ethan, you can come out now."

Jack turned off the forklift, glancing back at the three bound, gagged, and angry-as-hell Asians. At the base of the showroom wall were two more Caucasian corpses to go with the two under the tarp near the back door. Jack and I ducked into the front hall and came to a choice. We could go north into the showroom at the front of the warehouse or up the stairs to the offices above.

Jack paused. The building was silent. The four white guys Davis had mentioned had obviously been killed by the Asians Jack felled. There was no sign of whatever "girl in the suit" Davis had been referring to, most likely Paige, I thought.

Jack studied me. "Are you still too scared to be by yourself, or can we split up now?"

I flushed beneath my mask. "I can't believe you threw me into the line of fire. What the hell was that?"

He paused for a moment before responding. "You're in a bullet proof suit. I knew I'd get them before they killed you." I could have sworn I heard a slight jollity in his next word. "Probably."

"What?!"

He slapped me on the back and headed through the archway to the showroom. He pointed up the stairs. "You go that way."

I knew Jack would never have been so careless with me if I were in my female body. It was hard for me to get used to this aspect of being male. Everyone expected you to fend completely for yourself, and they enforced that by treating you as expendable. It was impossible to show fear. Jack ignored it, or worse, he tried to beat it out of me. It seemed there were some aspects of being male that weren't so fun after all.

"Damn it," I whispered.

I steeled myself with a deep breath and went up the dark stairs. At the top there were two rooms. Both had thick steel doors with reinforced windows. On my left, the room was dark. I tried the handle, but it was locked. On my right, the room was lit. In hindsight, I should have been warier. As it was, I pushed open the door and walked right in.

The room contained three long aisles of black metal cabinets, almost ceiling height, resembling gym lockers. The floor beneath my feet seemed to be white rubber and had little holes all over it. The north wall opposite the door had three industrial-sized cooling fans, all silent. Several cabinets were ajar. I pulled the nearest one open. It was empty, except for a computer cable abandoned at the bottom.

I moved west, to the front of the room, and pulled back a corner of the window blinds to peek out. Streetlights illuminated an empty parking lot. The guard booth at the warehouse gate was vacant. I contemplated the motionless wall fans on my right. A crisp breeze flowed, winding through the aisles of empty cabinets. In spite of the draft, I imagined it would be sweltering in here if all the racks were filled with running computers.

I checked randomly inside the nearest row of cabinets. The first two lockers I looked at were empty. The third was full of shelves about every three inches. I slid one of the shelves out. It contained a metal box. I opened the lid. Inside, molded gold-colored foam contained an array of thirty-two little holes. All the holes were empty except for tiny metal pegs peeking out from their center. The pegs weren't sharp; they were more like something to hold whatever got inserted into the box.

"Hm."

I pulled out the rest of the shelves. All contained the metal boxes with thirty-two holes. I looked more closely at one of the boxes. Its lid contained the same squishable, dense foam on the underside, and I saw thirty-two circular indents where the holes would be when the box was closed. Some indents had subtle patterns left over from whatever had pressed against them. I thought I recognized a tiny anchor and the wing of a bird.

I decided to try to take one of the boxes to show Goom. It was screwed into the shelf and hooked in to the back of the rack with a fat computer cable. I searched around in my waistpack for something that might work as a screwdriver.

Whump.

I whirled, gun out and ready to shoot. No one. The sound had been faint, inarticulate and short-lived. Had I imagined it? I crept to the wall of fans and peeked east down the aisle. At the end, a monitor, keyboard, and mouse sat on a small desk with a large computer tower underneath it. I approached slowly, gun first. The computer monitor was blank, either sleeping or off. I tucked my gun back into my waist pack and crouched in front of the desk, squinting into the darkness underneath. There was a thumb drive hanging off one of the desktop's USB ports. I pocketed it.

Click.

I froze. That had been right next to my ear. Something solid was pressed to my temple. A familiar female voice spoke quietly yet clearly.

"Don't move."

It was Paige, I thought. I stood, slowly, raising my hands and turning toward Paige as I did. She didn't blow my head off, which I took as encouraging. Instead, she stepped back, leveling the gun at my chest. She was in a black supersuit like mine, except hers had gold trim and accents, and she wasn't wearing her mask. Her long black hair and piercing blue eyes gave me an unwelcome thrill.

Paige sneered. "Who the fuck are you supposed to be? Batman?"

"Batman has little ears on his mask."

She craned her neck back and forth to get a better look at my headgear. "No ears. Okay, then, No Ears, give me one good reason not to blow your head off right now."

The gun she pointed at me looked like a .22. I thought I could handle a .22 to the chest. Or so I hoped. I responded with as much confidence as I could muster. "Give me one good reason not to dump you on your ass."

Paige snorted. "Just try it, No Ears."

"Not a good reason."

Before Paige could blink twice, I popped the gun from her hand and shoved her, hard. She careened backward and fell on her ass. I was rewarded with some choice Mandarin swearing.

I theatrically unloaded the gun, arcing the cartridge through the air and catching it with my other hand. I snapped the breach back to eject the last round, then threw the whole kit at Paige's feet. Awesome. I thought I really looked like a tough guy. Now as long as I didn't follow it up by falling on my face, maybe Paige would believe I was a match for her.

Paige sat where I had thrown her, seething mad. I moved toward her. Belatedly, it occurred to me I should search her. Before I could get close enough, she whipped out a gun from her leg holster and pulled the trigger.

Bam!

It was like being punched really, really hard in the chest by a very small but extremely fast-moving fist. The wind left my lungs, and I doubled over, toppling onto Paige. Paige sprawled beneath my weight, swearing and yelling at me as I caught my breath.

"Get off me, you stupid loser!"

I managed to roll off her into the narrow corridor between the tall racks and the wall fans. I pulled myself to my feet as Paige twisted and brought the gun up to shoot again.

Bam! Bam!

Paige's bullets zinged by and embedded in the steel lockers. I ran down the aisle toward the door, fumbling with my waist pack to get my own gun out. Paige leaped into the aisle, and I shot the ground at her feet, sending her back toward the computer desk.

I heard Paige run down the aisle toward the exit. I got there first and cut her off with a warning shot. Paige screamed, returning fire. We both turned and raced back down our respective aisles, toward the fans.

I poked my head out and almost got it shot off as Paige rounded the cabinets. I shot back. Paige took off down her aisle toward the door again. I whirled and ran similarly down my aisle.

"Paige, stop shooting at me!"

"No! You stop shooting at me, asshole!"

Once again, we met near the door and cut each other off with opposing gunfire. Then, again, we both ran back toward the fans, matching each other's speed. At the fans, Paige fired wildly, and I shot the ground near where I thought Paige would be. Paige swore viciously.

"I guess we can keep this up all day, if you want," I yelled.

"*Quh chi dan biahn!* Give me back my thumb drive, you jerk!"

At that moment, Jack yelled, "Mhei-Mhei!" It sounded like he was in the room, probably in Paige's aisle near the door. Shots followed, echoing off the metal lockers.

Jeez. Did Paige just shoot at her dad? I turned in time to see Jack leap into my aisle. He rolled, then flattened himself against the cabinets beside me as more bullets ricocheted around the room.

As the last pop faded, I turned to him. "Your daughter's trying to kill us, Jack. What did you do to her?"

He faced me, unreadable beneath his mask. He rested a hand on my arm. "No guns."

"You've got to be shitting me. She's the one shooting at us."

He said nothing. Paige made no detectable sound or movement.

"Is she gone?" I whispered.

At that moment, Paige jumped out at the fan end of our aisle, gun brandished. She screeched something in Mandarin and pulled the trigger. I threw my hands over my head.

Click. Click. Click.

Jack was on Paige in an instant, snatching the gun from her hand. She screamed at him in Mandarin, trying to punch his daylights out. He blocked her strikes, then slapped her. Not hard, but it shut her up. He grabbed her shoulders and shook her. "What are you doing here?"

"Fuck you! Give me back my thumb drive. Where's Jun Lo?"

She stamped her heel down, almost catching Jack's instep. As he shifted his weight to compensate, she sucker-smacked him, catching him clean in the groin with an unexpected thrust. He doubled over, and she whipped around in a 360-degree circle with her fist out, whacking him in the head and knocking him against the steel racks.

She bolted.

I was stunned. I couldn't believe Jack's tiny daughter had practically beaten him up. I gaped stupidly at Jack as he regained his balance.

"Don't just stand there," he said, "cut her off!"

I raced to the end of the aisle, emerging as Paige was launching herself through the doorway.

"Shit, Jack, she—"

A whistling interrupted me. It sounded familiar. An image of University Hospital right before the bombing flashed through my mind. I froze.

Jack yelled, "Incoming!" He threw himself at me and knocked us both past the doorway.

Wuff!

An explosion ate the air around us. The blast blew the door across the stair landing clean off its hinges. It warped and scraped through our doorway with such force that the nearest rack buckled in its wake, leaving a glob of burning steel blocking the doorway.

I stared at the twisted metal behind us. "Jack, th-the door's burning!"

"Mhei-Mhei!" he yelled.

The radio on Jack's hip crackled. Davis's voice came through a barrier of static: *Colonel ... surrounded ... police—*

Jack grabbed the transmitter. "Retreat! All hands. Retreat!"

We dropped to the floor and scrambled to the windowed wall overlooking the main warehouse floor, ending up at the computer desk. Fire crackled, and smoke filled the air above us. We were trapped.

I coughed acrid particles from my lungs. "We're totally screwed. And what's 'may-may' anyway? Is that Mandarin for 'stop shooting at us'?"

Jack sighed. "Mhei-Mhei is her given name."

"That's—"

The entire building shuddered as another of whatever-the-hell-that-was exploded near the south wall of the inventory floor. When the shaking stopped, I could hardly breathe. The air around us was opaque with sweltering radiation. The walls on the door side of our room were sagging, and the paint seemed, amazingly, to be melting off. I peeked through the window above me. The southern half of the warehouse was almost entirely engulfed in flames.

"Holy crap. Jack, what do we do?"

He seemed unbelievably calm in the face of disaster. He reached under the desk, dragged the computer tower out, and hefted it into the air.

"What are you—"

He hurled it into the nearest window. The glass shattered. The computer smashed to smithereens amid raining shards on the concrete below. The building shook with another explosion, nearly knocking us off our feet.

"Come on." Jack leaped onto the top of the desk.

I was coughing. My lungs were clogged. "What? No. No!"

Jack launched himself through the broken window, landing cleanly about ten feet below and rolling expertly. He ran to the northernmost aisle next to the loading bays, where I saw Paige struggling with Jun Lo's bindings.

"Ah, crap."

I jumped out after Jack, landing well and executing a neat roll about where he had. I scrambled to my feet, but they were tangled in the computer innards and I fell on my face. "Shit!"

Paige screamed at Jack. He whipped out his big knife, unfolded it, and sliced the men's zip-ties off.

Thunk.

I threw my arms over my head.

Wuff!

A tidal wave of hot air blasted over us. After it passed, I watched the entire south wall slide off its frame, opening a gaping maw through which I could see flaming trees beyond. A small secondary explosion dampened all noise around us. In that incongruous moment of peace, a blob of something fell, *splat*, on the floor in front of my face. It sizzled and bubbled and seemed to be burning right through the concrete in front of me. I was sure my heart stopped for a couple of beats.

"Wh-what in the hell can do that?"

The roaring of furious flame renewed. I was lying on the smashed computer. I recognized a hard drive sticking out of a bent dock. On a whim, I tugged at it, but it didn't release. Jun Lo was up on his feet, screaming at Jack, who was fiddling with a huge padlock on the nearest loading bay. Jack had his .45 out and shot at the lock.

The building shook under another explosion, and Jack missed.

I finally loosed the hard drive and shoved it into my waist pack. I struggled to my feet and hobbled over to the group. One of the two youths accompanying Jun Lo grabbed me and started yelling at me in Mandarin. I thought I answered amazingly calmly, considering the world was ending.

"Yeah. Can you yell at me again, in English, but only after we get the fuck out of here?"

Jack shot the lock again. His aim was better, but the padlock didn't give. He swore at it.

Despair flooded me. Then, Paige yelled at us from the next loading bay.

"This one's open, you useless excuse for a father!"

Jack's jaw clenched under his mask. He ran to Paige, ripped the chain from the mooring, and rolled the bay door up.

Everyone froze.

Twenty or so yards away, beyond the rows of shipping containers, about a million cops were arrayed behind cars and barriers. They were in the adjacent lot, but parts of the fence had been knocked down. A police helicopter hovered between the warehouse and the regrouping SWAT lines, its searchlight sweeping the area. Behind us, a loud, protracted crash heralded the fall of another of the floor-to-ceiling shelving units. The warehouse would probably collapse on us any second.

"Ah, crap," I said.

* * *

Did we all stay frozen and throw our hands in the air like good little arrestees? Of course not.

Paige and the three Asians jumped off the loading dock and ran east. Jack and I leaped off simultaneously and ran northwest, diagonally toward the truck trailers. The helicopter seemed to be chasing the others, behind us. Someone picked up a megaphone and yelled at everyone to stop and throw down their weapons.

Jack and I were almost to cover when I heard a whistling *crack*. A hole peeled open in the side of the trailer right in front of us, and a projectile slammed into Jack's chest, knocking him back into me.

"No!" I screamed.

We flew backward and crashed into the tarmac. I rolled, grabbing at Jack. He was moving but didn't seem able to get up.

Something deadly punched the pavement next to us. I grabbed Jack's suit at the shoulders and dragged him toward the rows of semi-trailers. It wasn't far, but Jack weighed around two-forty, even without all of his gear, so I struggled in spite of my brother's strong arms. Another shot echoed as it pierced steel trailer walls nearby. Excruciating moments passed before I finally got us to the cover of the trailers. I pulled desperately at Jack, getting us between two rows and hopefully out of the sniper's line of sight.

Jack seemed to be gagging, and his hands grasped at his chest. "M-mask," he whispered. "M-mask. . . off."

I ripped the black rubbery material from his head. Blood was coming out of his mouth. "Jack. Jack! Oh God. Please, *please* don't die on me."

He nodded, his chin eclipsed by sticky, red fluid. "Take my. . . gear off. All. . . of it."

"Oh jeez." Tears blurred my vision, and I removed my own mask so I could see him better.

He shook his head and took a labored breath. "You need to leave. . . need to take my gear and mask. . . can't be found with them."

I liberated his waist pouches and slung them over my shoulder, then stuffed his mask into my own waist pack.

"Now. . . *go*!"

"No." I wiped my eyes ineffectively with sooty gloves. "I can't leave you." I stripped off one of my gloves and cleared the tears and gunk from my eyes with naked fingers.

Jack glared at me. "*Go*," he reiterated.

"J-Jack."

I found myself caressing his smooth head. I leaned in and pressed my lips to his, ignoring the revulsion creeping through Ethan's gut.

Jack squirmed and turned his face away from my kiss. "No," he said. I pulled back. He stared at me, disgust and astonishment on his face. "*No*!"

I ran my fingers gently down his face and cleared some of the blood from his chin. "It's not what you think," I whispered.

He bucked and smacked me, pushing me away with surprising strength. "*Go!*" he yelled. "Damn you!" His whole body shook as he worked to suppress a series of racking coughs.

I moved back, terrified he was dying right in front of me.

"Go! Now!"

Distant sirens wailed continuously—more law enforcement on the way. Movement caught my eye, and I saw black-clad legs dashing between trailers, only a row to the north of us and closing. They looked like SWAT legs, but I couldn't be sure. I pulled my mask and glove back on and stood. I cast Jack's limp form a last rueful glance, then abandoned him to the chaos.

— 22 —

Captured

♀

The next morning I had to drive two hours through the pouring rain to Fort Gordon where Jack had been transferred from the Atlanta Hall of Justice. My skirt felt too tight, and my shoulderpads were smushed. How was I supposed to appear professional when I was having suit failure?

From the information I'd been given at the military base's front gate, I hoped I was nearing site block A5, the nearest infirmary. I had no clue what I'd do when I got there. Goom had faked legal credentials for me the previous night, but it had been months since I was in law school, and I didn't remember much. I had no trial experience and definitely no military court experience. The idea of a court-martial sent shivers down my spine.

Inside A5, my heels clicked across linoleum, and I tried to shake my umbrella away from myself so I didn't get my skirt wet. An officer with blond hair tucked into her beret waited for me at the reception desk.

"Judith Gold?"

"Yes."

"Warrant Officer Connor. I'm the Colonel's martial counsel, here to liaise with your civilian expertise."

I managed to not laugh out loud at her use of the term *expertise.*

"Right."

"Let's go see him."

* * *

Jack was propped up in a hospital bed, having a whole room to himself. His ribs were bandaged, and I could see breathing gave him some difficulty. Several other people crowded into the room, including Julian. I smiled uncertainly, and he nodded to me, no return smile gracing his lips.

Connor introduced me to everyone. Alicia Fisher was the Fulton ADA. She was a petite, buxom woman with cornrows and dark, smooth skin. Her brown eyes seemed to spark with fiery indignation. A tall man with auburn hair next to Julian was introduced as Officer Dahmiel. He was in a dark suit and blue tie, and I wondered what he was an officer of. He looked government. Finally, a portly, salt-and-pepper-haired gentleman with big lips and dark skin was introduced as Colonel Cox. From the dynamics in the room, I felt like Cox was leading these proceedings.

An anonymous man with caduceus insignia on his fatigues was looking over Jack's chart.

"Doctor, is he all right?" I asked.

"The impact fractured several of his ribs, but no organs were punctured. He'll be fine in a few weeks, but he needs to rest in the meantime."

I thought that was probably like asking a racehorse to keep it to a trot.

Colonel Cox looked at everyone under hooded eyelids. "That'll be all."

The medical man clicked his heels together and left.

Colonel Cox said, "All right. We're here because ADA Fisher requested Lieutenant Colonel Xiah be returned to the jurisdiction of Fulton County."

Fisher spoke up. "There have been not one, not two, but three unprecedented paramilitary attacks on Atlanta in the past weeks."

I wondered briefly at that, then I realized the ADA must be including the firebombing of my house. I felt slightly honored that Fisher put my poor residence on par with a hospital and a big warehouse.

Fisher continued. "Xiah is obviously involved. If he's not handed over, we'll throw the book at him: trespassing, felony arson, and tampering with a crime scene, for starters. After we're done with him, I'm sure our federal counterparts will want to debrief him."

Colonel Cox huffed into his mustache. "And your evidence?"

Fisher handed him a manila folder. Cox considered it.

"What does his counsel say?"

Everyone looked at me. I looked at Connor.

Connor said, "Everything is circumstantial." She turned to Fisher. "Did you actually find anything of substance on his person?"

"His accomplices escaped with the evidence. But we'll catch them. And when we do, I'm sure we'll match the gun he used to bullets at the scene."

I wondered how they'd manage to do that when the scene was a bubbling pile of melted steel.

"You have trespassing. A misdemeanor at most," Connor said.

"The fact remains, Xiah was behind enemy lines during a major criminal attack within city limits. We need his cooperation to stop these assaults. They've killed three of ours already, and who knows how many more will die before these episodes stop?"

Colonel Cox was silent.

Fisher put her hands on her hips. "Come on, Colonel. We all know what's going on."

She was wrong there. I, at least, had no clue.

Cox responded without much consideration. "I'm sorry ADA Fisher. Colonel Xiah is involved in," he paused, as if making this up on the spot, "a delicate and important operation for us. We simply can't give him up on threat of a misdemeanor or two."

Fisher's eyes narrowed. She turned to Jack. "In that case, I must ask Colonel Xiah to come forward of his own accord and help us. How many more of us must die before this stops?"

Jack frowned.

* * *

All the civilian law enforcement left the room leaving just me and the military types. Wait. Had Colonel Cox just winked at me?

"Got yourself a good lawyer, Xiah, as smart as she is gorgeous." His smile was on the lecherous side of friendly.

I blushed and bit my lip. What response should I affect? Flirtatious confidence? Indignant anti-paternalism? I couldn't decide, but Cox saved me the trouble by turning to Jack and ignoring me completely.

"Doc wants you to stay here for a couple days."

"I would prefer to return to the city," Jack said in a raspy croak.

"Of course you would." Cox chuckled. He left the room. As the door swung shut, I caught a glimpse of Julian at a water fountain down the hall.

"So are they letting you come home or what?" I asked Jack.

He nodded.

Connor said, "I'll help him get ready and we'll meet you outside."

* * *

Julian was already outside when I got there, standing with Officer Dahmiel by a large navy SUV that screamed government. They both acknowledged me with nods. The rain had stopped for the moment, but clouds hung thick and threatening over us.

I said to Julian, "So is this your partner?"

Dahmiel smiled.

Julian said, "No, Officer Dahmiel is NCS."

"NCS?"

They exchanged glances. "CIA," Julian said.

My mouth dropped open. "Why is the CIA interested in Jack?"

Dahmiel frowned.

Julian grabbed my arm, steering me away from Dahmiel. "I'll walk you to your car."

Halfway there, he tightened his grip on my arm. "ADA Fisher was really pissed the DOD stole her prime witness, huh?"

"I guess so. You sound pissed too. What does the FBI want with Jack?"

Julian didn't answer. We watched Jack exit the building, supported by Warrant Officer Connor.

Julian's grip softened as he turned to me. The gold in his eyes glittered for a moment as the sun showed through a break in the clouds.

He said in a low voice, "I was hoping you'd let me take you out to dinner. Sort of an apology for my behavior the other day. Also, maybe we can exchange some more information."

"Really? You'd do that?"

He glanced around. "Long as no one else gets wind of it."

I looked at Jack, whose jaw muscles clenched with the exertion of settling himself into the Battle Buick. Thin droplets of sweat appeared on his crown, shadowed with over a day's worth of ebony hair.

Julian's smooth voice brought me back to him. "Judith?"

"Okay, then. Sure. Let's go out."

"I'll pick you up at five."

* * *

Once Jack and I had cleared the base's exit, I breathed my relief into a long sigh. I'd been vaguely afraid someone would change their minds and have us gunned down as fugitives.

"Jeez, Jack. That was freaky. I'm not up to this lying-to-the-authorities stuff. I mean, Goom just faked my credentials last night. I hardly remember my law classes."

"Faked your credentials?" Jack's faux-shock was palpable. "In that case, I'm only paying you half your normal rate."

I chortled, surprised at his easy joviality. "Well, half of zero is still zero, so I guess I haven't really lost any ground there."

He smiled.

"The worst part was when they called you Xiah. I mean, I didn't even know who they were talking about at first."

He chuckled. "I'm sorry we didn't keep you better informed, Judith."

He turned to stare out the window at the gray hills, mottled with oases of stark autumnal color where the leaves hadn't completely fallen. The clouds parted for a minute, and the sun steeped the world in amber, endowing my fiancee with a dreamy bronzed hue that ended in the blackness of his bottomless eyes. I found I couldn't stop glancing at his stark profile.

"Is that your full name? Jack Xiah? They don't go together very well."

"Jack is my father's name. My real name is Xiah Lahngxian."

It was sonorous coming off his lips. I wasn't even going to attempt it.

"It's beautiful. But I'm afraid I'll have to stick with Jack."

He smiled. A subtle ache, an odd self-consciousness, pulsed under my ribcage while he gazed at me. Soon, he faced forward and settled back against the seat. After some moments of silence, I realized his eyes were closed. He slept the whole way home, only opening his eyes again when we pulled up outside the shop.

I touched his bare arm. "Have a good nap?"

He turned at my caress but said nothing for several moments. Then he said, "I'll need to debrief both of you this evening. We have a charge from Colonel Cox."

"Wait." I blinked rapidly. "You mean there actually is a 'delicate and important operation'? I thought Cox was just making that shit up."

"I'm quite certain that if I wasn't in a particular position to be useful, he would have been more than happy to let me rot under whatever charges ADA Fisher desired."

— 23 —

Black Room

♂

I eased myself off of the couch I had been sleeping on. I was sore from last night's exertions, but otherwise none the worse for wear. I was happy I hadn't managed to get Ethan's body seriously injured in all the ruckus.

I came downstairs and saw Goom was at his desk, typing away, his focus on his monitors. Jack sat on the big leather sofa, massaging his temples.

"What up?" I asked.

Goom snorted. "Your sister takes a nap, and you wake up. Gee. What a coincidence."

I yawned, stretching toward the ceiling.

Goom persisted. "How come we never see you and your sister at the same time?"

I stretched my neck, and it cracked loudly. Goom winced. I said, "I'm a vampire, remember? I can only come out at night."

Goom looked toward the sliding glass doors where the late-afternoon sun was peeking through the clouds, steeping Jack's pond in golden light. "It's afternoon, fucknugget."

I shrugged.

Jack had his hands steepled before him. "Where's the gear?"

I tilted my head toward their laundry room. "In there."

"Bring it." Jack stood, slowly. "I will require your assistance."

"All right." I went into the storage room and hefted my backpack, the supersuit Jack had lent me, and both of our loaded waist packs. I shouldered everything and returned to the computer room, where Jack had opened the ornate door leading to the White Room. I followed him inside. He closed the door behind us, moved so his back was against it, and contemplated me in silence. I stopped in the middle of the room and glanced around. Jack didn't seem inclined to continue. I let my gaze drop to the floor and studied the pristine white tile beneath my feet. It didn't take long for the silence to become uncomfortable, not to mention the weight I was holding. I shifted from foot to foot. As the moments passed into the excruciating zone, Jack finally motioned with his head toward the north wall, where I knew the secret door was.

"Third screwhole from the top on the second shelf rod," he said quietly.

I counted and found it with my eyes. "Yeah."

"Punch it."

I resettled all the gear so I had a free arm, walked over, and smacked it. Nothing happened. I looked at Jack.

"I said the second rod. You hit the third."

I looked more closely at the wall. Instead of being a particularly thick shelf support, the second white metal rod nailed to the wall was actually two rods, snugly adjacent. I reached up and tried again, on the outside rod. I heard a click, and the two rods separated, maybe by half an inch. I squeezed my fingers in and pulled. The door came away easily. I saw that the inner shelf rod overlapped the door opening by a quarter inch or so, completely disguising it from sight. I was impressed.

"Neat. But can't anyone who's suspicious just knock around until they get lucky and hit it?"

"No. I have to enter a special code to activate the mechanism. If I enter an abbreviated code, the White Room is accessible, but the hidden door won't respond."

"Oh. Wow."

Jack moved gingerly to the opening and slid through, an injured yet still supple cat. I followed, lagging behind a couple of arm lengths. When I made it to the secret room, Jack was on the other side of the wooden table and had switched the overhead bulb on. Its downward illumination cast most of his face in shadow, emphasizing the darkness of his eyes and the prominence of his brow.

One hand rested on the table. With the other, he pointed to its surface. Dutifully, I laid the gear on the table and pushed it toward the middle so he could easily reach it. I folded my hands behind my back. My bare toes curled against the cold stone floor, and a chilly draft circled my naked torso. I was in pajama pants, nothing more.

Jack reached forward and pulled his waist pouch toward him. He extracted his .45. My heart thudded in my chest as I had an insane split second where I was afraid he might shoot me. A trickle of sweat left my forehead and slid down my cheek. I studied the tabletop intently.

"So, Ethan," Jack said, unloading and stripping his weapon expertly. "We need to discuss your... performance last night."

I grimaced. "Do we have to?"

He paused, his eyes glittering in the harsh light. "Yes."

My gut churned. "I, um... I'm straight. I didn't mean it."

His eyes narrowed. "What?"

"The, um... the kiss." I felt my face burn.

"Oh." He frowned. "I wasn't talking about that."

"You weren't?"

"No."

Mental facepalm.

"But since we're on the subject... "

I winced, closing my eyes. Jack remained silent. I opened my eyes again to find him staring at me. His face was unreadable under the glowing severity of the hanging bulb.

"You need to know that my taking you on as my student precludes any sexual contact between us. I realize your kiss was actually from your sister, but you need to work to keep her out of you when we're together. I require your full attention and yours alone."

I squirmed. He didn't understand how my power really worked, of course, and that what he asked was impossible.

He said, "Is that clear?"

"Yes."

He was leaning with both fists on the table, the gun parts arrayed in front of him. He straightened up, rasping through a difficult breath, then pulled a gun kit off a nearby shelf. He set about carefully cleaning, wiping, lubricating, and inspecting his .45.

"Clean yours as well, Ethan."

"Oh. Okay." I fumbled my waist pack toward me, found my gun, and started unloading it carefully.

"By 'your performance,' I was referring to your continued disobedience of my commands."

"Uh." I stopped to consider that. "Any command in particular?"

He'd finished with his maintenance and reassembled the gun. "I ordered you to leave me. Take my gear and leave. You refused."

"Oh." It only took me a couple of seconds to remove the spring and barrel lock from my Beretta. I reached for the brush and oil.

Jack returned his unspent ammunition to the box, then housed his gun in its special case, which, in turn, he placed in its dedicated shelf spot.

"How come yours stays in here?"

"Military issue," he said simply.

"Oh."

"Your gun is civilian. It belongs in the White Room."

"Right."

I had finished cleaning and drying the chamber and bore, and turned to the spring assembly. I started to lubricate it, then bungled my grip—it sprung violently from my hands and flew across the table. Jack snatched it out of the air. Slowly, he turned his hand over and opened his fingers, revealing the long, thin metal piece. He stretched his arm across the table.

I took up the wayward part. "Um. Sorry about that."

He closed his hand and brought his fist down on the table, hard. Everything on it jumped. So did I.

"You will not disobey me again during an operation."

I stared at him with my mouth open. I was probably trembling a little. The knuckles of his fist gleamed white against the tabletop.

"It's one thing to joke around and disrespect me in the dojo, it's another to do it in the field." He leaned forward, pointing his index finger at an invisible line between us. "Do it again and there will be consequences."

I swallowed hard. I wondered what those consequences would be and if Jack would risk alienating my female self to discipline my male self. Still, there was only one thing to say to that.

"Yes, sir!"

— 24 —

Mission

♀

After my embarrassing dressing down from Jack, I decided to hide in my own body for a while, even though I'd only been up in my brother for an hour or so. It took me a while to settle down so my consciousness could make the switch.

I found Jack and Goom in the kitchen. The setting sun cast long shadows on the porch outside the sliding glass doors. I slid into the chair across from Jack. He was sipping tea and reading a Chinese newspaper with a large picture of the burned-out warehouse on the front. Goom was at the stove concocting dinner.

Jack smiled at me. "Good evening, Judith."

"What does the paper say?"

He frowned. "Nothing useful."

I shook my head. "That was insane. What kind of missiles were they shooting at you guys? The same as at the hospital?"

Jack let the newspaper droop and watched me over it. "The same as at the hospital but not missiles, apparently. Simply an anti-materiel rifle using high-explosive incendiary rounds. Probably the same weapon as the Russians used on your Decatur home."

My eyebrows raced up my forehead. "A. . . rifle? Not a freaking tank? Or a rocket launcher?"

Jack cocked his head. "It looks like an ordinary sniper rifle. The rounds are about," he held up one hand, measuring perhaps six inches, "that big. They're .50 caliber."

"That's insane."

Jack returned to the paper. I studied his head over the broadsheet.

"And the round that hit you? What was that? A peashooter?"

He pulled back a corner of the paper to look at me. "Ordinary sniper ammunition. Also .50 caliber."

I shuddered. "It went through the truck trailer before it hit you."

Goom said, "Good thing it did, or we'd be talking to a ghost." He set a steaming heaped bowl in front of me.

I sniffed at it. "So, um, what is this stuff?"

"Just try it, sweet-nuts. You'll like it." He plopped a large serving bowl filled with rice in the middle of the table and sat down next to Jack.

The idea that a simple rifle could do such damage had killed my appetite. I watched them eat for a couple of minutes.

"So what's the mission Colonel Cox was talking about?"

Jack put down his fork. He sipped his tea and swallowed his mouthful.

"Someone's been walking off our bases with state secrets and selling them to foreign governments."

I started. "State secrets? Like what? Experimental weapons blueprints? Troop positions? Gym locker combinations?"

Goom snorted.

Jack continued, expressionless. "Everything seems up for grabs. So far the most damaging information to show up in the hands of our enemies were the access codes and exact location of one of our Predators."

"Predators?"

Goom stopped shoveling food into his mouth and stared at me. "Don't you ever watch the Discovery Channel? Bubblebrain. A Predator is one of our elite drone planes."

That rang a bell. "You mean like the one over Afghanistan that disappeared last month?"

He mimed a gunshot with his pudgy little fingers. "Bang."

I was sure my complexion dropped several more shades toward pasty. "That's not good."

Jack said, "No, it isn't. Colonel Cox thinks it might have been redirected into China."

"Crap."

Jack nodded somberly. Goom resumed eating.

My brow furrowed. "So Colonel Cox thinks someone inside leaked those codes? And we're supposed to find out who it is? How do we do that?"

Jack stared into the distance. "It seems more complicated than that."

"How so?"

He sighed. "They're sure it isn't a mole. And they're sure it's not a leak in their network. All of their security measures are intact and functioning."

"And yet, somehow the information got out to bite us in the ass."

"Yes."

Without really meaning to, I spooned a bit of Goom's whatever-it-was into my mouth. I worked it around my tongue and realized I loved it.

"Wow. This is great."

It was a heady mix of spices with an underlying touch of sweetness. I could have sworn it had some good old Tex-Mex chili undertones, but the overall taste was something distinctly more exotic. Asian? African? Who knew? Who cared? I wolfed it down in earnest.

Goom scraped the last bits from his bowl. "No offense, but why'd they pick you, Lahngxian? I assume they got plenty of intelligence working it."

Jack sat back and crossed his legs. "Of course. But apparently Bead and Dahmiel have narrowed it down to something being run out of the warehouse we worked over. We're smack in the middle of that mess, so that makes us their 'inside men,' so to speak."

Goom grimaced. "And they don't know we don't know fuck all about fuck all, right?"

Jack sipped his tea. He looked at me. "I'll need to talk to Ethan. We have a charge for him."

Goom said, "We do?"

Jack nodded. "I want him to question Paige. I feel she must know more than she'll tell me."

"Yeah, get the redneck to question her. She likes him."

Tears ran down my face. I managed to choke out, "Likes him? At the warehouse, she shot him in the chest. Point-blank."

Goom chortled. "Yeah, you should see what she does if she doesn't like someone. And what the hell's wrong with you, sugarface?"

I had my hand over my mouth and was bright red. "Water," I croaked.

Neither of them moved quickly enough to get me some, so I jumped up from my chair, ran to the sink, turned the water on full blast, and stuck my face underneath, lapping at the stream desperately.

Spray reached the table and sprinkled Goom. "Hey, watch it! That's why you're supposed to eat it with the rice, dummy."

When the fire in my mouth had subsided, I returned to the table. Goom rolled his eyes theatrically. There was a restrained but unmistakable smile at one corner of Jack's mouth.

I was wet but relieved. "That was fantastic. You got any more?"

— 25 —

Hard Drive

♂

About eleven that night, I was in the top of a towering magnolia tree with a great view of Paige's room on the second floor of Dragon's mansion. Jack had lent me infrared field glasses, and I was sweeping the area, trying out all their cool settings.

Beep. Bee—

I frowned. The noise had been slight and squelched immediately, but it was close. I looked around. I found a pair of FBI agents with surveillance equipment trained on Dragon's villa. They were nearly invisible, tucked into the undergrowth on a slight hill, and I would have stepped on them before seeing them if I hadn't heard the beep. Since they had the front of the house covered, I went in the back. Dragon was having a dinner party. He must have had his alarm system turned off because I was able to sneak in through the kitchen while the cooks' backs were turned without any random goons coming to kill me.

There were a dozen rooms on the second floor. I could almost smell the vast hordes of money Dragon was sitting on, and it mingled with the carpet freshener and filtered through my mask, making me want to sneeze. No wonder Paige donned a costume and ran amok all night. The suffocating wealth was making me antsy to clamber up tall buildings, and I'd only been there five minutes.

Finally, I heard Paige. She was behind a locked door, talking vigorously in English. I listened for several moments and realized she was talking on the phone. I rapped on the door and ducked into the room across the hall.

"What?" Paige yelled.

After a minute it was clear she wasn't coming out. I emerged, rapped again, and hid.

"What!?"

Paige swore as she unlocked her door and yanked it open. She stuck her head into the hall and looked around, then ducked back into the room, slamming the door behind her.

I sighed.

Rap, rap, rap.

This time, Paige came all the way into the hall. She said into her phone, "I gotta go. Some asshole is banging on my door. Probably one of the fucking party idiots."

After she hung up, I reached out and grabbed her. I pulled her into the room with my hand over her mouth. She tried to smack me in the nuts and struggled fiercely. I held her tight. I whispered into her ear, "You know the FBI are watching the house, right? Is there someplace we can talk?"

She went perfectly still at my voice.

I lifted my hand from Paige's lips. "Don't scream." She said nothing. After a moment, I said, "Paige?"

What normal person has a stun gun attachment for their phone? I belatedly realized I should have taken the damn thing away as I felt a biting current in my thigh and one side of my body began to clench in response.

The instructions on those things say it can take "up to five seconds" to fell a determined attacker. I knew I had to get the fucker off my leg before my five seconds were up and I turned into a useless ball of cramping muscles. I spun Paige around and smacked the phone from her hand, then raised an elbow and caught her square in the face so she flew across the room and crashed into a shapeless blob of furniture. For me, it was like being stung by a dozen killer bees in one spot on my thigh. I lurched sideways, then Paige was back on me and broke a lamp over my head, sending me flat to the floor.

She raced to the wall and flipped the overhead light on. "Next time you come to kill me, at least do me the honor of bringing a gun, you dickless asshole!" With that, she ripped my mask off.

I laughed at the surprise flooding her gorgeous silver-blue eyes. I yelled back at her, "Lord, Paige, you are such a pain in the ass!"

She seemed thoroughly confused. "My father is sending his sidekick to kill me now?"

"I'm not here to kill you. I just wanted to talk."

"Are there really FBI outside?"

"Tons. I'm amazed you haven't noticed them. They've got everything on your ass short of an eighteen-wheeler with the word *inconspicuous* stenciled on the side."

Her face dropped. "Fuck." She helped me up and whispered in my ear, "Come with me." My traitorous body felt a tickle of desire at her nearness.

She led me down two flights of stairs into a cool limestone basement. We went through a wine cellar that probably contained more inventory than many vintners and ended up in a narrow white-washed room that smelled of fresh laundry and cement. Paige flipped a switch, and a ceiling fan began to lazily circulate the air. The room had everything in small nooks: a sink and mini-fridge, a desk and computer, a bed and toilet. It also had a big-ass steel-reinforced door, which Paige closed with difficulty. The door looked like it should have a bank vault behind it.

Clank.

"Now, redneck, we are alone. No FBI. No interruptions. We can talk."

I frowned. Paige's wicked intonation and threatening smirk scared me.

She came at me, and I threw my arms up and crouched to block whatever attack she was going to throw at me. Instead, she laughed and took my gloved hands in hers, pushed them apart, and gave me a big sloppy kiss right on the mouth.

So that's what the intonation and smirk boded. Yikes.

I held Paige at arm's length. "What the hell were you doing with that warehouse computer? What's on there?"

She batted my arms away and snuggled up to me. "Sex first. Talk after."

She grabbed my face, sucked on my lips, and pushed her tongue between them. I found myself kissing back, even though I didn't want to. From the way Ethan's body was responding, it was clear I didn't have much conscious choice in the matter. Fear shot through me. What if I couldn't perform properly? Paige had me on the bed with my suit half off and ran her tongue over my naked torso. I was frozen completely solid, concentrating on not embarrassing myself by finishing before we even started. All I needed was to be known as the hair-trigger redneck.

Paige tore off her robe, revealing a stunning nakedness underneath. This was going to get worse before it got better.

* * *

"That was different."

Paige had her head propped on one bare arm and was staring at me. I felt sluggish and stunned. I couldn't believe I'd just had sex with Jack's daughter in my brother's body. And she had called it... *different*? I had decided to do stuff to Paige that I liked when I was in my female body and hope for the best. Apparently, that made it *different*.

She seemed to be waiting for some kind of response. I frowned. "I assume that's a compliment."

"I'm very afraid now."

"Yeah? Why?" I looked at her and felt a little thrill at her blue eyes.

"If you make me feel like that again, I will have to fall in love with you. Most guys can't even find the tweety bird, let alone make it sing."

Great. I had turned Paige away from the dark side with my super-fantastic loving, and all I wanted to do was run away screaming. Out loud I said, "So does this mean that the next time you see me, you won't shoot me or stun-gun me?"

She laughed. "Maybe."

"I hope the FBI outside are blushing after hearing that."

"Oh, they can't hear us in here, redneck. Definitely not."

I glanced around. "They can't? Walls too thick?"

"This is my father's panic room."

"His what?"

"Panic room. He built it so when the other mobsters come to kill him, he can hide until his reinforcements get here to kill them."

"Wonderful."

She batted my chest. "So what did you want to talk about?"

My mind was clouded. I forced myself to focus. "What was on the warehouse computer? And the thumb drive?"

Her eyes narrowed. "You still have my thumb drive? Give it back."

"I might if you tell me what's on it and what you were doing."

She sighed. "It's a rootkit."

"What's that?"

She scoffed. "Don't you know anything? It's how you hack a computer."

"I'm a redneck. I don't know stuff like that."

Paige sat up and pressed her back against the wall, not bothering to cover her nakedness. My eyes raked her body; desire climbed within me. I found myself thinking about the countless puny male spiders who impregnate a female and get themselves eaten for their trouble. I didn't think spiders were in the human genetic line but maybe something of that intrinsic stupidity had intruded nonetheless.

She studied me. "I was getting IP addresses for Jun Lo."

I played dumb, since I seemed to be so good at it. "Who's that?"

"Jun Lo Pii. My cousin. He's an idiot. But he's gorgeous."

"Right."

Paige reached out and rested her hand on my shoulder. "Don't be mad, redneck. You're twice the man he is. I could really fall in love with you."

I sat up next to Paige, shoulder to shoulder. "So why did you want addresses from that computer? Addresses for who?"

"Not regular addresses, IP addresses. Computer addresses. And Jun Lo's botnet controller. It's the only copy. We wanted to get it back before the Russians stole it. Or destroyed it."

" 'Botnet controller'?"

"Yeah. Jun Lo made it for his brother, Shun Yan, a while ago. Months before they killed Shun Yan."

"The Russians, you mean."

"Yes. We think they killed him over it."

"Why would they kill your cousin over a computer program?"

"It's very clever. We needed to get lots of information back to China but without your American snoops getting into it."

I hoped I managed to sound indifferent. "So? What's it do?"

"You know what a botnet is, redneck?"

"No fucking clue."

"It's a ton of hacked computers all over the world. Jun Lo hijacked over a hundred thousand at last count."

"Wow. And they are wired up to send stuff to China from the U.S.?"

Paige smiled. "Not directly. That's the clever part. Usually botnets send out spam."

"Oh, so they're responsible for those penis enlargement ads and crap?"

She chuckled. "Yeah. But Jun Lo modified this botnet so we could send out coded stuff. It looks like a generic spam attack on mainland China, but really, taken together, we could send anything—any message, big or small. And your spies would never find it."

A chill crept down the back of my skull and settled into a knot of tension in my neck. "Whatever. You shot me and your dad over some stupid scam."

She smacked me. "Shut up, redneck. It's brilliant, just brilliant. Jun Lo has a way with these things. He's really smart."

"I thought you said he's an idiot."

"Yeah, well, it's a different kind of smarts. I think he's autistic."

"So did you manage to rescue his great contribution to science then?"

Paige frowned. "Well, no. You and my fucking father stopped us, didn't you?" She held her hand out. "Now where's my thumb drive?"

"I don't know. Goom probably has it with the hard drive."

Paige's mouth dropped open. She got up and left the bed.

"You have to leave." All of a sudden, she looked terrified.

I sat forward. "Why? What's wrong?"

"You have the hard drive."

I shrugged. "It's warped and busted. It's probably unusable."

She put on her robe and tied it. "You have to leave. Now."

She thrust my underwear at me, and I put them on. She dragged my supersuit over, and I put my legs into it. Then she was at the door, fiddling with the big lock.

"What's wrong, Paige? Where are you going?"

"When Dragon finds out you have that hard drive, he'll rip your skin off and make eggrolls with it."

"Uh. . . " I pulled my suit on then clicked my waistpack into place.

"My idiot father should have told him you have it. I will tell Dragon you came on my father's behalf, and maybe he will forgive you if I beg him."

"Jeez, Paige. It's just a wrecked hard drive."

"You really have no clue, do you?"

"Well—"

Paige came forward, grabbed my face, and kissed me. I kissed her back and was lost momentarily in the subtle floral scent issuing from her hair.

She stopped abruptly, jumped back, and slapped me—hard. My hand leaped to my stinging cheek. "Ow! What in the hell was that for?"

"For making me feel this way." Paige swung the heavy door open. "Now get out. And don't come back."

* * *

When I returned to Jack's, I rapped on the sliding glass door to the basement, and it only took him a moment to get there and open it. The room was dim. Goom was at his computer and shot me a worried glance.

"What?" I asked. "What's wrong?"

Jack said, "We got a call from Suhn Yihxian."

"Who?"

"You know him as Sam."

"Dragon's man?"

"Yes."

"What did he want?"

"He wants us to meet him at Chin's at 0700 this morning."

I checked the time in one of Goom's monitors. "That's in four hours. Why so early?"

Jack motioned to the couch, and I sat. He sat down in one of the armchairs and steepled his hands in front of him. His voice was low and deliberate. "Why don't you tell us exactly what transpired with you and Paige. Don't leave anything out."

I crimsoned. The last thing I wanted to do was tell Jack I had wild and protracted sex with his daughter.

"Well, I found Paige in her room. I got her to come across the hall because the FBI guys were watching the front of the house."

Goom said, "And you know that how?"

"I found a couple of them nearby with some listening equipment aimed at the house."

Jack sat motionless as a statue, watching me carefully.

I twiddled my thumbs. "Anyway, she stun-gunned me. . . "

Goom chortled. "Nice."

". . . and then broke a lamp over my head."

Goom was laughing full out now. "See? I told you she likes you."

I fingered him. "Just shut up."

Jack was silent.

"Anyway, then she told me there's a rootkit on her thumb drive."

Goom stared at the tiny black box sitting next to him. "A rootkit."

"Yeah, so she could hack Shun Yan's computer. Apparently Jun Lo had written a program she called a botnet controller that sends American secrets to China."

Goom quizzed me for several minutes about what Paige had said about the computer program. I told him all the terms she had used and explained as much as I could.

After we'd finished, Jack said, "That's it?"

I stared at the coffee table. A computer magazine cover proclaimed the miracles of miniaturization. Apparently there were computers people could wear now on little clips. I didn't know why anyone would want to wear a computer when we all had smartphones.

"Yeah. That's it," I said.

Both Goom and Jack frowned. Goom said, "You were there for four hours. You talked about computer shit the whole time?"

I nodded. "Basically."

They stared at me, and I fidgeted.

Goom said, "You fucked her, didn't you?"

I glanced across the coffee table at Jack. He was sitting very still. His lips were pressed together, but so far he showed no sign of flying across the room and strangling me with his bare hands.

Goom chortled wildly.

I said, "Settle down, Goom-boy. I didn't really have a choice in the matter. It was the only way I could get her to talk to me."

"I told you she likes you."

"What's the big deal anyway?" I shook my head. Then, suddenly, I cringed. "Wait. Wait. Do you think that's why Sam wants to meet us? Would it bother Dragon that I, uh. . . I mean, we. . . "

Goom looked at Jack.

The big man frowned. "I doubt that's the reason. What else happened?"

"Well, nothing. I mean, she jumped up and threw me out, and I came back here."

"She threw you out?" Goom snorted. "What'd you do? Misfire or something?"

"No, shithead. But after I mentioned we had the hard drive, she got all testy and told me to leave. And she said Dragon would be furious we didn't tell him we had it."

Silence.

Goom's mouth hung open. Jack's eyes seemed frozen wide, about forty percent larger than usual.

"What? What is it about that stupid hard drive? Every time I mention it to someone, they seem to go into cardiac arrest."

Jack jumped up and started pacing in short, angry circles.

Goom's face had gone greenish-gray. "You are so fucking stupid I wish I had my gun."

"What? Goddamn it. What?!"

"Dumb shit-for-brains. You were supposed to get information from her, not blab our secrets all over the place."

"How in the hell is that a secret? Why didn't anyone tell me?"

Goom facepalmed. "It's obvious, you useless sack of stupid."

Jack stopped and contemplated the bent and charred hard drive sitting on Goom's desk. "At least now I know what he meant when he told me to bring 'the item' with us."

"Jack. You're not going to give it to them, are you?"

"You've really left us little choice, Ethan."

"That thing probably has American secrets on it. You can't give it up."

"Considering we pulled it from Shun Yan's computer, they probably already know what's on it. They just don't want it to fall into other hands."

"Other hands?"

Goom said, "Yeah, like Agent Bead's."

"Or, the Russians," Jack said. "After they pry it from our dead fingers."

I shuddered.

* * *

When we pulled up to Chin's, Goom's dash clock read 6:52. Two other cars were in the lot, a fancy sports car and a VW bus.

"Wow," I said. "An actual VW bus. I thought those died with the sixties."

"It's Guan Ho's," Goom said.

"Wax Man?"

"Who?"

"When I first saw him, he was so still I thought he was made of wax."

Goom snorted. "Great. Dipshit."

Inside, Guan Ho was at the stove with three woks sizzling around him. He bowed to Jack.

Jack bent and hugged him. "My friend. Thank you for preparing us such an elaborate meal so early this morning."

Wax Man nodded, his beard and mustache drooping from the searing heat and steam.

We pushed through the swing doors into the main dining room. Our usual table in the back was occupied by Jun Lo and three pals, including one I recognized from the warehouse who had a bandanna on his head and a huge black eye. Jack looked at them through narrowed eyes. They ignored him. Jack stepped toward the table, and Jun Lo looked at him then, making as if to rise. The other three youths reached into their pockets, waistbands, or jackets.

I froze. Goom stepped back slightly so I was between him and the men. Adrenaline trickled from the base of my neck down my spine.

Guan Ho had followed us from the kitchen, and now he neatly interceded. "Lahngxian," he crooned, "please come sit at the table I have prepared for you and your friends."

Jack allowed himself to be led away. Jun Lo sat down and returned to his food. His buddies put their hands back on the table in plain sight, and someone told a joke. Raucous laughter followed Jack, Goom, and me up the aisle to our new table.

Guan Ho placed a large teapot in the middle of the table and spread cups out. I poured everyone tea.

"So," I said quietly between sips. "Is everyone else in here about to whip out a gun and shoot at us?"

Goom surreptitiously cast his eyes about. "Probably."

Jack sat ramrod straight, but his face betrayed no sign of anxiety. He said nothing. His back was to Jun Lo's table.

Goom squirmed in his chair, wringing his hands. I fidgeted and checked my watch. 6:58. I jumped as Guan Ho banged out of the kitchen door. He walked up the aisle and set small plates in front of us: eggrolls. Dread settled heavily onto my shoulders. I stared at the innocuous little delicacies. Goom picked one up and nibbled at it. Jack sat back in his chair, crossed his legs, and placed one, whole, into his mouth. I wasn't sure what my face registered, but I'd completely lost my appetite.

"Eat, fuckhead. What's your problem?" Goom said.

"It's what Paige said. She told me Dragon would rip my skin off and make it into eggrolls."

Goom raised his eyebrows and looked at Jack.

Jack, naturally, remained nonchalant. "It's a coincidence. Eat up."

The front door chimed, and a man darkened Chin's doorway. It was Sam. He was dressed impeccably in a perfect-fitting, dark gray suit and tasteful green-and-silver striped tie. He walked to our table and bowed low. Jack stood and returned the bow. I stood too, and Goom likewise slid off his chair.

"Good morning, Sh'fu," Sam said. "Thank you so much for agreeing to meet me on such short notice." He bowed to Goom and me. We lowered our heads in response. "Please." Sam waved his hand at our table. "Continue eating. I will join you in one moment." He headed to the back of the restaurant and engaged Jun Lo.

The three of us resumed our seats. "Seems like he's in a good mood," I said quietly.

"Huh?" Goom glanced at Sam. "Why?"

"He's so polite."

Goom snorted. "He's always polite. In fact, if he gets more polite, we should all head for the fucking hills."

"What?"

Jack sighed. "If Suhn Yihxian starts to whisper an apology in your ear, you'll be dead before he finishes."

I swallowed heavily. The eggroll I'd bitten haunted my throat.

Loud Mandarin reached us from Jun Lo's table. Whatever Sam was saying to him, Jun Lo didn't like it. He slammed his fist on the table and shoved his chair back, standing abruptly. His buddies got up with him. They threw open the kitchen door, and all four stomped off. Moments later, an engine roared. It continued, distantly, around the side of the building, then I saw the sports car from the back parking lot shoot by the front window. I doubted they were obeying the thirty mile-per-hour speed limit.

Sam strolled back to us.

I whispered to Goom, "Should I be more worried now? Or less?"

Goom and I both looked at Jack, who smiled. "You shouldn't be worried at all." The smile dropped from his face. "It won't help."

Sam was disturbingly obsequious toward Jack as he pulled out the fourth chair and sat across from him.

"My apologies, Sh'fu, for the unenviable timing of my little brother."

I froze with my teacup halfway to my lips. This was the first I'd heard that Sam was Dragon's nephew, too.

Jack's eyes narrowed. "Suhn Yihxian."

"Please," Sam said. "Yes?"

"I will not tolerate disrespect from Jun Lo."

Sam swallowed and lowered his head. "My greatest apologies, Enforcer. I will see to it he is properly instructed in courtesy."

Guan Ho shuffled over with more eggrolls and cleared our empty plates.

Jack said flatly, "Dragon is aware of my commission?"

Sam bowed slightly. "There is speculation." He spoke using an equally bland intonation. He chewed the tip off an eggroll.

"Then you understand the position I am in."

Sam said nothing. Silence descended upon them. After Sam finished his eggrolls, Guan Ho immediately removed his plate. I was impressed with such quick service from the old guy.

After Guan Ho retreated, Sam said, "Have you made any progress determining the killer of Shun Yan?"

"We have," Jack said. "It is as Dragon suspected."

"His philandering has caught up with us."

Jack nodded slightly.

Sam frowned. "It was the Russian woman who started this?"

Jack nodded again. It was merely a quick inclination of his head. "She had help. Volkov."

Sam exhaled heavily, eyes narrowed.

Before he could respond, Guan Ho came out with a huge tray and set up a folding stand. He placed large bowls in front of us that appeared to contain watery, steaming rice. He then set plate after plate in the center of the table, each containing a strange delicacy.

There was something that looked like yellowed, pickled brains. Another plate had egg slices arrayed like flower petals, except the egg white was tar black and the yolk was equally dark but with a greenish undertone. A third plate held what looked like beef jerky, only oranger. After the orange jerky, Guan Ho set down a plate with a heap of something that looked like a cross between thinly shaved onion slices and sawdust. Finally, he set down a handful of smaller bowls containing chives and sauces, one of which looked vaguely like ketchup. He bowed deeply. "Mahnmahn chi," he intoned, then disappeared entirely for the duration of the meal.

Goom, Jack, and Sam started eagerly spooning various accompaniments on top of the rice slush in their bowls. I stared at the food, not moving.

Goom was the first to notice my consternation. "What's the matter, tard-nugget? You never seen congee before?"

"Um."

"C'mon," he prodded. "It's good." He pointed to one of the dishes. "That's—"

"No, no, don't tell me. I'll guess."

Goom raised his eyebrows. Everyone eyed everyone else with varying degrees of suspicion.

After a moment, Jack parked his spoon in his bowl and waved his hand over the table. "Go ahead, Ethan."

"Okay." I took a deep breath.

I pointed at the yellowed, cortical-like mass. "Pig brains." I indicated the black eggs. "Eighty-million-year-old dodo eggs." I waved my hand at the jerky-like slices. "Oranged panda-gut meatloaf. And, to top it off," I nodded to the pile of sawdust, "sun-dried Komodo dragon skin shavings."

Silence.

"Oh, wait, I forgot a couple." I pointed at the ketchup-like sauce. "Vampire bat blood." I pointed to the chives. "Freeze-dried crabgrass." I made a show of looking over the table, as if to be sure I'd hit everything. "Oh yeah." I pointed to the bottle of Kikoman's. "And soy sauce."

More silence. I cleared my throat.

Goom piped up. "Not bad, for an imbecile."

"All right." I rubbed my hands together. "I'm starving. I'll try a bit of everything." I took a fat spoonful of the sawdust-like stuff, dumped it on my rice soup, then switched spoons and stuffed it into my mouth before I could lose my nerve. "Mm." I crunched the mouthful down. "Wonderful."

Jack watched me without speaking, but there was mirth in his eyes.

Sam broke the ice further by chuckling aloud. "Pass the bat blood, please." Goom obliged, shooting him an evanescent smile.

"You forgot one," Jack said. He pulled out a small plate that had been hidden from my view behind the teapot. On it was piled little cubes of fermented white cheese-like stuff in a golden sauce. "Pickled snake eggs."

"They're square," I said.

"Your powers of observation never cease to amaze."

Everyone but Jack laughed out loud, and even he cracked a smile, the edges of his mouth drifting upward ineluctably.

* * *

Sam was the last to put his ceramic spoon down. The ping as it hit the bowl had barely ceased before Guan Ho appeared. He cleared the table with record speed, then settled a new teapot near the center of the table and handed out fresh cups. He bowed deeply and disappeared once more, leaving a plate of oddly shaped fried dough pieces behind.

I snapped one up and ate it. "Wow. What a meal."

Sam bowed his head low toward Jack. "This has been a very great pleasure for me as well." He paused, then raised his head and continued. "I am afraid I must return to business for one moment."

We were silent. I sat back so as not to impinge Jack and Sam's view of each other. I studied a random spot on the tabletop.

"This destruction of Shun Yan's warehouse."

After a moment, Jack said, "Yes. That was an unfortunate occurrence."

"It was an insult," Sam hissed with surprising feeling. He took a breath, and his voice returned to its inflectionless, urbane tone. "We would like to see the mastermind punished."

Jack's eyes narrowed. "This may be difficult. Such a man would not be easy to reach."

"In this endeavor," Sam said, "our interests may be once again aligned."

Jack bowed slightly. "They are."

"In that case," Sam stated deliberately, "we will naturally pursue the execution of justice with utmost zeal. In fact, I can assure you, *double* attention will be paid to this matter."

Jack's head bowed further. "You honor me."

"No, Enforcer, it is you who honor us with your invaluable assistance."

Without looking up, I glanced at Jack, then at Sam, from the corners of my eyes. I felt like something had been decided but could not for the life of me say exactly what.

Sam bowed his head so deeply his forehead almost contacted his teacup. "I greatly regret, Sh'fu, that I must put the most grievous of insults upon you at this time of agreement."

Jack exhaled deeply. "Regret not, Suhn Yihxian."

Jack pulled a small black anti-static bag from a pocket on the inside of his jacket and slid it across the table toward Sam. My heart sank. It had to be the hard drive.

Sam took the package, without raising his head, and slipped it into his own jacket pocket. "I am eternally in your debt, Sh'fu."

"As I am in yours." Jack balled one hand, placed the other over it, and bowed quickly toward Sam, who returned the gesture identically.

Sam rose then. Jack stood as well, and Goom and I followed suit.

"Please. All of you have a most pleasant day," Sam said. He straightened his silky tie and walked up the aisle toward the front door.

Guan Ho appeared out of nowhere and raced after Sam to open the door. They bowed to each other, and Sam was gone. Guan Ho flipped the sign back to *open*, and I felt like a great weight had been lifted from us—or a horrible outcome had passed us over by a hair's breadth.

— 26 —

Safety

♀

I wore a simple black tube dress that came halfway down my thighs. I stepped from Jack's room. He was training and stopped midpose.

"Judith."

I fingered the snake pendant at my neckline. "Do you like it?"

He smiled. "Gorgeous."

Goom sat in a pile of pillows against the opposite wall with his laptop on his knees. He said, "Yeah, that thing really shows off your tits."

Jack barked a quick phrase in Mandarin, and Goom hid behind his computer. I laughed. Jack followed me out to the mudroom to wait for Julian. We stood in the dimness of setting sunlight filtering through paper blinds.

"This is a bad idea," Jack said. "Are you sure you won't reconsider?"

Li Jong's battered body had turned up in a landfill that morning. In light of that, Jack didn't want me to leave his sight. I was pretty sure it also had to do with Julian. Jack didn't want me to go with Julian, in spite of not admitting it openly.

"I'll be fine. No one's going to attack me with an FBI agent there. Plus, what would I tell him?"

"Tell Agent Bead something's come up. Or tell him you're sick."

I bit my lip. "I want to try to get more information out of him. Like, on that Wolf guy."

Jack shook his head. “It’s a dangerous game. You don’t need to play.”

I fidgeted with my purse straps. “Julian’s not going to do anything to me. I’m practically his daughter.”

Jack moved forward slightly and dropped his head to mine as his hands slid around my waist. He kissed me. I was completely paralyzed. He pulled back, and I stared at him. He released me and bowed his head. “Please forgive me. I misunderstood.”

“Dummy!” I grabbed his face and pulled it to mine, kissing him urgently. I was losing myself to the intensity when he abruptly pulled away and stared at a point near the ceiling over my shoulder. Above the front door, the first of several tiny LEDs was flashing.

“He’s here.” Jack ran his finger down the side of my face, tucking an obstreperous curl behind my ear. “Be careful.”

The doorbell sounded. My attention turned to the thick red door. When I glanced back into the dojo, Jack was nowhere to be seen. Glowing light penetrated the paper panes of his worship room.

Knock. Knock.

I jumped. “Jeez.”

I pulled the front door open. It was Julian, of course. He was in black jeans, a crisp white button-down shirt, and a gorgeous tan suede jacket with fringe across the chest. He was freshly shaved, and his silky black hair was pulled back into a neat ponytail.

“Um, hi.” I stepped outside and closed the door behind me.

“Hi, gorgeous.” Julian grinned. He leaned over and plopped a kiss on my lips. I returned it, but by just a peck. I felt my cheeks burn.

Julian’s eyes narrowed. “You okay?”

“Yep. Yeah. Of course. Let’s go.”

“All right.” He put his hand on my elbow and led me away from Jack’s house. “I hope it’s okay that I chose a different restaurant.”

"Um. What one?"

He smiled. A sunbeam caught his eyes, turning them to translucent gold. "It's a really nice one some ways north, overlooking a lake. I'm told the food is exquisite, more than worth the drive."

"Oh. Well, okay. Sure."

* * *

Of course, by the time I became suspicious, it was too late. We left the interstate at Gainsville and turned north on Route 129, a two-lane road that wound upward into the heart of the Appalachians. I watched the dark forest race past, punctuated by the occasional porch light.

"Where's this fabled restaurant. Canada?"

Julian ground his teeth, saying nothing.

I crossed my arms. I could feel my lower lip jut out in prime pouting position. I felt like an insolent teenager again.

Julian eyed me askance. "You have no idea what that bastard got you into, do you?"

I glared at the glove compartment.

"Fine. I'll enlighten you. Do you want me to start with the mob war or the treason?"

I scoffed.

"Or maybe I should start with the useless band of vigilantes running around Atlanta beating people senseless."

Useless. That was a bit harsh.

"Does he think he's Robin Hood? Or. . . Batman?"

I stared at the tan ceiling.

"Why is Volkov in America?"

I frowned. Why was he asking me?

"Is it to kill Pii Jiang Lee? Or was his nephew the target?"

Julian thought the Wolf killed Dragon's nephew? As far as I knew, Jack suspected Msti. Was she even still alive?

"Or did Jack kill Shun Yan? To start a succession war?"

I furrowed my brow. Either Julian was toying with me, or he was clueless about what was really going on.

"Jack didn't kill anyone," I muttered.

Julian snorted. "Sure. And I'm the Virgin Mary. How in the *hell* did you get messed up with the Tongs?"

"The 'Tongs'? What are those? Aside from a barbecue implement."

He smacked the wheel. "Don't play dumb with me, young lady."

I sighed. I guessed it would be better if I didn't say anything.

"Tell me how you met him."

"What?"

Julian ground his teeth for several moments. His eyes raged. "Colonel Xiah. How did you meet him?"

"Oh. Um."

I thought back to the first night I met Jack. I almost laughed out loud as I remembered Ethan's less-than-stellar bout of fisticuffs with Goom. It seemed like ages ago. And there was no way I could tell Julian the truth.

"It's hard to explain," I said quietly.

Julian breathed deeply, and I thought he was attempting to calm himself down; his anger seemed to ebb accordingly. "We have time," he responded softly.

I guessed a half-truth was better than nothing at all. "Jack's my Wushu personal trainer."

He glanced over at me. " 'Wushu'?"

"Kung Fu. Self-defense, basically."

He drove for a while, staring straight ahead. I squirmed. I watched the blurred forms of trees race past in the darkness, embraced by the stone faces of mountains rising around us in the moonlight.

Julian cleared his throat. "Are you seriously trying to tell me you're taking private self-defense lessons from a decorated special ops commander? And he's letting you stay at his house out of what? A sense of civic duty?"

"Well, yes." I bit my lip. "I mean, I don't know."

He snorted loudly. "Where on God's great earth did you find him? Does he advertise self-defense services for perky Atlanta women in *Soldier of Fortune* or what?"

I frowned. "Actually, his, uh, friend, Goom—I don't think you met him—owns a comic book store. It's close to my neighborhood and, uh. . . "

Julian was shaking with laughter.

I crossed my arms. "Yeah," I mumbled.

More laughter. "You must think I'm a complete idiot." He wiped his eyes. He looked at me, shaking his head. "How much does he charge?"

"Well, at the moment, it's really more of a trade. His Wushu for my, uh, legal representation."

He broke out simply guffawing.

"Calm down, Julian. It's not that funny."

"Man alive, Judith. You're absolutely priceless."

* * *

After a tiny town called Clermont, we turned off onto something called Old Cleveland Road and followed it for a while. I checked my watch. We'd been on the road for almost ninety minutes. Shortly we came to something claiming to be a town called Mossy Creek. Actually, it was little more than a stop sign amid the overshadowing peaks and woods. Julian went east, then north on a dirt road. After less than half a mile, he turned into a gravel drive tucked among tall evergreens, stopped, and cut the engine.

We sat in silence for several moments. I was so angry I couldn't bring myself to speak.

Beside us was a chalet-style cabin. It had thick walls of white stucco arrayed with fat log ends and a high, sloping roof with wide eaves. The lot seemed to abut a stream, or perhaps a river, down a sloping hill. A pale-faced woman with curly black hair and a navy suit came out the front door onto the stoop.

"Who's that?" I muttered. "The maitre d'?"

Julian scoffed. "No, that's Agent Becker."

I frowned. "Where in the hell are we?"

"It's a safe house, Judith. I'm going to put you here until you're no longer in danger."

"Shit."

I wrenched the door open and bolted. I got a couple of car lengths back down the gravel driveway when I stopped. Where the hell was I going to go? Also, I doubted I could successfully wrangle with the big black strapping agent who emerged from the trees near the end of the drive.

"Where would you go, Judith?" Julian called after me. "We're in the middle of nowhere, and there's a price on your head. Now get back here, and I'll introduce everyone."

My hot breath erupted into thick mist when it hit the cold mountain air.

"You bastard."

I threw my purse at Julian. He deflected it and started toward me. When he got in range, I tried to slap him. He grabbed my hand. I brought the other one up, fast, and manged to clip him on the chin before he grabbed that one too.

"Don't make this harder than it needs to be," he said. I tried kneeing him in the groin, but he was too close. I struggled and screamed at him, writhing one arm free. I aimed carefully and stuck my fist into his nuts.

"Ahh," he yelled, his grip loosening.

I ripped free and followed up with a kick to his kneecap. He deflected most of it, doubling over. I went nuts, slapping him. I was like a windmill, whacking him repeatedly on the head and shoulders, screaming like a banshee too. Out of the corner of my eye, I saw the black-haired woman pull out some kind of fat gun with two prongs sticking out of its mouth. I realized it must be a Taser. In that case, I wanted the woman to stun me. Hopefully it would knock me out so I could switch to Ethan. I whipped around and flew toward Agent Becker.

"No! Don't stun her!" Julian yelled.

The woman's eyes widened, but her trigger finger hesitated. I smacked the weapon from her hands and slammed into her, knocking her backward against the house. I bounced off, then came up swinging, punching her in the face. Julian jumped me from behind, knocking me to the ground. I screamed and flailed. He had handcuffs and tried to work my arms behind my back so he could cuff me. I bucked and kicked.

"Judith, stop," Julian yelled. "You'll hurt yourself!"

"No!" I put more effort into my struggle.

The big agent at the end of the road had come forward. The three of them worked together and had me subdued pretty quickly. I was disoriented; my head had hit the gravel more than once. My hands were cuffed behind me. Julian dragged me to my unsteady feet. "Let's get her inside," he said. I went completely limp, and they nearly dropped me.

"Damn it, Judith."

Julian and the other man hooked their arms through mine and half-carried, half-dragged me inside. Two more agents had appeared at some point during the melee and joined us in the kitchen. I was bawling loudly and cursing Julian for all I was worth.

The house had an open layout. The front door led to the kitchen and dining area, which continued to the living area. Vaulted ceilings rose above us. On the left, a staircase wound up to an open balcony overlooking the main floor. They dragged me past the staircase to a walled-off room at the back of the house. It contained a plush couch along one wall, flanked by oversized armchairs in pretty floral fabric. There was a plant, a large window, and several soothing pictures hanging from the walls.

They left me face down on the carpet and slammed the door closed so I was alone in the darkness.

Once my heaving breaths had abated, I heard Julian murmuring on the other side of the door. I went ballistic. I struggled to my knees and threw myself at the door.

Wham.

"Ow! Fuck!"

"Judith, stop," Julian yelled from the other side.

"No! Let me out!" I turned around and kicked the door.

Wham! Wham! Wham!

They flung the door open, smacking me. "Ow! Police brutality!"

Julian flicked the overhead lights on, and the strapping dark-skinned Agent knelt and grabbed me. I struggled, but he held me fast. "C'mon, girlfriend," he said softly. "We're not going to hurt you."

A broad-chested white guy came in with a hypodermic needle. "Hold her still," he said, flicking the thin, exposed tip.

"No," I yelled, struggling harder. "What is that?" I looked desperately at Julian. "No!" The guy with the needle came closer. "No, no, no! Julian!"

"Judith," Julian said, standing clear. "It's just a tranquilizer."

I couldn't do a thing. The needle was eased into a vein, and the plunger pushed. Warmth immediately spread out from where whatever-it-was had entered me. I tried to fight, having no clue how to do that. Adrenaline poured down from my pituitary to compete with the invader, but was overcome. Whether I wanted to or not, I relaxed. My motions became weak and slow. My heart's pounding slowed, and my breath deepened. They released me, and I spread out along the carpet like a puddle. I coughed, but even that felt subdued and half-speed.

"Damn you," I whispered.

"What did he do to you to make you act like this?" Julian was saying. "Did he brainwash you? Put you in a room and deprive you of life until you thought you loved him?"

His words came to me as if through a thin, gauzy curtain I couldn't push aside. "Wh-what?"

"Did he—" Julian stopped and stared at the ground. A dark flush spread over his cheeks. When he looked at me again, his eyes narrowed. "Did Xiah make love to you? Tell you you're a goddess?"

My mind was as sluggish as my body. I looked at the black-skinned man and black-haired woman hovering over me. They were unreal, having vague halos of illumination around their faces, as if they were saints.

Julian continued, speaking low and intently. "Judith."

I tried to look at him. He was a blurry figure standing somewhere that seemed inordinately far away.

"Xiah has no boundaries," he insisted. "No conscience."

I realized my eyelids were being pulled back by the barrel-chested man who'd injected me. I blinked desperately, trying to clear my view. The man stood and nodded to Julian. Everyone but Julian left.

Julian traded the harsh overhead light for the dim glow of a standing lamp. He helped me to my feet, removed the handcuffs, and led me to the couch. I sat. I was actually more slumped than sitting. Julian sat in the nearest armchair and opened a second button on his shirt. He smiled.

"Jeez, girl. You really threw us for a loop there."

I was having trouble holding my head up properly since my neck was so relaxed. I laid my head back against the couch and closed my eyes...

I started awake. I was sweating heavily and squirmed in the suffocating wool of my dress. I looked at my feet and realized Julian had taken my sandals off. A pulse of fear rose weakly within me. I had passed out. Why didn't I switch to Ethan?

"Was I out?" I asked Julian, who was sitting quietly in his armchair, contemplating me.

He turned his arm and looked at the watch face on the inside of his wrist. "Almost ninety seconds."

I sat forward, panting noticeably. "What is that stuff?"

"It's just a benzodiazepine. It'll wear off soon."

"Why am I shaking?"

"I had Agent Thompson cut it with an eugeroic to keep you with us."

"What? A 'huge heroic'?"

He smiled. "A mental stimulant. It'll probably make you feel happy."

"My dress itches."

He looked at me. "It'll pass. Tell me about Jack."

"What about him?"

"Who did he meet this morning?"

"What?"

"At Chin's," Julian said. "You know, the Chinese restaurant."

"We had bat blood." I giggled. My hand flew to my mouth. "Jeez. This stuff is making me loopy."

"You had 'bat blood'?"

"Well, not really. It might have been ketchup. Or chili sauce."

"Okay. Who else was there besides you?"

"Goom. And Jack, of course. And... Sam."

"Sam. Is he a friend of Jack's?"

"No, he's Dragon's deputy."

"Dragon," Julian repeated. "You mean Pi Jiang Lii."

"Yeah. Jack told me to call him Dragon. His name sounds like a swear word to me, and if I pronounce it like that, he might rip my skin off and make it into eggrolls." I chortled.

Julian's face had been expressionless, but he grimaced at that. "Jack told you that?"

"No, his daughter told me. Do you have any wine?"

"Wine?"

"Yeah. I feel like drinking."

"I'll see what I can do in a minute. Paige Lii told you Dragon might rip your skin off?"

"Yeah. But aren't you the big anti-mobster guy? How come you don't know all this stuff already? Your guys were watching her house."

His expression was unreadable. "We know some of it. What else do you know? Everything?"

"Well, yeah. And I know the Wolf blew up my house. And Shun Yan's warehouse. But he's not Asian. He's Russian, right?"

"Yes."

"Why does he want to get me?"

"I guess he thinks you know something. Or maybe that you have something he wants."

I scoffed. "You mean, that stupid hard drive? The idiot was trying to get me before we even had that stupid thing." Everything since Ethan's accident seemed completely unreal. What did it matter if I told Julian everything? It was all a dream anyway.

"Hard drive? What hard drive?"

"We got it from Shun Yan's warehouse. Why don't you know that? For a know-it-all you're not very knowledgeable." I laughed at that, far more than it was actually worth.

Julian waited for my spate of hysteria to pass. "So Jack managed to get a hard drive out of the warehouse before Volkov destroyed it."

"No."

He started. "No?"

"I mean, I'm not going to say anymore until you do something for me."

Julian took a deep breath. "What's that?"

I smiled. "Come over here." I patted the couch next to me.

He stared at me for several seconds. "All right," he finally said. He crossed the space between us and sat next to me. "Now what?" he asked.

"Now... kiss me."

He closed his eyes. "Judith." He reopened them. "Let's talk more."

I leaned over, resting my hand on his thigh. He placed his hand on top of it, holding it still. I pressed against him and found his lips with my mouth. I climbed into his lap, and we necked for a while. It didn't really seem to be going anywhere. At least I had his shirt open. I ran my hands around the bare chest underneath. "Make love to me, Julian."

"God, Judith." He closed his eyes again and took another deep breath.

"What's wrong? Don't you like me anymore?"

"Of course I like you. But I want to talk some more."

I laughed. "Sex first, then talk," I said, Paige's command ringing in my memory. "Isn't that funny?"

"Hilarious."

"Mmmm." I licked my lips, then pressed myself against him. We kissed some more, then he laid me down and covered me, pushing me into the soft cushions. "Oooh," I said, already practically orgasmic in spite of still having all my clothes on.

He considered my flushed face. "So Jack took a hard drive from the warehouse. Did he pass it along to Dragon's deputy this morning?"

I gyrated against him. "Yeah. It had Jun Lo's program on it. But Dragon already knew about it. Do you have any idea why he was so insistent on getting it back?"

Julian blinked a couple of times. He didn't answer.

I realized I was sweating so much that my dress felt soaked. "I need to get out of this dress. It's wet. Help me out of it, Julian." I licked my lips.

"In a minute," he said. "Did Jun Lo tell you about his program?"

"Jun Lo's an idiot." I scoffed. "He disrespects Jack. He's a stupid little pipsqueak with some dumb ass gang-bangers for friends. We hate him."

Julian sniffed. "Really."

"He totally rubs me the wrong way. Unlike you." I pulled his face to mine, and we kissed again.

Afterward, he pulled back and smiled. "I'm not so good at computer programs. But I hear Jun Lo knows his way around them."

I huffed. "Autistic little geek. Paige told me he runs their botnet. A hundred thousand computers, all over the world. So they can encode American secrets in spam."

"In spam?"

I shrugged. "Paige sure seemed impressed. But if he's such hot shit, why don't they just rewrite the program?"

"It would take them a while to compromise that many computers again."

"Well, maybe that's why the hard drive is so important. Jun Lo had to steal it for the computer addresses, and the Russians blew up the warehouse with their big gun so the Triad wouldn't get it."

Julian was completely still. "You were at the warehouse?"

"Well, don't worry. I got out in time."

Julian looked like he'd been slapped. "Xiah brought you with him to the warehouse? What in God's name was he thinking?"

His horror made me realize I'd said something wrong. "Um. No. No, I wasn't there. He just . . . told me afterward."

Julian lowered his head and nuzzled my neck for several seconds.

"God, Judith," he whispered. "How did I let you get into this mess?"

"Are you crying?"

"Not quite." He raised his head. Concern and grief were brimming in his eyes. "But I'm not far away."

"Oh, Julian." I caressed his face. "I love you."

He grimaced. "I wish you'd say that when you're not drugged."

I furrowed my brow. "What did you really shoot me up with?"

"Just what I told you." He seemed regretful, which made me doubt him. "You probably won't remember any of this by tomorrow."

"Really?" I grinned. "Then I guess you can do anything you want to me. Without consequences."

He sighed. "There are always consequences. I just want to talk."

"So we're talking." I yawned. "Jeez. Now I'm getting tired."

Julian studied me. I studied him. He lowered his head and gave me a last kiss, long and mournful.

"What was that?"

He smiled. He peeled himself off me. The entire front of his clothing was soaked and wrinkled. He rubbed his eyes and shot me a sheepish glance. "I'll need to change."

I frowned. "What about me?"

— 27 —

Hide

♂

I flailed around on the couch in Jack's media room, barely catching myself before falling off. I leaped up, rushed to the door, and exploded into the dojo. I ran through the room, into the mudroom, and down the stairs into the darkened basement. Goom was curled up on the couch, napping.

"Goom," I yelled. I ran over and shook him. "Goom!"

He snorted and waved his arms around. "What? Fucking what? Ethan? What you on about?"

"Where's Jack?"

"How in the hell should I know?" He shook his fists at me. "At least he's not down here scaring the shit outta me!"

I saw on one of Goom's computer screens that it was 0146. "We need to get out of here. Now!"

"What?" He rubbed his eyes. "What's wrong? What happened?"

"Julian kidnapped Judith. She's in a safe house in the mountains. She told him everything."

Goom's complexion drained to pasty green, the striking color change apparent even in the dimly lit room. "Oh, for fuck's sake!" He ran to his computers. "We are fucking boned!"

I was already scrambling up the stairs, yelling, "Jack!"

* * *

By 0221, FBI teams were swarming over the bungalow and comic book store, and Jack and I were standing on the roof of a church half a mile away. The rise in terrain gave workable line of sight to Jack's, especially since the intervening trees had lost most of their foliage.

We contemplated the two Russians at our feet. When we scaled the church, it's hard to say if we or the Russians were more surprised. One had been looking through his sniper scope when we waylaid him. It was still trained on Jack's kitchen window, through which I could see a couple of agents milling around.

"Nice," I said.

Jack was crouched beside me. He nodded silently. He'd been going through the Russians' wallets and handed them to me. I looked at the wallets while he searched their duffel bag. I held one in the air so the uplights on the side of the church illuminated it clearly. "'Yve-g ... geny Viktory ... vich Lebed ... Lebedov-sky.' Jeez. Why can't these people have pronounceable names?"

Jack stopped to look at me. If he hadn't been wearing a mask, I thought I would probably have seen his you're-an-idiot expression. It wasn't so much a change in his implacable face as a set in his jaw and resignation in his shoulders. "*Viktoryevich.* It means his father was named Viktor."

"Oh." I considered the Russian's shadowed face: a slender, wolf-like nose, high cheekbones, and angular jaw. Finally, I got it. "Jeez! 'Viktor' as in 'Viktor Volkov'? It's the Wolf's son?!"

"Perhaps." Jack had finished rifling through the duffel and zipped it closed. Apparently he hadn't found anything interesting.

"So what do we do with them?"

"We'll leave them for your friend, Agent Bead." He pulled one of Goom's untraceable flip phones from a waist pouch and started composing a text message. With his free hand, he tossed me a couple of zipties. I secured the men's hands behind their backs. Afterward, Jack showed me the phone. "What do you think?"

His message read: *Gresham All Saints, on the roof. Happy hunting.*

I laughed. "He'll appreciate that. Especially the 'happy hunting' part."

Jack sighed. "It's only humorous if he doesn't find the Black Room."

I grimaced. "What happens if he does?"

"It's wired to the gas mains. If we see fire in the sky, he found it."

* * *

Half an hour later, Jack and I were in the basement of Blaze's mom's boyfriend's cousin's newly purchased funeral home. Ownership of the funeral home was technically still mired in red tape pending review of the bankruptcy petitions filed by its former owner. Nonetheless, it was spacious, well appointed, unoccupied, and there was no way Volkov or Julian could trace anyone to it. Or so we hoped.

Blaze came down the stairs and saluted us. "Hey, guys. Is this perfect or what? When you told me you needed a place to lie low, I knew right away this was perfect for you."

We contemplated Blaze's arrangement. She had several iron candelabras placed around the dank room. In the middle sat three plush coffins. Two were full-sized, and one was half-sized.

"Those actually look pretty comfy," I said.

Jack remained stone silent.

Blaze smiled broadly. "The little one's for a larger family pet, but it looked just the right size for Jack's midget."

We started coughing into our hands to avoid falling to the floor and rolling around screaming with laughter.

She turned back to her arrangement, beaming at her own cleverness. "I even drilled little air holes in them, near the head. I wasn't sure if you guys need to breathe while you're regenerating, so I hope that's okay."

Jack recovered first. "They're perfect."

Blaze smiled shyly at me. Suddenly, the smile dropped from her face. "Oh! Ethan, I forgot. Msti came to the junkyard and asked about Judith."

I started. "What?! When?"

"Uh, a couple of days ago. She didn't even stay for a drink or anything. And she didn't look so good. Skinny and haunted. She wouldn't tell me where she's staying, just asked about Judith and gave me a hug and left."

I shuddered. "It's not safe for you at home. You'll have to stay here."

Her eyes widened. "What?"

Jack nodded. "Starting now. And your mother?"

"Oh. Well, mom and Dwane are in Kentucky this weekend at a monster truck rally." Dwane was Saldene's boyfriend, the one with the cousin trying to buy the mortuary we were in at the moment. Blaze lifted a finger to her mouth and bit into the nail. "Do I need to call them and warn them?"

Jack frowned. "Might be a good idea. But they are probably safe there."

"Who's safe where now?" Goom tottered down the stairs and joined us.

"Ah. Gumbah Sarbloh," Jack said. "Blaze has thoughtfully provided us with comfortable resting quarters." He waved his hand, indicating the three coffins arrayed before us.

Goom looked at Blaze's layout, and his mouth dropped open. It took him a while to pull himself together enough to speak. "What the fuck's that little one? Is it for dead kids?"

Blaze piped up. "Technically it's for pets, but it's plusher than the kids ones he's got in stock at the moment."

Goom's face grayed. "I ain't sleeping in no dog coffin. No way in hell."

We all looked at him.

"I want a full-sized one. With red satin." He snapped his fingers at Blaze. "Get on it."

* * *

Upstairs, Goom unpacked his computer and set it up in one of the cushy receiving rooms. I sat on the couch, unsuccessfully attempting an aging Rubik's cube. Jack was somewhere unknown, probably checking over what gear we'd managed to pack in our mad rush to hide. Goom's voice rumbled out from under the big walnut desk where he was pulling cables and connecting equipment. "What'd you want to ask me, dickweed?"

"Huh?"

Goom snorted. "Ethan, put that fucking thing down and concentrate. You said you had a couple of questions about the case."

"Uh." I had to shift mental gears to get back on track. "For starters . . . why didn't anyone tell me Sam is Dragon's nephew too? How many of them are there?"

"Just the three. Sam's got a different mom."

"Oh, so he's a half-brother."

"Yeah."

"Previous wife?"

Goom slid out from under the desk, sat up, and contemplated me. "Chinese familial relations. You know anything about them?"

I blinked several times. "If they're different than ours, then no."

He sighed. "Sam's mom is the favored concubine. That puts him below Jun Lo and Shun Yan, but above the other concubines' kids. He's third in line for Dragon's empire. Well, second now, I guess."

I could feel my mind starting to boggle. "Who has concubines in this day and age? What century is this guy from?"

Goom snorted. "Ignoramus."

"Wait." I frowned. "Dragon has no kids of his own?"

Goom shrugged. "None that count."

"What's that supposed to mean?"

"He's got a daughter in Hong Kong. She's some kind of beauty product CEO or some crap like that. Rich and nasty."

My brow furrowed. “And she doesn’t count?”

“She’s a girl, stupid.”

“Well, that’s a little shortsighted.”

Goom hopped into the voluminous leather desk chair, pulled out his keyboard, and started typing. I returned to my Rubik’s cube. I knew how to do them; I had worked one many times as a kid, but somehow I couldn’t remember the trick.

Goom poked his head out from behind the monitor. He chortled. “You trying to solve that thing or make it worse?”

“Just shut up.”

“Give up now, retard. What was the other thing?”

“Huh?”

“The other thing you wanted to ask. You said there were two. Asslick.”

“Oh. Right.” I set the cube on the end table next to the couch. “I found something in the warehouse. I wanted to ask you about it.”

“I’m all ears.”

“It was a bunch of metal boxes screwed to one of those computer racks. About this big.” I held my hands out, a foot-and-a-half apart. “The boxes had gold foam inside and little holes.” I closed my eyes, visualizing what I’d seen. “Thirty-two little, round holes.”

I opened my eyes. Goom had rolled his chair out from behind the desk and was staring at me. “And?”

“That’s it.”

“Metal boxes with thirty-two little holes.”

“Yeah.”

He frowned. “How in the hell am I supposed to know what the fuck they were? Did you get a picture?”

"Uh. Not really." I cursed myself. Why didn't I take pictures?

He snorted. "Dumblenuts. No fucking clue. If they had foam, maybe it was to store something delicate."

"They had little needles sticking up in each hole."

"Needles?" His eyebrows slid up his forehead.

"Little, pointy metal things. Not sharp though. More like to hold something in place."

He thought for a couple of moments. "Maybe some kind of contact? Was the box cabled to the rack? Or just screwed in?"

"No, it had a thick cable going off the back. Like . . . this one." I pulled a wide, gray computer cable out of Goom's box of parts.

"Huh. It could have been some kind of reader. For uploading stuff from something in parallel, thirty-two at a time."

" 'Uploading stuff from something.' What 'something'? Circular thumb drives? Big marbles?"

He rolled behind the desk again so the monitor hid him completely. "How the hell should I know? Next time get me a fucking picture, brainiac."

I sighed. "Crap."

Goom rolled back out again and studied me. "But since we're asking questions, I have one for you too."

I felt a minor jolt of fear at that. "What?"

"Are you really telepathic with your sister?"

"Um."

"Oh, come on. It's not a trick question. Jack thinks you are. I think you're full of shit."

I stared at the dark red carpeting around us. "I'm not full of shit."

"So what's it like then?"

"What?"

"Being a girl."

I squirmed on the couch. "It's surprisingly similar to being a guy."

Goom rolled his eyes. "Oh, right. That socialist crap about how we're all the same."

"No, really. It is. Sure, there are physical differences, but it feels basically the same."

Goom snorted. "Some great insight. You're useless."

A rush of anger rose in me. "You want to know what the biggest difference is, little buddy?"

"Don't call me that."

"It's the same as being three feet tall and black."

His face darkened with red. "Screw you."

"Bet you can't guess what that difference is."

The corner of Goom's lips lifted in a sneer. "So tell me, oh wise one."

"It's easy. The biggest difference isn't being short or tall, or black or white, or male or female."

"Fine. So what is it?"

"It's the way other people treat you."

* * *

"Let's go over it again," Jack said. "Exactly what happened after Agent Bead picked your sister up?"

"Um. Well." I licked my lips. My mouth seemed awfully dry. Whenever Jack interrogated me, I had an unsettling vision of him standing over me with his .45 in his hands. I realized that was probably intentional. "Julian said there was a change in plans. They were going to a distant restaurant overlooking a lake."

Jack nodded.

"They came to the safe house."

Jack's eyes narrowed. "Ninety minutes of driving?"

"Yes."

"Then Agent Bead drugged her?"

"Well, she was freaking out. They almost tased her, but Julian told them not to. Instead, he had them shoot her up with something. Ben . . . bendo . . . bendoz-something."

"Benzodiazepine."

I snapped my fingers. "Yeah. That thing. And something else. It made her loopy. Happy and loose-lipped."

Goom snorted from behind the desk. "Great."

Jack seemed lost in thought. "Did he mention what it was?"

I sat for a moment, trying to recall the other term Julian had mentioned. "It sounded like 'huge heroic'?"

Jack exhaled deeply and closed his eyes.

Goom slid his chair out to look at us. "Fucking great. What's that mean, Lahngxian?"

Jack opened his eyes. "It was probably an amphetamine."

I grimaced. "It made her feel hot. And sweaty. And—" My eyes wandered the room. "Uninhibited."

"Yes." Jack's mask of equanimity was back.

I opened my mouth to continue, but Goom cut me off. "So basically your sister's FBI buddy kidnapped and drugged her, and she blabbed all our secrets."

I glared at him. "More or less."

Goom sneered. "And you know all this because you're telepathic."

"Ye-es. Basically."

Goom facepalmed. "We just sent Pike into the wilderness to look for this safe house. You'd better not be setting us up, asshole."

I frowned. "What do you mean?"

Jack uttered a quiet Mandarin phrase at Goom.

Goom crossed his arms. "He's playing us, Lahngxian."

I started. "What?"

Goom glowered at me. "Did y'all plan this before your sister left? Is the idea that we'll run up there and walk right into your pal Agent Bead's trap? Is that it?"

"No." I looked at Jack. He remained silent. "It's not like that at all. I'm not lying to you."

"Look," Goom said. "I get a kick out of your stupidity and all, but people aren't telepathic. Somehow you and your sister are shining us on."

What could I say? "No. We're not. It . . . It's hard to explain."

Goom snorted. "Yeah. I'll bet."

"It's the truth," I said quietly.

Goom rolled his eyes. "The only reason I don't shoot you both in your fucking sleep is because I've known Lahngxian here for my whole life and he's all I have. And he believes your shit."

Jack uttered another quiet Mandarin phrase.

Goom scoffed loudly. "Yeah, yeah. I know." He turned to me. "Your sister wags her perky little titties at him, and he thinks she's the goddess Nuwa. He's always been a sucker for pretty ladies. It's gonna get him killed this time."

Jack responded in Mandarin. He didn't move, his face didn't change, but he sounded distinctly angry. Goom flinched, like he'd been slapped. He fell silent. I thought his eyes might have been watering, but he looked away before I could really tell. I squirmed in my seat.

"Tell us about the link, Ethan," Jack said.

"Link?"

"With your sister."

I swallowed. "Well, when I'm asleep, she's awake, and vice versa."

"And when you wake, you remember everything that happened to her. And she you."

"Yes." Once again, I didn't bother trying to explain the reality. If it was hard to believe we were telepathic, I figured it would be impossible to believe I was actually a different person inside. Plus, from the outside, how could anyone tell the difference anyway?

Goom scoffed. When I looked over at him, he was shaking his head, but he kept quiet. He stared at the ceiling.

For some reason, it mattered to me whether Goom believed me. I frowned. "Goom-boy. If I was making this shit up, don't you think I'd give myself a better superpower? Like claim I could fly or read minds or something?"

He sneered. He muttered something unintelligible that could have been about assjockeys and retards. Or maybe douchebags and foreskin lint.

I sighed. Jack was staring at me. I furrowed my brow. "So . . . uh. Jack."

He cocked his head. "Yes, Ethan?"

"Do you really believe my sister is your snake goddess?"

— 28 —

Breakfast

♀

I was thirsty beyond belief and had a raging headache. I guessed that was the aftermath of the crap Julian had drugged me with.

Agent Becker sat in a chair near the window. She had been reading, but now she noticed I was awake. "Morning. Sleep well?"

The woman had a nasty fat lip. I supposed that was my doing. "Um." I felt myself blushing. "Sorry about punching you."

"I've had worse." She looked at her watch. "Agent Bead will be here soon. Why don't you shower and come downstairs for some breakfast?"

A while later, Julian and I were on the back porch. He sat, watching me closely, sipping his coffee. I had my hands wrapped around a mug of hot chocolate. Even wearing the huge sweater Agent Becker had brought for me, I was freaking freezing. The sun peeked out over a nearby mountain, promising warmth later in the day. For now, I shivered.

Julian broke the long silence. "How did he know we were coming?"

My head snapped up. "What?"

"Your friend, Jack. How did you warn him?"

I glared at Julian. "What? Becker's cavity search wasn't enough? You know I'm not bugged. How could I possibly warn him?"

He drummed his fingers on the table. "Where is he now?"

"How the hell would I know?"

"Where's Blaze?"

"Blaze? What do you mean? Is she missing?" I hoped my feigned ignorance was convincing.

His eyes narrowed. He didn't answer.

I smacked the tabletop with my palm. "No, tell me. Did something happen to her? Is she all right?"

"Where's Ethan?"

I couldn't help it—my mouth dropped open. "What?!"

He rubbed his chin. "You told me he's in an urn on your coffee table. We found nothing in the refuse of the Decatur house."

I shut my mouth. My mind raced.

"Also, I can't find any record of his cremation. I've been diligently checking funeral homes within ten miles of Decatur."

I bit my lip. Julian was checking funeral homes. That wasn't good. "Well, I have no idea what's wrong with your CSI guys. He was right there. Although, it was hard to tell with the Russian mob blowing up the place."

"Oh, so you were there that night."

I swallowed. What did I just give away?

He drummed his fingers on the table again. "It would save us a lot of trouble if you'd fill me in on these things. I can help you. All of you."

I stared at my hot chocolate, saying nothing.

"Do I need to order another cavity search?"

"Asshole."

— 29 —

Decoy

♂

I knelt in what used to be Ethan's bedroom, noting that while 99 percent of the house was destroyed, at least one completely random and minor object in every room seemed to have magically escaped even the barest of fire damage. Here, I found the helmet that hadn't saved my brother's life. Once I pulled off the melted shreds of the effects bag, I turned it over.

On the outside, the helmet showed scant signs of the impact or the subsequent firebombing. Some scrapes ran across the top and back of the helmet, and a noticeable groove was bored into the left temple, perhaps a quarter inch wide and two inches long. Maybe from a pebble trapped between Ethan and the ground? I tossed the helmet back into the rubble.

"Wonderful."

I was here to find somewhere to hide Ethan's "cremains." It was brilliant. We'd forged an entry for him in the foreclosed funeral home's records, a cryptic, abbreviated note that wouldn't lead to anything concrete. We liberated a small urn, into which we put ashes from the crematorium after burning them with bits of Ethan's skin, hair, fingernails, and whatever else we could get off without permanently injuring him. Then we singed and cracked the urn. It plausibly could have survived the firebombing. Right?

Except, I had to find somewhere to leave it. Somewhere that would corroborate my story, but explain why the CSIs hadn't managed to find it before. I sighed.

As I stood, a moving shadow caught my eye. I whirled, ready to fight. No one. No sound except the crickets and occasional night bird. I waited for several minutes, poised to strike. No additional shadows disturbed me. I continued with my search of the ruins.

The ceiling had collapsed on the kitchen, so I dropped off the foundation and circled to the back of the house to check if there was another way to access the utility closet where we had stored our mementos in a metal lockbox. I supposed I could have been so distraught over Ethan's death that I had forgotten I'd transferred his urn to the keepsake box.

The closet was buried. But the stove was standing nearby, relatively unscathed. With a stretch, I might be able to reach the back, which used to have a wall behind it. Suppose I buried the urn in the rubble there? Could it have been perched on the stove, where it would have fallen and rolled under the oven as the wall collapsed?

* * *

As I was wriggling out of the contortions I'd needed to reach the spot, I heard a twig snap. I wrenched myself the rest of the way out and whipped my head around. There. A dark figure disappeared behind what was left of the garden shed. I ducked into the overgrowth and circled the shed, emerging silently behind the intruder. The woman was in a black-and-gold suit with a full face mask. Was it Paige? Why on earth was she poking around the remains of my Decatur home?

The woman turned and saw me a split second before I grasped her, then took off down the alley, running full tilt. I took off after her, impressed at how fast she was. She passed the most obvious route to the skies, which would have been the fence at the end of the block. Instead, the figure in black and gold rounded the corner and sped down the sidewalk. I was gaining, but the woman put on a burst of speed and leaped over some scrub bushes into the rail track. Where in the hell was she going?

My hand was no more than an inch from the scruff of the woman's neck when she abruptly swerved and jumped off a bridge. I skidded to a halt and looked over the side in time to see the woman roll neatly, glance up at me, and disappear into the tunnel underneath.

"Damn it."

I readied my gun, lifted myself over the short bridge wall, and dropped down to the middle of the street below. I was ready for a hundred mobsters to jump out in front of me, but I wasn't ready for what I actually saw. At the other end of the tunnel, illuminated clearly in bright streetlight, stood The Wolf, aka the Blond Smoker. He had the woman by the throat and a .45 to her head.

I stopped dead.

Saliva glinted on a silver tooth cap as Volkov smiled. "Hello, Enforcer."

"Wha—"

Thunk.

Something unyielding smashed into my skull, and I fell into darkness.

— 30 —

Breakout

♀

I flailed in the darkness and screamed. My arm connected with the lamp on the bedside table and swept it to the floor.

Crash!

Heartbeats later, the bedroom door opened, and a big man with a gun was silhouetted in the hall light. I screamed again and rolled off the bed, knocking the wind out of myself on the carpeted floor. The overhead light came on, and Agent Roberts dashed around the bed, noting me sprawled on the floor. He searched the window area and far side of the room, holstering his gun once he'd satisfied himself there were no monsters.

The big black FBI agent with the kindly face and salt-and-pepper beard knelt beside me, giving the all-clear over his walkie-talkie.

"You okay, sweetheart?"

I wasn't by any stretch of the imagination okay. "Where's Julian?" I jumped to my feet.

Roberts straightened up with me. "He's not here. What's wrong, honey? Nightmares?"

"No, I did not have a nightmare. I need access to the Internet, now." I glowered at him.

"That's not gonna happen, girlfriend. You want a cup of coffee?"

Agent Becker appeared in the doorway. "What's happening?"

I pointed at her. "I need Internet. I need it now!"

Becker's brow furrowed. "I'm sorry, that's not possible. You are incommunicado for your own safety."

"Okay, look." I glared from one to the other. "If you don't get me Internet access right now, someone very important to me is going to die."

They looked at each other. They looked at me.

I sprung onto the bed, launched myself at Agent Becker, and sent her flying backward onto her ass in the hallway. I rolled over Becker, jumped to my feet, and flew toward the stairs.

"Shit!" Becker yelled.

I heard Roberts on his radio. "She's running! Lockdown, now!"

I barreled down the stairs. Agent Thompson stepped out at the bottom. "Easy, sweetheart," he said. I didn't stop. I put on a burst of speed and jumped him, climbing right up his chest and vaulting over his shoulders.

Agent Howard leaped up from the kitchen table where he'd been playing solitaire. He got between me and the front door and pulled his Taser. "Sorry, sweetheart. No can do."

I scrambled onto the dining table, threw my arms up to protect my head, and dove toward the generously sized window above the sink as whizzing projectiles missed me by mere inches. One hundred fifty pounds of woman versus sheet glass: I went right through, impressing the shit out of myself and leaving the agents inside dumbfounded when I landed semi-cleanly and rolled head over heels without chopping myself open on the glass and without stopping the momentum of the jump.

Everyone was yelling at everyone else to stop me.

I swore bitterly at every single donut I had ever eaten as I ran for my life across the gravel driveway and jumped into the forest on the other side. Although we were far out in the boonies, there were neighbors. I crashed and cursed through prickly bushes and thick forest and emerged near another house. It was dark and looked empty, but at least I could trade the mud and roots I'd scrambled over for a gravel driveway, then a dirt access road.

Surprisingly little yelling came through the dense night wildlife noises. In the distance, I heard car doors slam and knew my captors would round the drive any minute and overtake me. I ran for all I was worth, even though it was pointless.

Adrenaline had my system in such an uproar that it took me a while to recognize the miracle in front of me. It was a car's headlights, moving along the road directly toward me.

The front bumper of the beat-up, brown hatchback stopped inches away. I was sure the driver was wondering what to make of the crazy lady in pajamas blocking the road. I ran around to the passenger's side, wrenched open the door and threw myself over the seat into the back. My legs sprawled around near the ceiling. A Caucasian bottle blond with an obvious tanning booth fetish sat in the driver's seat, a cigarette butt hanging from her open mouth. I managed to turn around and flatten myself out of sight, half on the backseat, half in the foot well.

"Please, please, drive," I said.

Bottle Blonde blew out a lungful of smoke, reached over, slammed the passenger door shut, and started up again like nothing had happened. Cars passed us almost immediately. It was a narrow road, and the woman nearly had to drive with two tires off the side to let the FBI sedans pass.

We drove in silence. I tried hard to think of some kind of plausible excuse for my predicament. Bottle Blonde finished her cigarette and lit another almost immediately. I was getting a nicotine high simply from being in the car with her.

Finally, she spoke. "Coot's is on my way to work. I'll drop ya there, honey, and maybe y'all can call someone to come get ya."

That sounded promising. "I don't suppose this 'Coot' guy has Internet?"

The woman laughed.

***

Cooters turned out to be a seriously crappy redneck bar in the middle of the Appalachian village near Julian's safe house. I might have been right at home, except I was in my pajamas and my feet were bare and bleeding. I strolled up to the bar, ignoring the roving masculine interest floating toward me from the dark figures nursing their drinks in the gloom. The bartender was a really skinny white guy with tattoos covering his arms and scraggly blond hair falling over his shoulders. His very existence in the place probably violated several health codes.

"Howdy," I said to him.

He looked me up and down. "Hey. What you want?"

"You got Internet?"

He lit a cigarette. "Do we look like a fucking computer cafe, or what, lady? We got beer. That's it."

I would have shot back a snarky remark, but I noticed a very interesting table of patrons. There were three young guys with ball caps, and miracle of miracles, one of them had an iPhone. I strolled over casually. I always showed up at hick bars in my pajamas, I was just that cool. I smiled.

"Dude, can I please borrow your phone? I just need to log into a site and leave a message. It'll be, like, thirty seconds."

The three of them gaped at me. The guy holding the iPhone grinned, obviously having several beers under his belt by now. I winced, bracing myself for the inevitable rude comment. He waved the phone at me.

"You want this? For thirty seconds?"

"Yes, please."

"Show me your tits, and I'll give it to you for a whole minute."

Big smile. Buddies laughing. Ha. Ha. I lifted my pajama shirt for a millisecond, then put it down again.

Silence.

I snatched the phone from his outstretched hand while he was still stupefied. Lots of laughter. One of his buddies called to me. "Hey, lady, if you show me your tits, I'll give you way more than just my phone." Eyebrows waggled all around the table. Whatever. I was already logged in to Goom's secure site, calling for help. I simply had to send Jack a couple of prearranged panic codes. Due to Volkov and Julian monitoring any communications, this is what we were reduced to.

I hit send, waited for confirmation, and handed Beer Belly back his iPhone. "Thanks."

"Anytime."

The cute one sitting beside my iPhone savior didn't look twenty-one.

"Lady, you want to have a drink with us? I'll buy a round."

I did vaguely consider it. They were staring at me with hopeful expressions. But no. Just no. "Nah, I got some friends coming to pick me up."

They nodded, returning to their posturing and beer drinking.

I wandered out to the front porch and sat on the stoop. The waitress was smoking a cigarette in the parking lot, no doubt enjoying her break from the stale, claustrophobic establishment behind us. My breath condensed in the frigid air. I wrapped my arms around myself and shivered.

It wasn't long before a state trooper pulled up. A pudgy white guy climbed out, donned his trooper hat, and muttered into his car radio.

He ambled over. "You Judith Gold?"

"Yep."

"Well, ma'am, I'm gonna have to ask ya to stay put here and wait with me." He horked up a glob of smokeless tobacco and spit it on the ground near the bottom of the stairs. "Ya got some people coming to get you."

"Yep."

The waitress finished her break. "Evenin', sugar."

I was pretty sure she was greeting the trooper and not me.

He tipped his hat. "Howdy, Sadie. Busy night?"

"Nah, jus' the regulars. Y'all want me to bring you somethin'?"

"A Coke'd be awful sweet of ya, honey."

And, so forth, and so on. Just another ordinary night in the boonies.

***

Julian pulled back a corner of the bedroom shade and peered into the front driveway. "If I didn't have such respect for your dad, I'd have you thrown into jail right now."

I was sitting on the bed. "If you're so sure Jack is coming to get me, why don't you just move me somewhere else?"

Julian didn't answer. After a minute, he uttered his checkpoint phrase into his radio.

A chill slid down my neck. "You're gonna try and catch him."

He said nothing.

"You can't do that!"

"How many men does he have?"

I fell silent.

Julian's eyes narrowed in the glow suffusing through the thin shade. "How did he know we were coming to his house yesterday?"

I frowned deeply.

"What message did you send him at the bar?"

I swallowed, saying nothing.

"I can have Agent Thompson cut you another cocktail if you prefer."

"Fuck you."

"Fine. If you're not going to help me, then keep quiet, or I'll have Agent Roberts lock you in the bathroom."

* * *

By 0438, my anger had given away to drowsy boredom. I almost missed the sudden darkening due to a power outage. Julian was on his radio. "Everyone hold your positions. Hold your—"

Headlights moved across the shade, flooding the front of the house with shining brilliance. Julian jumped up and looked out the window. He transmitted, "Pickup truck. Accost. Extreme caution."

I jumped off the bed, ran over, and peeked out the other side of the shade. Blaze's pickup truck was slowly making its way up the gravel in front of the house. What on earth was she doing? Blaze stopped near the house. I heard agents yelling.

Stop your vehicle! Step out of the vehicle!

The driver's side door opened. I counted at least three agents surrounding the truck, guns ready and trained at the cab. Blaze's hands emerged first. "Don't shoot!" she yelled. The rest of her came out slowly, and she nudged the door shut behind her with her rear, holding her empty hands high in the air. Aside from the grimace on her face, she was wearing a black military vest with what looked like about a dozen or so pipe bombs strapped to it. A huge man in a black suit and mask remained in the cab: Jack. Through the windshield, I could see his outstretched arm holding a .45 aimed directly at Blaze's torso. She stood motionless beside the pickup.

"Son of a—" Julian whirled. "Are they crazy enough to set those off and blow us all to kingdom come?"

I was shaking all over. "Uh. Maybe?"

A wavering voice came over the radio. "*Sir*?"

Julian replied, "I'm coming down. Move back. Okay? *Move back*. Get everyone back. And secure all the entrances!" He stalked across the room and pulled the door open. A tall, muscular figure in a black suit with red piping and a full face mask stood there, poised to strike. "Holy—"

Julian had no time to react before his radio was slapped away and Jack's open hand buried itself in his chest. Julian flew backward, stumbling across the room. He fell hard into the chair next to me, gasping for breath. Jack came in and closed the door behind him.

"Jack!"

I ran over and threw my arms around him. He winced; I remembered his tender ribs and eased up. He put his hands on my shoulders, then bent slightly and kissed me on the forehead through his mask. It wasn't super intimate, but I glanced back and saw Julian grinding his teeth.

"Xiah," Julian hissed. "You're . . . under . . . arrest."

Jack said nothing. He crossed the room, leaned slightly, and punched Julian, hard. The chair tipped over, and Julian fell to the floor.

I ran to them and grabbed at Jack. "Stop!"

Jack knelt on Julian's chest, holding him immobile. He pulled a thin tube from his belt and loaded a tiny dart into it.

"Stop! Jack! No. Don't hurt him. Please?"

I couldn't do anything. Jack raised the tube to his lips and shot Julian, point-blank. A tiny, feather-ended spike protruded from Julian's neck. I tried to reach Julian, but Jack blocked me. He bent quickly and plucked the dart from Julian's throat, tucking it carefully into his belt. He dragged me away, muttering, "Now he can see how it feels."

Julian moaned softly behind us.

I was helpless under Jack's iron grip, but that didn't stop me from struggling. "Jack, please! What did you do to him?"

Jack halted and lowered his masked face to mine. "Judith. Stop fighting me. He'll be fine. We need to go, now."

* * *

Agent Becker was bound and gagged, lying on the ground floor in front of the staircase. When I saw Becker, I squawked. My hand flew to my mouth.

"Shh," Jack warned as we stepped over Becker. As he led me toward the back door, he put his free hand to his ear. "We're coming out," he said, so softly I could barely hear it. A moment later, he shuffled me out the door. I saw Agent Roberts and another man I didn't recognize lying on the patio, bound and gagged just like Becker.

It didn't take long for us to clear the lot. The blackness of a rural night enveloped us. Jack pulled night goggles down from his forehead. We walked for what seemed like ages. I had no idea what direction we were going. I stumbled more than once over dense underbrush; finally, my feet simply gave up, scratched and bleeding from my two bare-footed trips through the tortuous undergrowth.

Jack took me in his arms and carried me, as if I were no more cumbersome than a small child. He said nothing.

The swaying of my body in Jack's grip had almost lulled me to sleep by the time we reached two vehicles parked in a clearing. I could hardly see anything, it was so dark. Jack helped me stand, and a shadowy figure came around one of the vehicles and held something out at me. I cowered as he waved it all over my body, arms, and legs while Jack supported me.

"She's clean," the man said. His face was impenetrably dark, and I realized he was wearing black face paint.

Jack nodded, then hoisted me into the passenger side of the familiar black Wrangler he borrowed from Captain Pike. We reached the main road a couple minutes later. Jack put his hand to his ear and said, "We're clear." He pulled his mask off, unhooked his earbud, and plopped them into the utility holder between the seats.

I studied my companion's profile in the dim glow of the dashboard lights. He was stone silent. It seemed odd, but up until that point, the whole vigilante business had been like a game. Dangerous and brutal, yes, but exhilarating and noble. Now, in the aftermath of my liberation, jumbled versions of Julian's warnings came back to me.

He's a stone-cold killer.

He has no conscience.

I winced, sinking back into my seat.

"Cold?" Jack asked. He'd been watching me from the corner of his unfathomable, jet-black eyes.

I shuddered. "Did you, or did you not, just roll an FBI safe house?"

He said nothing.

"I thought you were in the truck with Blaze?"

"That's a dummy in an old suit. A decoy to keep them occupied while we escaped out the back."

"Wow."

Jack was silent for several moments, watching the empty road through the windshield.

"Hostage liberation," he finally said.

"What?"

He faced me, his expression as neutral as always. "It's what I do."

— 31 —

Message

♀/♂

Piss, shit, and blood. A whiff of them from somewhere nasty is blessedly short-lived. On the other hand, being thoroughly saturated with their putrid, chemical stench—

I choked and shook my head, gasping for air. I tasted rusted metal steeped in antiseptic, and no matter how much I coughed and spit, I couldn't stop tasting it. Someone was screaming, and someone was yelling. I thought it was me screaming and Volkov yelling, but I wasn't sure. He definitely wanted something. He wanted me to wake up.

Wake up.

My eyes were crusted shut, and I couldn't get my hands down to help them. I finally willed one eye open and realized I was underwater.

No.

Not underwater. Freezing cold water was running down the chain I was hanging from and dribbling over me. I was naked. Hanging from a meathook. My feet were chained to the ground so I was stretched out, and my toes barely scraped the puddles underneath me.

Volkov was asking me something. A single word pushed through a curtain of agony.

Enforcer.

I snorted up an immense blob of disgusting body fluids and spit at him.

Splut. Direct hit.

He brought forward a black stick with blue lightning crackling at its tip and slammed it into my chest. A million angry fire ants swarmed me and every time one bit me the muscle would cramp so I was a ball of biting, swarming, cramping torment.

Nooo . . .

* * *

No. That wasn't right. I was screaming at Jack. He was restraining me for some reason.

"Judith," he was saying. "Come back to me."

My senses reeled. I was in the funeral home on the heavily carpeted floor in the receiving room. The door was closed, and Jack was kneeling beside me, bending over me, pressing down on my shoulders. My gaze settled on the tiny, black stubble protruding from his chin. His large thumbs delicately wiped my cheeks.

"Where is he, Judith? Where is Ethan?"

"I don't know!" Tears stung my eyes. This was it. It was all my fault. My brother would die a horrible second death, and it was only because of my hubris, my stupid, stupid arrogance that I could be a superhero. This wasn't a comic book. This was real life, and real life was vicious and unforgiving. Ethan was dying. I prayed that his unconsciousness was buried so deep inside that he wasn't feeling the torture; that he was in a place of calm and comfort. I shuddered. Everything was ending, and it was all my fault.

Jack shook me, gently but earnestly. "No, Judith. Don't give up. You must focus. Breathe."

"What?"

"Relax, Judith. Look at my eyes."

I looked at his eyes. They were impossibly black, as if the pupils had swallowed his retinas. "Deep breath. Take a deep breath with me." He put one hand on my chest. He heaved a great breath: in, then out. Another: in, then out.

Time slowed as I watched, the immediacy of my plight receding.

"Good girl. Now breathe all the way into your stomach." He moved his hand from my chest to my stomach.

I stared at him.

"Come on, I want to feel your stomach rise with the next breath. Watch."

He heaved another great sigh, the air traveling in with his shoulders and puffing out his entire chest and stomach, then deflating.

I was hypnotized. I breathed a voluminous, deep breath, causing his hand to rise and fall on my belly. I felt a coolness around my neck and realized Ethan's pendant was still with me, dangling onto the floor under my head. I reached up and brought it back to my chest. I stroked it, fingers running along the tiny obsidian bumps. It was a double S shape, and I saw it in my mind, all silver and black, glowing with Ethan's essence.

Jack said, "Very good. Now. Be calm. I need you to go back to him."

"I can't!" My breath caught in my throat. I clenched the pendant.

"Breathe, Judith. Breath is the divide between body and mind. Just breathe. Don't let your heart race." His hand returned to my chest, closing around my hands and the pendant, weighing into my sternum. I was sure he felt my desperately pounding heart. My head was heavy, and I felt as if I were falling.

"Wh-What? Jack?"

"Judith, I can make my heart stop. I can hold my breath for nearly ten minutes. It's not because I'm superhuman. It is practice. You can make your mind work for you. You can see Ethan and learn to control it."

"He's . . . " I swallowed thickly. "They're torturing him."

"Don't fight it. Just let it happen. And, when you come back, tell me everything."

I closed my eyes, aware of Jack's heavy hand resting on my thudding chest. I forced myself to breathe more slowly. More deeply.

This was what superheroes were actually made of. They were made of fearful breaths and the will to go on when reason failed. I could save my brother. Jack had said so. The pendant said so. I could save him because I was a superhero. Female or not, heroes were made inside with determination and guile. I would go back there and face Volkov. I would hold on to the pendant and know I was separate, something Volkov couldn't possibly know or plan for. I could do it.

The room disintegrated around me. All I had was my own breath.

* * *

I couldn't breathe. It was the end, because I couldn't breathe. I was underwater. I couldn't lift my head. The impulse to breathe was overwhelming, but I knew I couldn't inhale the bitter liquid. Darkness settled into every sense; I was moments away from death.

Then, someone pulled me out. Or had I dreamed it?

I wasn't underwater. I was back on the meat hook. Volkov was in my face. I had lost my rage somewhere in this journey, and all that was left was the purely animal need to exist for another moment. And then another.

And . . . yet another.

Through a watery veil, I saw a slender figure in black emerge behind Volkov. The woman in the gold-and-black suit. With her mask off. Cold betrayal sloshed in the pit of my stomach. In retrospect, I supposed it was obvious. I coughed the woman's name.

Msti.

Volkov's eyes narrowed. He turned to his evil associate. They conversed in unintelligible, guttural syllables for several moments.

"You see," Volkov turned to me. He gripped my chin, squeezing my cheeks together. "I thought you were this 'Enforcer' we seek. But my comrade assures me you are not. You are a dead man. Come back to life. Only to die again." He laughed.

Msti cursed at him and spoke vehemently, gesticulating wildly.

"Nyet." He dropped his hand from my chin. Then he brought it up again, fast, and socked me across the jaw.

Ow. I tasted fresh blood.

"I think you do know Enforcer."

Msti threw her hands up and stalked from the room.

Volkov gritted his teeth. "Very well, we shall see."

He brought up his pain stick and pressed it to my underarm. Great, savage screams echoed throughout the cavernous room. My screams. Yet they were oddly distanced, as if my ears had detached and I heard them from afar. Volkov retracted the stick, but it took several seconds for my insides to stop shuddering. I flailed in my bonds. Blood trickled down my arms from where the chains cut into my wrists. I couldn't feel my hands.

"F-f-fuck you." In spite of the water running over me, I couldn't seem to find enough liquid in my mouth to spit at him.

"Hm," he said blandly. "Well, we've only begun, my friend." He moved to a steel table next to us. He set the pain stick down and retrieved a syringe filled with clear liquid. He held it up to the light and flicked the needle. "We have only just begun."

* * *

The terror in my blue eyes was reflected in miniature in Jack's bottomless irises. He was gripping my outstretched arms. Tears were flowing down my cheeks. "He's killing him. Volkov is killing my brother."

"Yes. What did you see?"

"He's hanging from a chain. It's a big room. Metal floors. Dark walls. One light, just a bulb, overhead. A metal table with," I swallowed heavily, "instruments."

Jack nodded. "Was there a window? A door?"

"A door . . . " I remembered the cheap plywood slamming behind Msti. I gasped. "Msti was there! You were right."

Jack frowned. "Were there any markings? Dirt on the floor? A grate?"

I buried my face in my hands. "No. I couldn't see. I can't see anything." Sobs wracked me. My chest burned with despair. "It's . . . k-killing . . . me."

Jack was silent for several minutes, holding me through my fit of despair. Once my wailing subsided, he took his phone from his breast pocket and held it out. "Text your friend Msti. I'll dictate."

"But—"

He waved his hand.

I entered Msti's number and waited.

He said, "Tell the Wolf Enforcer will deal."

* * *

"You're back," a voice said. I heard footsteps clank and a door open, then muffled voices in Russian.

I blinked and blinked, trying to clear the cloudiness from my eyes. I was in the same room, but secured to a chair, with my arms behind my back. Volkov and some anonymous thug I hadn't seen before came through the plywood door. Thug Boy closed it behind them and stepped to one side, loitering in the shadows while the Wolf greeted me.

"You do have an annoying tendency to leave us just when it's getting interesting." He pulled my eyelids back one by one with his thumb and studied my eyeballs.

Assclown, I thought, inwardly chuckling.

I felt like laughing every time Goom called me that. It was so rude, yet it felt like a happy word, like scruffling a shaggy, faithful dog's head under a brilliantly sunny sky . . .

Huh?

Volkov was asking, ". . . and how do you feel my friend?"

"Farking fabulous," I said. My mouth seemed stuffed with cotton. My tongue felt fat. I chortled. "I feel fat."

He smiled. "Good."

Something tickled my mind. Something I was supposed to remember?

He pulled a chair over. It scraped and whined on the flooring. I shuddered. The din lingered in my mind, echoing for several seconds after it stopped. When the sound had finally died, I realized Volkov had sat down. He leaned against the back of the chair and crossed his legs.

"So, my friend. Talk to me. Has Enforcer abandoned you?"

Something oozed over my upper lip. I tasted it. Not blood, just snot.

Volkov lifted a finger. He waggled it around as he spoke. I followed it with my eyes, transfixed. "He has thrown you to the wolves, so to speak."

I shook my head to clear the image of that finger. "Maybe. But he is just pretend. Like Batman and Robin."

"Oh. Are you Robin?"

"Yeah, I am." I snorted. "Sometimes I get to ride in the Batmobile."

Volkov grinned. "Happy little sidekick. And what does he call you?"

"I'm just a dumb redneck. I can't understand the names he calls me."

Volkov lit a cigarette and inhaled deeply. I marveled at the glowing ember, a spot of blinding orange that followed my gaze around the dim room. There it was in front of the ceiling when I looked up; a visual memory.

Memory.

I frowned. I was supposed to remember to tell Volkov something. Smoke curled around him. He held the cigarette in one hand and was fiddling with his phone with the other.

I started. "Your phone!"

His eyes narrowed. "What?"

The door banged open, making Volkov jump. As the sound reverberated through my addled mind, Msti emerged through the curtain of smoke.

I gasped. "Her phone. Check her phone."

— 32 —

Raveland

♀

Jack, Goom, and I were in the black Jeep in the parking lot of a nightclub called *Raveland*. The setting sun cast long shadows on two massively muscled bouncers guarding the door. The queue wound around the building three people wide, merry partygoers of all sexes and persuasions cavorting in a haze of dying rust-colored light.

Jack handed me an earbud which I inserted and arranged my hair to cover. "No need to hide it well," he said. "They'll expect it." He adjusted a tiny microphone attached to a miniature plastic box and handed it to me. He looked away as I tucked it into my bra. Inside my purse, my phone rattled. I had only turned it on a couple of minutes ago, but I already had a message. I saw it was from Julian. I hit play.

". . . telemarketer?" Goom was saying from the backseat.

"Shh," I warned him. "I'm trying to listen."

"I said, who is it?"

I shook my arm at him, motioning to shut the hell up. Meanwhile, Julian's rambling voice stuttered from the phone. I couldn't understand most of what he said. It sounded like part of it might have even been Cherokee. If I didn't know better, I'd have thought he drunk-dialed me. I cut playback off midsentence.

Jack sat with his hands folded in his lap. Goom pecked at his laptop.

I cleared my throat loudly. "Jack."

The big man faced me. "Judith."

"What did you do to Julian?"

Silence.

"Tell me. Now."

Jack sighed. "I put him into outer space."

I huffed. "And that means?"

Goom piped up. "He shot him full of acid."

"What!?"

Goom snorted. "Acid. You know. LSD."

"You—" I couldn't believe it. I stared at the phone in my hand.

Goom chortled, hardly attempting to suppress his jollity. Jack eyed a speck on the windshield, his face blank. I couldn't help myself. I burst out laughing. I could only guess what poor Julian was going through.

* * *

I managed a flippant, broad smile for the bouncers, ignored the queue, and handed the bouncer my VIP ID. He looked at it, checked a list on his smartphone, then held the door for me. "Enjoy your night."

Inside, my eyes and ears had to adjust to the darkness and din. Now what? Suddenly, Msti was beside me. Like me, she was dressed in club clothes: A shimmery blouse and tight miniskirt. She kissed me on both cheeks, as if we were just a couple of best friends meeting for a night on the town. I felt vaguely nauseous.

"What now?" I had to yell over the raucous beat.

Msti smiled. "Come, chickadee. Let us sit."

She led me to a small booth near a crowded platform and dance cage. Ordinarily, I was as big a fan of the club scene as any twenty-something. Not tonight. A waitress in a leather bustier and hot pink miniskirt came over. I started to wave her away, but Msti stopped her and ordered something. How could Msti be so calm and ordinary? I realized I didn't know Msti at all. How could I be her friend for years and not know her at all?

"You have always been good with me, Judith," Msti yelled. "Looking after me, listening to my stories."

I nodded. The waitress came back with a colorful drink, and I asked her for water. My mouth was dry as wool.

It was irritating to have to yell everything. But at least there were so many people around I couldn't see Volkov starting a firefight. On the other hand, if he bombed a hospital, why not a nightclub? I shuddered.

Msti was laughing. The sound was lost to an intense bass riff. "Friendship is why you are not dead in jail for killing rat-turd Russian." Her throaty voice didn't seem to penetrate the music any better than mine. What was she talking about? Before I could ask, the waitress interrupted, dropping off my water. I filled my mouth and slid the liquid around, trying to douse the parched disgust from my palate.

"What does Enforcer have to deal with us?" Msti yelled between sips of her drink. She eyed me keenly.

"Him for Ethan," I yelled back.

Msti's eyes narrowed. She sat for a while. I realized Msti was probably hooked up to Volkov the same way I was hooked up to Jack.

"We're both puppets," I shouted.

Msti nodded gravely. "It is that simple?"

"That simple." My yell barely rose above a creshendoed refrain. The music ceased for a heartbeat, then the pounding aural melee continued.

Msti finished her drink. "I go to bathroom."

"I stay here."

Msti nodded, exiting the booth. I eyed the pretty silver clutch purse she'd left on the tabletop next to her empty glass, wondering where Msti had gotten the delicate accessory and how much it cost.

After a few minutes, I became concerned Msti might have left and abandoned me and forgotten the purse. And what was Ethan suffering in the meantime? I fingered my cold, slimy water glass.

At last, Msti returned. She sat heavily and slid a piece of paper across the table. I picked it up. Neat slanted handwriting included an address and numbered instructions.

"This is how trade works," Msti yelled.

I nodded, slipping the paper into my own purse. This was good-bye, I guessed. Msti lifted her empty drink glass to me in a mock salute and sipped the dregs of melted ice. I felt powerless and incredibly saddened.

"Good-bye, Msti," I muttered. I was sure my farewell was lost in the sea of cacophony.

— 33 —

Exchange

♂

I couldn't lift my head. I was still sitting in the chair, arms cramped and tied behind me, but now I wore a collar. It was attached to the floor, keeping me doubled over. Suddenly, someone released it, freeing me to raise my head. Through puffy, bruised slits, I saw Volkov carrying a big fucking scythe. He wore a long, black, hooded cloak, and his face was skeletal and ashen. He raised the blade, sweeping it toward my head. I prepared to die, keeping my eyes open out of spite.

Instead, I dropped in a heap at his feet.

Somehow, I had confused Volkov with the Grim Reaper. And he wasn't wearing a cloak; I'd imagined that too. Instead, he wore a simple, neat suit in dark brown heathered wool. It fit well, and he crowned it with a slick pastel pink tie. What a fashion magnate. He heaved me up over his shoulder, and I was impressed he could carry someone of my brother's size so efficiently. Or maybe I wasn't big. Maybe I was a waif, like a woman. Maybe I was as tiny as Goom. I smiled. A mini-superhero. I'd never be able to do Parkour again if I was only three feet tall.

Cool wind bit my buttocks. My ass was up in the air being winded on. That was different. Usually it produced the wind. The turnabout was so hilarious, I had to laugh. It came out as a pitiful, choked snuffle. Had they cut my tongue out? I didn't recall anyone doing that.

We were in a graveyard in the crisp air of midnight, threading our way through headstones and monuments. A masked figure in black and gold walked on our left. Msti. She strode rigidly, arms at her sides. Her gloved hand carried a large silver handgun. I guessed that meant they were taking me out to shoot me. That was oddly disappointing. I survived all that torture only to be shot? Losers. Unimaginative losers.

Volkov dumped me on the grass in front of a headstone. In my stupor, I wondered why they'd spelled my name so wrong. So very wrong.

I was lifted to my feet, and something silky and warm was pulled around me. A kimono. With snakes on it. Someone very large was holding me up. A giant in a black-and-red bodysuit. Batman. No. Jack.

Behind me, Volkov was talking. I tried to pay attention.

"Well, Enforcer. We meet at last."

Jack was silent.

Volkov laughed. "This is all there is to the great Enforcer. I am not impressed." He reached into his lapel and pulled out his gun.

I lurched backward in Jack's arms.

"Careful," Volkov warned, leveling the gun at my face.

I froze. At least, I froze as much as I could, considering I was shaking like crazy. Jack seemed unarmed and alone. This was the great liberation plan? I couldn't believe it.

"It will not be quick," Volkov was telling us. "I will play with your boy here some more, then make him watch you die."

Msti was standing slightly behind Volkov. I didn't even see her move. Her shot exploded into the silence around us. The retort echoed off stone gravemarkers, off iron mausoleum gates, off granite statues, and around my head, an imagined aftermath reverberating long after its source died away in the distant night.

Volkov had a single moment of consciousness remaining. I saw enlightenment and disbelief before the evil burning in his eyes extinguished. His body slackened; he crumpled and hit the ground hard, throwing up a faint outline of dust into the moonlight. Msti lowered her gun and nodded at Jack. He pulled a small object from his belt and held it up. A key. His voice was low, almost inaudible.

"Train station. Assuming we leave alive, your gift awaits you."

We turned away. I needed Jack's help to move. I expected to feel searing lead burn through my back at any moment, but there was none. When I glanced behind us, Volkov was alone, face down in a pool of deepening shadow. Msti was nowhere to be seen.

— 34 —

The Wolf and the Fox

♀

Goom was at his desk in the funeral home receiving room. When I slid off the couch, he spun in his chair to face me.

"Where do you think you're going, sugarbutt?"

"Out."

He pulled his Glock. "The man told me to keep you here."

I shrugged. "Go ahead, then. Shoot me. How do you think he'll feel about that?"

"Well, I don't have to shoot you anywhere important." He lowered the gun, clearly aiming at my feet.

"Piss off and die."

I sat back down, wondering if Goom would actually shoot me. I crossed my arms and stuck my lower lip out. Foiled. I glanced at the Rubik's cube on the table beside me. It had taken me less than two minutes in my female body to solve it, an oddity that piqued me. Someday, when mobsters weren't imminently wrecking my life, I'd have to sit down and think about the fact I was the brains and my brother provided the brawn.

Goom's eyes narrowed. "What're you thinking about, candylips?"

I didn't answer.

"That look in your eyes. It's fucking creepy. I hate that look. That's the 'I'm about to fuck everyone over' look. Shut those evil eyes and go back to sleep, 'cuz I ain't letting you leave."

"Think fast!" Blaze's voice erupted behind Goom, and he turned just in time to see the heavy brass urn she had launched toward his head.

"Fu—"

I jumped up and bolted.

Crash!

I glanced back to see a puff of whitish powder, most of which was on Goom. His screaming followed me down the hall.

"Ahh! There's dead people all over me! Ahh!"

I was smiling as I flew down the front steps and threw myself into the Battle Buick. I gunned the motor, slammed it into reverse, and screeched out of the mortuary. At the next red light, I thumbed my smartphone and entered the code for the tracker I had pushed into Msti's wallet between a credit card and her driver's license. I was pretty sure Jack had been referring to the Amtrak station downtown. The direction Msti was headed seemed to confirm my guess. I drove as aggressively as I dared, hoping Msti wouldn't have retrieved her "gift" and left before I even got there.

* * *

Msti was looking through a large black backpack when I climbed into the passenger seat next to her. She reached for the gun in her purse.

"Uh, uh, uhh." I waved my own gun. Msti froze. I snatched the purse and dropped it into the backseat, well out of arm's reach. "Let's have your hands where I can see them, like on the steering wheel."

Msti settled her hands at three and nine o'clock on the steering wheel, as if undergoing strict driving lessons.

"Tell double-crossing cunt-eyed bastard he can suck my left tit."

For once, I didn't find Msti's colorful slurs funny. "I'm not here on Enforcer's behalf."

Her eyes narrowed. "Then why? You wish to escape with me?"

I hadn't even considered that. What a strange idea. It gave me brief pause, but then I shook my head. "I'm here to get some answers. I don't understand what just happened. In fact...I don't understand anything that's happened in the entire last three weeks."

Msti looked at me. I looked at Msti.

Msti said, "What part did your puppetmaster not tell you?"

I scoffed. "All of it?"

Msti laughed. "Oh, Jude. You poor little kitten. How on earth you got messed up in...this." The bangles on her wrists jingled as she waved her hands. She dropped her hands back to attention on the steering wheel and shrugged. "Enforcer made me offer I can't refuse. Freedom. A new identity and cash, so I am at last away from Satan's bitch pig."

"Who? Volkov?"

Msti snorted. "He was my husband."

"What?!"

"Oh, yes. He picked me from group and shot my friends before my eyes. 'You are too beautiful to die,' he tells me." Her voice was a malicious hiss.

"Then he drag me to compound and fuck the life from me. I belong to him then. My family, dead. My country, gone. And still I live. I live as slave, as useless whore to Russian special forces."

She smacked the steering wheel. "But, I survive. I please him. And," she lowered her head and rested her forehead between her hands on the steering wheel. "I inform on my neighbors. I help the devil. And he lets me live. I don't deserve to live. He should have killed me."

I shuddered.

Msti's head jerked back up, and she faced me directly, shaking a red lacquer-clad finger for emphasis. "But, at last, I have vengeance. I shoot him in back of head. And your master pays me for it." The backpack Msti had retrieved from the train station sat open on her lap, fat wads of twenties clearly in evidence. I thought I saw the navy blue corner of a U.S. passport peeking out as well.

"So Enforcer paid you to off the Wolf," I said. "Where did he get to you? When you went to the bathroom in the club?"

Msti nodded. "Viktor is stupid, rash. Angry. Incredible angry that I hide from him. He blows up Triad warehouse, so Enforcer is set on us. I tell him, 'Go back to Russia and hide,' but he does not, of course. He says, 'We kidnap girlfriend, kill him back.' You see where that got us."

I frowned. *Kidnap girlfriend. Enforcer is set on us.* What had I been denying to myself all this time?

Msti said slowly, "Surely you know, hand that plays you is top Triad assassin. Viktor fears *nothing.* But, he fears the great Enforcer."

I felt like the stupidest person who'd ever lived. Of course Jack was Dragon's prime hitman. It was obvious, in retrospect. Blindingly freaking obvious. I couldn't speak. I could hardly breathe.

Msti started, as if she'd just thought of something. "But, Chickadee, can you imagine my shock and how joyful I was to see your brother alive? It is miracle."

I nodded. I didn't want to make a big deal of Ethan's incredible "recovery." I just hoped Msti wouldn't broadcast it to anyone.

Msti frowned. "I am so sorry I could not stop what he did to Ethan. Your beautiful brother."

I felt it prudent to change the subject. "And now? What about the American secrets? Will they stop being leaked?" I had no idea if Msti knew about the breach of state security. If she didn't, I supposed I had just become guilty of treason for telling her.

Msti eyed me. "He tells you nothing."

I glared through the windshield at nothing in particular.

"I am to flee. I will set myself up in Europe, somewhere this money will buy me a new start. And I will wire your master the details of our inventions."

"You will?" I furrowed my brow. Could we trust her?

"Of course. I want, it is finished. Done. No more."

"Then tell me now."

"No. How can I think Enforcer is not sitting around corner waiting for me?" Msti gestured at the half-empty parking lot around us. "Or our friend, Special Agent Bead?"

I sighed. "Jeez, Msti. How on earth did the Major get messed up in all this? Did he know you were already married when he brought you over?"

Msti shook her head. "My poor Walter. It is big mess."

I waited.

Msti swallowed heavily. "I push him too much. I have one too many boyfriend."

"He found out about you and Shun Yan Pii?" If Msti was surprised I knew her lover's name, she didn't show it.

"Yes. It was last straw."

"Then he started to assemble a divorce case against you. I bet he got one of his former detectives to help him."

She nodded slowly. "Big, big mess."

"Then the detective finds out you and Shun Yan are running a spy ring out of his shops. And that you're not exactly who you said you were." I would have loved to be more specific, but at this point I had crossed into pure speculation.

Msti frowned. "It was brilliant plan. Make us fantastically rich. We can go away and buy island. Live free forever."

"Who? You and the Major?"

Msti was silent.

"Or you and Shun Yan?" My mouth dropped open. "You were hoping to elope with him? Wow."

Msti wiped a tear from her eye with the back of one hand. "He was smooth talker. Smoothest. Or maybe I am old woman. I lose mind and believe donkey shit he shovels at me. Yellow man, yellow heart."

I huffed. "So you interrupted Shun Yan with Li Jong and killed him."

Tears flowed freely now, and Msti wiped them off with one hand, then the other, alternately, leaving a hand on the steering wheel in between.

"My Walter confronted me. I run to Shun Yan, I beg him to leave with me. I find him with little Asian bitch. Rat-pig deserves bullet in brain."

I grimaced. "Jeez. And who killed Li Jong? Volkov? Or you?"

"That bastard, the Wolf, of course. How can you think I would bother to kill worthless whores? Viktor, he said she must not inform on me. So he kills her after he plays with her."

I shuddered. The two of us waited in silence for some time while all the revelations bounced around in my mind. I felt a creeping sadness pervade me.

"Good-bye, Msti," I murmured at last, returning my gun to my purse. My farewell floated lazily in the silence between us.

"Good-bye, my chickadee," Msti replied softly. She leaned over and hugged me, kissing both cheeks as a send-off.

* * *

I stormed into the mortuary receiving room and found them. Jack sat cross-legged in an armchair with his eyes closed.

"You *bastard*!" I screamed at him.

Goom had been pecking on his computer. He peeked out from behind the screen. "Oh, here we go."

I whipped out my gun and shot the floor near Goom's desk.

"For fuck's sake!" Goom leaped up and stood on his chair.

Jack was on me lightning quick, on his feet and across the room faster than I would have thought possible. He snatched the gun from my hand, unloaded it, and tossed it on the couch. He said nothing. He folded his hands and stood at ease before me, looking down at me.

I punched him. I didn't just slap or backhand him. I hauled off and socked him in the face with all my might.

Smack!

He was preternaturally fast, of course, and snapped his head backward as my fist came forward. Nonetheless, I was gratified to feel cartilage give beneath my knuckles.

"Ow!" I shook my hand out, my knuckles and wrist flaming with pain. "Ow! Crap, that hurts!"

"Holy fuck! The bitch has flipped." Goom cowered behind his screen.

I growled at him.

He dove from the chair and scurried under the desk so he was invisible in its depths. "Stay away from me, you crazy flake!"

Jack straightened up, eyes blazing. He touched his hand to the side of his nose and looked at the blood that resulted. His eyes narrowed, but he said nothing and returned to his stance, standing stock still with his hands folded in front of him, daring me to hit him again. I could see the red swell of bruising at the edge of his nose and the corner of his lip. He didn't move and made no attempt to either defend himself or assault me.

I stomped my foot. "You're a fucking, lowlife hitman!"

Goom's whiny voice issued from beneath the desk. "How in the hell is this news to you?" He poked his head out. "God, what is it with you and women, Lahngxian? How do you pick these psychos?"

He scrambled for cover when I pulled a bottle of hairspray out of my purse and hurled it at the desk. Jack remained expressionless and unmoving. Only his eyes betrayed his ire.

"Answer me!" I yelled at the big man, hands on my hips.

Jack's eyes closed. "What do you want me to say?"

"You paid Msti to off Volkov! Did Dragon foot the bill? How much was your cut?"

His eyes opened. He was silent.

"Why didn't you tell me? Why don't you tell me anything?"

Goom piped up. "It might be because you're an overemotional nutcase. Did you think of that?"

I grabbed the next thing from my purse I could get my hand around and threw it at him. It was a wad of tissues. It unraveled halfway to Goom and floated in useless strips to the floor.

"God damn it!"

Goom retracted his face, probably to hide his smirk so I didn't tramp over and whack him to death with my purse.

"You can hit me again if it makes you feel better," Jack said quietly. "If it helps you . . . accept me."

"Accept you?!"

"This is who I am, Judith. Our lives are intertwined now. That is your doing—and your brother's—not mine."

I remembered when I'd pursued Jack and insisted he give Ethan martial arts lessons. "You're a fucking mobster! I thought you were a superhero!"

"There's no such thing as Batman."

"What!?" I stamped my foot again.

"Christ! You're making the floor shake," Goom cried from his bunker.

"Shut *up*!"

Jack's shoulders heaved up and down with his angry breaths.

I shook my fist at him. "You kissed me! How dare you!"

Goom muttered something unintelligible from within the desk's depths.

"You punched me," Jack said, ignoring Goom. "You shot the floor."

He had me there. My actions hadn't exactly been the pinnacle of rational adulthood. "Damn you!"

A cellphone buzzed. Jack's jaw clenched.

I searched my purse, but it wasn't mine. Goom came out from under the desk and felt around on top of it until he found the offending instrument. He looked at the screen, then tossed it to Jack, who handily caught it. Jack glanced at the screen, then pressed the answer button.

"Report."

Everyone was silent except the phone, out of which came a tinny, warbling woman's voice. Vaguely familiar? I frowned.

"Acknowledged."

Jack silenced the phone and tossed it back to Goom.

"That was Connor," he said. "Msti was found at Hartsfield with a bullet in her brain."

— 35 —

Mail

♂

The day Msti was found was a Sunday and the last evening of reprieve before we all were due the next morning at FBI headquarters for a full report. Jack thought it likely he would be arrested, stripped of all his privileges, and sent to prison indefinitely. In the meantime, we drove out to Decatur to check on the burned-out husk of my home and pick up my mail. The house was flattened. The mailbox was untouched.

Jack stared out the Mustang's passenger window at blackened rubble. He said, "Ethan, most of my assets are in Gumbah Sarbloh's name. He will take care of you and your sister. You can rebuild or move elsewhere."

I scoffed. "Goom will take care of us? He hates us."

Jack's jet-black eyes glittered in the evening sunlight. "He will. Because it is what I want."

I grimaced, as much because I ached all over as because of what Jack was saying. Either way, I felt like crap. "This sucks. It's not your fault Msti got herself killed before she could tell us how the scheme worked."

Goom opened the passenger door and hefted a fat tote bag off the curb. Jack took the bag from him and passed it to me in the backseat.

"You sure you got it all?"

Goom snorted. "Everything that was in your mailbox, assmonkey." He toddled around the car and climbed into the driver's seat. I zipped the bag open and started sorting through the contents while Goom fiddled with his driving stilts.

"Oh . . . shit!"

"What?" Goom and Jack said simultaneously, both craning their necks to look at me.

It was a large manila envelope. I held it up. "It's to Judith. From Msti!"

"Well, open it, for fuck's sake," Goom yelled.

I ripped the top off and quickly scanned the contents. At first, I didn't understand what it meant. I passed it to Jack.

"What?" Goom looked from me to Jack and back. "Someone tell me what the fuck that is. Did she send the info? We good now? Please tell me we're good now."

Jack's brow was deeply furrowed. "It's a firearms report. And fingerprints."

"What? What the fuck does that mean?"

I frowned. "Are they—"

"From the motel where the Russians held your sister," Jack clarified. "And a note from Msti." He held up a little Post-it note. " 'Ethan did good. These are sole copies. I delete all others. Be at peace, chickadee.' "

Goom and I gaped at Jack.

He replaced the envelope's contents. "You have a lighter? Matches?"

Goom didn't seem to hear him. "The crazy Russian chick covered up for you killing that Russian? Why would she do that?"

"She's Abkhaz, not Russian, you dorkwad."

"Whatever."

Jack nodded. "She did us an immense good, Ethan. If this was officially known," he held up the envelope, "it would have been impossible to fight."

"I don't get it." Goom was scratching his head. "She's a good guy? I thought she was one of the bad guys. Why would she protect you?"

My mind raced. I could only think of one possibility. "She always said criminals deserve to die."

Jack opened the glove compartment and searched through it. Goom rifled through the backpack in the seat well. "Here, Lahngxian." He passed a butane lighter to Jack.

Jack immediately started the lighter, held up the envelope, and touched the flame to one corner. The three of us watched in silence as he turned it around and over, coaxing the fire to consume every last bit. I was amazed at his proficiency. Not a single ash fluttered loose to mar his black T-shirt. Finally, he opened his door, dropped the last burning bit to the pavement, and watched to make sure the destruction was total.

Jack closed the door and slipped into his seat belt. "Let's go."

Goom fired up the Mustang, and we pulled away from the curb, leaving the last obliterated detritus of my previous life behind us.

— 36 —

Disclosure

♀

That was Sunday. Too soon, Monday arrived and, with it, our delayed comeuppance. The Battle Buick merged smoothly onto the 403. We were minutes away from FBI headquarters on Millennium Parkway—and whatever punishment awaited us for being too stupid to solve the mystery of the stolen state secrets.

"So basically we're gonna meet your spy bosses, and they'll chew us out for losing Msti?" I wanted Jack to go over our predicament with me again, more carefully.

"Yes, Judith," Jack said simply, then fell silent.

So much for small talk.

Dark clouds were gathering in the east, rendering the morning light wan and diffuse. I supposed if we were really lucky, a freak tornado might touch down and wipe out FBI headquarters before we got there. I frowned.

"I still can't believe you're a hit man. And a mercenary. This is your own damn fault for working over a bunch of FBI agents with your little soldier buddies."

Goom snorted loudly from the backseat. "They can't prove it was us, so cool it, sugartits."

"Do not call me that!" I twisted in my seat to glare at him.

"Car! Car!" He jerked his stubby finger wildly toward the windshield.

I slammed on the brakes just in time so we didn't ram into backed-up traffic. "Oops."

"Fucking lunatic."

"Sorry!" I yelled. "I'm upset. I'm not real good at this spy shit. Being a superhero was supposed to be more . . . innocent."

Jack frowned deeply, revealing the wrinkles in his forehead. "I kill for money, whether it's on a government salary or Dragon's payroll. How can that be innocent?"

* * *

Julian was one of three grim personnel who met us in the lobby. We removed everything we carried, plus our shoes, and went through the X-ray setup. Then we walked through detectors even more sensitive and elaborate than post-9/11 airports.

There was silence in the elevator on our way to the eighth floor.

If the mood hadn't been so oppressive, I would have broken out laughing at the two anonymous agents accompanying Julian. They wore identical dark suits, dark ties, earbuds, and somber expressions. They reminded me of every Hollywood lampoon I'd ever seen about the government's secretive intelligence agencies.

Once again, life imitated art. And life was the absurder.

In the eighth-floor lobby, Goom and I had our fingerprints taken and were carefully lined up for digital pictures. Apparently, it would take some time to check our backgrounds, in case either of us had randomly decided to join a terrorist group on the way over. Goom grabbed a coffee, sat in a chair, and picked up a magazine. They wouldn't let him keep his backpack, his laptop, or even his smartphone. He looked lost without his technology.

Jack stood like a statue near Goom with his back to a wall. One hand held his hat; the other was folded behind his back. His expressionless gaze wandered over our surroundings, hovering on Julian from time to time. The mass of medals on his dark blue Army dress uniform winked and undulated with each breath.

Julian finished a discussion with the agent running the checks on Goom and me and motioned me over to him. When I got there, he grabbed my arm and hustled me down the hall. He pushed me into his office and slammed the door behind us, flipping the deadbolt locked.

"Ky—" I got out before he grabbed me again. He gripped both of my arms and shoved me into a chair, then dragged another opposite me and plunked himself into it, his knees brushing mine.

"Wha—"

He lifted his index finger to his lips. I shut my flapping mouth. He shook the finger at me. "Not a word. Not a damn word."

I blinked back tears and crossed my arms and legs, whacking his knees in the process.

"Do you have any idea what my last thirty-six hours have been like?"

I looked at him more carefully. His eyes were sunken and bloodshot. He was sweating noticeably. His normally impeccable shirt was wrinkled, and he had the top button open under his yellow tie. In short, he looked like hell. I bit my lip.

"That bastard shot me full of LSD. LSD." His voice was a growling whisper. "You know my history. Do you have any idea of the trouble this causes me? They're doing an internal investigation on me, for Christ's sake."

I blinked furiously with my head lowered, fighting not to burst out bawling. I hardly understood what he was telling me.

"You told him. How could you."

My head snapped up, and I stared him in the eyes. "What? Told who? What did I tell?"

"You told that criminal about my past. About my alcoholism. How could you? That crossed the line, Judith. That really stinks. In this whole, big mess I've tried to do right by you. I would never have done that."

My mouth dropped open. "What?! I did not! I didn't tell him a damn thing!"

"Then how did he know the trouble something like that would cause?"

I shook my head. "He didn't. I wasn't part of that at all. I only found out afterward. He doesn't actually tell me anything."

Julian considered me. "You didn't tell him about my drinking?"

"No! Of course not. Besides, you're not a drunk. You don't do that anymore. Right?"

"Four years, Judith. Not a drop."

"Then why are you worried? Let them investigate you."

He flushed. "You saw that dart. It didn't leave a mark. They think I doped myself up and screwed the safehouse defense."

"That's crap."

"Are you going to tell them that? Tell them you saw the dart Xiah shot me with? Testify against that bastard?"

I stared at the floor.

He scoffed. "That's what I thought."

"Well, if it comes to that, I'll think of something," I mumbled.

He shook his head. "Judith, come stay with me. You can have your own room. He'll get you killed and probably me too."

I felt rotten about Julian's troubles. But how could I possibly leave Jack? Especially since he was the only person in the universe who knew my deep, dark secret. Or at least the only person who knew something close enough to help me with the whole mess.

I sighed heavily. "I can't."

"Do you want me to beg you? Ask you to marry me? I will, you know."

I had no idea what registered on my face. I felt an odd mixture of horror and hope wash over me. "M-m-marry . . . "

He got down on his knees and grabbed my hand. Before he could say anything else, I jumped to my feet and snatched my hand away.

"No!"

"No?" His face deflated; his shoulders drooped.

"I mean, maybe."

"What?"

I shook my head. "I can't think. I can't answer. It's not no, but it can't be yes. Not n-now. Arghhhh." I pulled at my hair. I was engaged to Jack. How could I even be contemplating Julian's offer?

"I know it's bad timing."

"Bad timing? Bad timing!? Why don't you just take out your gun and shoot me?"

"Judith . . . "

I could hardly breathe I was so upset.

"Okay, forget I said it." After a moment, he added, "I wasn't 100 percent serious anyway."

"You weren't?"

"Well, no." He stared at my feet, flushed and uncertain.

"God, Julian. Do you love me?"

"Of course," he said easily. "Do you love me?"

My eyes widened. "Yes."

"You hesitated."

I stamped my foot. "Of course I hesitated. My life is crazy. Ever since Ethan died, it's been one horrible calamity after another. I can't even begin to think of what 'normal' might be after all this crap."

"Fair enough."

I stared at him. He looked meek and unhappy. I stepped forward, grabbed him, and pressed my lips to his.

A minute later, our passionate kissing was interrupted by a timid knock and a voice calling through the door. "Special Agent Bead? Sir?"

Julian pulled his head back. For just a minute, I had forgotten everything else. But with the voice on the other side of the door, our predicament came rushing back. "We're coming," Julian called.

I grimaced. "How bad is this meeting going to be?"

He sighed. "I'm not sure. Xiah screwed up. We lost our informant. Nothing's left of the warehouse. The director of National Intelligence will be there, and he'll need a head to roll. I just hope it's not mine."

"Or mine."

"It definitely won't be yours. But I can't say the same for your friend."

***

In the crowded lobby, everyone but Goom and me was wearing a business suit or decorated military outfit. I threaded through a couple of military guys and emerged next to Jack.

He nodded. "You all right?"

"I suppose."

His eyes held a distinct question.

I frowned. "You really fucked Julian over with your little dart trick."

Jack's brow furrowed, but he said nothing.

"They're investigating him," I whispered. "He might lose his job."

He seemed surprised. "Really."

"Yeah." I crimsoned. "Very funny."

"That was not my intention." He studied me. "What else did he say?"

I flushed deeper. "Nothing."

Lieutenant Connor came over to us. I hadn't even noticed her before that moment. The woman nodded to Jack. "They won't let your friend in. But she can attend." She indicated me with a tilt of her head.

"What? Who won't they let in?" Judith asked.

"Gumbah Sarbloh, apparently," Jack said.

I looked at Goom. He thumbed listlessly through another magazine.

"He didn't pass the background check?"

Connor turned to her. "He did. But the DNI doesn't want to allow non-intelligence persons into the briefing." She turned back to Jack. "He's really pissed you're insisting Ms. Gold attend."

Jack was stone-faced and unmoving. "The DNI is an ass."

"Yes," Connor agreed. "But he's a powerful ass. Be cautious, Colonel."

* * *

There were eight of us, sitting around a huge oval conference table of polished walnut. At the head of the table sat Richard Grant, introduced as the fabled director of National Intelligence, or DNI. He was so self-important, and everyone else so deferential, that it was clear he was the big mucky-muck. I immediately disliked him.

Clockwise from him sat Julian's boss, Special Agent Michael Ross, and then Julian. Continuing clockwise, there was a quiet, brooding man in a very dark navy, almost black, uniform, introduced as Lieutenant General Devon Howe, NSA director. Next to Director Howe, opposite DNI Grant, was a woman in a dark green uniform with two stars on her epaulets, introduced as Major General Ruth Herschel. I was so intimidated I didn't hear the woman's title properly, but it was director-something-something of Army intelligence. I was next to her, then Jack, then Officer Dahmiel, sitting on the other side of DNI Grant, across from Julian's boss.

I was literally quaking in my sandals after Julian made the introductions. I couldn't believe all this brass was in Atlanta, and I was sitting around a table with them. I was torn between fleeing from the room screaming and simply peeing myself on the spot.

Jack had been watching me out of the corner of his eye. He surreptitiously took my hand beneath the table and leaned toward me.

"Don't be afraid," he whispered. "They're just titles."

I nodded quickly and bit my lip. Julian glared at us across the table. I slid my hand from Jack's gentle grasp and folded my hands on top of the table. Jack returned his hand to his lap and leveled his gaze at Julian.

The DNI cleared his throat.

"Thank you for the introductions, Special Agent Bead. Perhaps you would be so kind as to begin this briefing with a run-down of events to date concerning this matter."

Julian nodded. He took up the charge smoothly, but I could tell he was nervous.

"Early this year, we began suspecting leaks in Military Intelligence. Compromised information seemed to be sporadically leaving our control, prompting an investigation by General Herschel and her team."

Julian paused, looking at General Herschel.

The general nodded. She said, "The leaks seemed unconfined to any single base and utterly asynchronous. Some were outdated logistics. Others were, incredibly, snippets of recent conversations with high-ranking security personnel.

"Naturally, we suspected covert surveillance. All bases involved conducted a thorough search of property and surroundings, as well as tightening security protocols for individuals attending confidential events."

She frowned. "Our efforts turned up nothing."

Julian waited a moment to be sure the general had finished. He turned toward DNI Grant and continued. "On October tenth, one of our Predators was rerouted from its path along the Wakhan Corridor during a routine reconnaissance. We lost track of it a hundred miles past the Chinese border."

A gasp sounded at the table. It belonged to me.

Officer Dahmiel piped up. "Naturally, we were unable to verify receipt of the Predator in China. Their government insists no such aircraft was detected or found."

Julian coughed. "Shortly afterward, Officer Dahmiel and colleagues discovered there had been a breech in protocol for the Predator, consisting of an override code that came out of Fort Gordon."

I started. "Someone in Fort Gordon sent our Predator to China?"

Everyone turned to look at me. DNI Grant looked like he'd found a bug swimming around in his coffee. I flushed beet red.

Julian cleared his throat. "Actually, only the codes used to initiate the override were traced to Fort Gordon, to a major general."

I nodded, shrank back in my seat, and resolved to stop saying anything.

Julian continued. "The general's codes were issued a week prior to the breech. He and all his staff were, of course, thoroughly investigated. The results of the investigation became available in early November."

Everyone looked at Julian. He looked at General Herschel.

The general sighed. "Negative. Not a shred of evidence linking anyone at Fort Gordon to anything. We accounted for the major general's whereabouts for literally every second since he'd received the codes. Everywhere he'd been, everything he'd touched."

More sighing around the table. I fidgeted nervously. So far it sounded like we were totally screwed.

"And now," DNI Grant was addressing Julian, "you're going to tell me the good news."

Julian adjusted his tie. He glanced at the NSA man, Howe, to his left, and said, "It so happens that, in an unrelated project, Director Howe was overseeing new techniques in searching for steganographically encoded information in email."

I had no clue what that meant. Julian looked at Director Howe. After a pause, Howe spoke up. "We decrypted a match for the override codes among a coordinated spam attack on mainland China. The attack occurred forty-eight hours prior to the aircraft redirection."

I frowned. *Spam attack.*

Howe kept going. "The attack originated from a botnet we'd had our eye on for some time. We received a tip the botnet was run from a central source right here in America. We traced the ancestry of the botnet program to an IP address in a warehouse in Atlanta, belonging to an Asian businessman by the name of . . . " He paused, shuffling some papers around in front of him.

"Shun Yan Pii," I said aloud. I hadn't meant to. Everyone looked at me. I lifted a pad of paper I'd been doodling on and hid behind it.

"Yes," Director Howe said. He cleared his throat. "We contacted this Atlanta office, and Special Agent Bead assisted us from then on." He turned to Julian. "Please, continue."

Julian sat forward and opened his mouth.

Before he could say anything, DNI Grant interrupted. "I'm sorry, but I have to ask. This . . . woman." He waved his hand in my general direction.

I looked behind me to see who he was referring to.

"Judith Gold," Julian said immediately.

"Yes." DNI Grant sniffed. "What, exactly, is her role?"

"Uh. Well, sir, I will be getting to that soon."

"Why don't you jump ahead and give me a quick summary."

I watched Julian, curious.

He rubbed his chin. "Ms. Gold witnessed the assassination of a retired Atlanta police major. He was shot at a local hospital."

"Poisoned," I corrected. Why could I not keep my mouth shut?

Julian grinned. "Yes, of course. Poisoned. That's what I meant."

Beside me, I saw Jack's hand fly to his forehead. I couldn't see his expression behind it. A chill ran through me. What, exactly, had I given away? Then it hit me. I'd just confirmed for Julian that I had been in the hospital during the attack. I barely restrained myself from facepalming.

DNI Grant harrumphed. "I see. And this qualifies her to be a party to the information in this room."

Julian frowned. "The murder is intimately tied up with the espionage."

"I see."

I felt like the temperature in the room dropped ten degrees every time the DNI said that. If this kept up, I'd have to wear a fur coat just to be in the same building with this asshole.

Grant cleared his throat. "So she is here at your behest, General Herschel." It sounded like the accusation of a crime.

General Herschel didn't bat an eyelash. "Yes." My respect for the woman, which was pretty high anyway, considering the medals on her chest and stars on her epaulets, ratcheted up another notch.

The DNI sat back and turned to Julian. "Then, please, continue. Let us have full disclosure."

Julian was silent for a moment, probably trying to recall where he had left off. Then he continued. "Shun Yan Pii had ties to organized crime."

DNI Grant interrupted. "Had?"

"Pii was shot and killed the week before we received Director Howe's collaboration request."

"Wait." DNI Grant held up his hand.

Everyone waited silently while he pondered.

At last, he said, "There was a lag? Between our decrypting the codes in the spam emails and linking them to the aircraft override?"

There was an awful lot of fidgeting in response to that.

General Herschel spoke up. "The codes themselves appeared in my report. Your deputy director has an unusually good memory. He recognized them among Howe's search results, but only last week."

Everyone considered that for a minute. I could have sworn DNI Grant uttered some choice swear words under his breath. Aloud, he said, "So basically, if it wasn't for the fortuitously eidetic memory of my deputy director, we'd still be . . . how should I put it . . . being fucked up the ass by the Chinese?"

I blushed at Grant's blunt summary. There was an awful lot of squirming now to go with the continued fidgeting around the table. I glanced at Jack. Even he showed a slight crimson hue beneath his perpetually unflappable expression.

"Please." Grant's voice was a low hiss. "Continue, Special Agent Bead."

Julian swallowed. "We had Pii's warehouse under surveillance."

DNI Grant looked at him sternly. "And?"

Julian cleared his throat. "Perhaps Colonel Xiah would like to continue."

All eyes turned to Jack.

He began, "Independently, I had been looking into security concerns for the site. An operative and I responded to a break-and-enter and found several individuals had been shot and killed on the premises."

Julian sighed, but said nothing.

Jack frowned.

DNI Grant looked at him, expectantly. "Yes?"

Jack said quietly, "Special Agent Bead and I were, at the time, unaware of each other's jurisdiction."

Julian snorted.

Grant's eyes narrowed. He looked from Julian to Jack and back. "What the hell is that supposed to mean?"

Julian cleared his throat. "My apologies." He nodded at Jack. "Please go on, Colonel."

Jack went on. "We suffered casualties during a subsequent paramilitary attack on the building. The site was destroyed, but we managed to retrieve a valuable piece of evidence in spite of this."

There was silence while everyone digested that.

DNI Grant spoke up first. " 'Piece of evidence,' you said. Will somebody please tell me what that is?"

After a moment, Jack said, "It is a hard drive. I believe it is in Special Agent Bead's possession."

Julian started, but said nothing.

"You removed the drive from my home two nights ago," Jack said.

Julian's eyes narrowed. "We did." I wasn't sure whether it was a statement or a question.

DNI Grant harrumphed. "And?"

Julian turned to Grant. "The disk Colonel Xiah is referring to is in great disrepair. Our team is still working on retrieving information from it."

Grant scoffed.

Julian glanced at me. "We have a tip that it contains the control program for the botnet."

"I see," Grant said. There went the temperature again.

I leaned over toward Jack and whispered, "I thought you gave the hard drive up to Sam."

Jack leaned symmetrically toward me and whispered back, almost inaudibly. "It did look like that, didn't it?"

I twisted my head around to look at his face. It was impassive, as usual, but his eyes watched me intently.

Julian was looking pointedly at Howe, who piped up. "It could be the control program for the spam attacks containing our leaks."

A light seemed to go on in Director Grant's eyes. "I see," he acknowledged. "But we still have no idea how these leaks are being perpetrated in the first place?"

Silence.

* * *

We recessed about ten o'clock. There were coffee and donuts in the reception room. I elbowed my way up to the table, grabbed a couple of cream-filled specimens, and shoved one in my mouth.

I was standing in a corner, watching everyone else converse and sipping a cup of coffee, when someone appeared at my elbow.

"Ms. Gold?"

I started, sloshing a bit of coffee onto my blouse. Great. "Yes?"

It was Officer Dahmiel, the CIA guy. He extended his hand. I stared at it. I knew my hand had powdered sugar all over it. I shook Dahmiel's hand anyway, briefly and limply.

He wiped his hand on his lapel, leaving a trace of white.

I blushed deeply. "Sorry."

He smiled. "No problem. I wanted to mention, your mom was my mentor for my first year of training. We lost touch, but I'll always remember her. An amazing woman."

"Uh. Thanks." Amazing and probably dead, having disappeared over a decade previously in some godforsaken hellhole in the Middle East. They never even told us which country she was in.

He was still smiling, regarding me with obvious appreciation. Him and every other straight male I'd ever met. I returned his smile. Maybe I could gain from his predisposition. "You had a really interesting, uh, folder you were looking at."

"Oh?" His pale, neatly trimmed eyebrows rose.

"I don't suppose I could... see it?" Big, wide smile. And a little eyelash batting. Don't forget the eyelash batting.

He laughed. "Seeing as how you're a party to these proceedings anyway, I don't see how it can hurt. C'mon." He motioned for us to return to the conference room.

* * *

I was in the ladies room. Dahmiel had said we needed to be quiet about my having his folder, and this was the quietest place I knew. Considering almost everyone around was male, there was hardly anyone who might come inside in the first place, let alone loiter to bother me.

The most interesting documents had to do with Msti. I devoured what I could find with all due attention.

Some of it I knew, like the fact Msti had grown up in Abkhazia.

"Svetlana Mik-hail ... ova Loeb ... Loebachev ... sky." Apparently, Msti was born under that annoyingly unspeakable name.

There was a record of Msti's marriage to Rogov, who wasn't Volkov yet. I winced reading the certificate, reminded of how Msti had characterized her relationship with her abuser.

I live as slave, as useless whore...

There was a birth certificate. Mikhail Viktoryvich Rogov. I started. The man on the church roof, the one who was somehow familiar. It must have been Msti and Volkov's son.

"Wow," I whispered.

I shuffled through more papers, reeling at the idea Msti's son was still out there and probably holding a grudge against whoever set up his father's death. If I were in charge of leading the investigation into Msti's death, I would have started with him.

I skimmed partway through a transcript before I realized what it was. An ICC complaint against Volkov. I had been confused because "Svetlana

Loebachevsky" was listed too. On page thirteen of the convoluted legalese, there were excerpts from victims. My hair stood on end as I read.

The woman lured us in . . .

She threw my baby into a corpse-filled pit and told us we were pigs . . .

"Oh, Lord." From the testimonies, it sounded like Msti was at least as much of a sociopath as Volkov. My only hope was the stories were exaggerated, or maybe there was another side to them.

Right. Another side, which explained how a seemingly principled woman could throw a wriggling little baby into a pit to die.

I closed the folder.

* * *

Fresh pads of paper had appeared at our places around the conference table. I doodled absentmindedly on mine. Dahmiel's cursed folder of knowledge was back at his place. Someone slid into the seat next to me as I stared morosely at the innocuous manila folder. I wished I hadn't seen it. I wondered when our break would be over.

"You all right?" Jack's voice was whisper-quiet.

I shifted in my seat so I could look at him. "Yeah."

He didn't pry, but his gaze seemed to hold a question.

I sighed. "Msti's name is actually 'Svetlana.' She was basically as evil and vicious as Volkov. I guess since she's dead now, it doesn't matter."

Jack's brows dipped toward his dark eyes. "Sorry."

I snorted. "Well, it's not your fault. I sure know how to pick my friends."

"She came here to get away from Volkov. She joined the force and, as far as we know, assisted with many police cases."

"I guess so."

He lowered his voice even further, so I could barely hear him. "She also saved Ethan from a devastating identification."

Meaning, she had no scruples about purging the official database of Ethan's horrible crime. How was I supposed to feel good about that?

People were trickling in. The generals took up their places.

"How did Volkov find her again?" I asked Jack.

He was silent.

"I mean, she got away from him by running away and marrying the Major. So how did he track her down all the way in Atlanta?"

Jack frowned. "When the Major was investigating her for the divorce, he probably ended up initiating an ICC request for information."

I remembered the ICC report in Officer Dahmiel's folder and that Msti had acknowledged the Major was having her investigated.

Jack said, "I would not be surprised if such channels were monitored."

Monitored. Monitored by the Russian mob? By the Russian army?

I shuddered. "So Major Fairholme signed their death warrants when he initiated the divorce investigation."

Jack nodded.

* * *

The three directors were blaming each other for everyone's lapse in intelligence. It was noon, and we were no closer to unraveling the puzzle.

My stomach rumbled. Everyone seemed to be concerned with the question of which agency was the most incompetent. General Herschel was under particular fire. It seemed Military Intelligence was going to be the scapegoat of choice.

As the tension crescendoed, I let my gaze wander around the room, feeling oddly piqued. There had to be something I was missing.

General Herschel studied a point over DNI Grant's shoulder as he said, "...understand correctly, that we lost a hundred thousand dollars of taxpayer money and a new identity to this woman and received nothing?"

I started. Msti got 100k for shooting Volkov? Maybe I should take up shooting war criminals in the back of the head for a living.

Herschel frowned and picked at a thread that had come loose near one of the buttons on her jacket. "These operations do not . . . "

I was so distracted by the glittering golden circle next to the general's fingertips that I missed the rest of her reply. I leaned toward Jack and pulled his arm back so I could study the front of his jacket.

"The buttons," I whispered.

He looked down at his chest. "Buttons?"

"The ones on the uniforms."

He turned toward me, and I pulled the front of his jacket nearer so I could see them more clearly.

"They're eagles," I said. "With tiny, spread wings."

He nodded.

I asked quietly, "Are they all eagles like that?"

He frowned. "Well, these are the Army ones."

The feeling of impending revelation that had begun as a silent burp in my subconscious was now working its way out, bubbling up slowly, inevitably, toward the surface of realization.

"Do the Navy ones have anchors?" I asked, expecting the answer yes.

"No."

"Shit."

He leaned closer. "The ones with anchors are Coast Guard."

There was a lull in the recriminations. I interjected, softly but clearly, "I know how they're getting the secrets off our bases."

Seven faces turned to stare at me. Without exception, each contained some degree of astonishment.

— 37 —

Nibble

♂

It was Jack's idea to "reward" Blaze for her diligence and sacrifices.

We heard her truck pull up to the funeral home and saw headlights sweep the small casement windows facing the parking lot. Jack, Goom, and I stood near our coffins, in full vampire regalia.

Jack wore a long black kimono over his dinner suit, the suit having a white collar inset that seemed appropriately head-vampire-like. I was also in a black silk suit with a mandarin collar and butterfly buttons. It had a flowing shape and intricate snakes subtly embroidered in silver thereover. We even had Goom in a mini-suit of black and red. He looked like a little monk, arms folded in front of him, hands tucked into his open sleeves, and a skullcap pushing down his dreads.

I frowned. "You sure this is gonna work? These stupid fangs are biting into my gums. I don't know if I'll taste Blaze's blood, but I taste my own."

Jack turned to me. "Ethan, you have to keep your jaw open as far as possible beneath your lips."

"I know, but I keep forgetting."

Goom shushed us. "She's coming down now."

A moment later, Blaze stepped off the stairs and rounded the corner into the room. She looked haggard. When she saw us, a broad smile crossed her face. "Hey, guys!"

We nodded in unison. I pressed my lips together. Just. Don't. Laugh.

Blaze looked around the room, noticing our formality. "Um." She averted her eyes at the pressure of us three men staring at her. Red color rose in her cheeks. "What's goin' on?"

I cleared my throat. "You okay? What's the verdict?"

Blaze's wonderment was replaced by a thoughtful frown. "Well, I have to report to a city shrink twice a month for six months. But other than that, I think I'm okay."

I guessed that was what happens when you fend off a bunch of FBI with empty cigar tubes taped to your vest.

I lowered my voice to a somber monotone. "Blaze. . . we're very pleased with the loyalty you've shown us. You have expressed an interest in formally joining our order. Do you still wish to?"

Our "disorder" was probably more like it. I cleared my throat again and noticed Blaze was trembling. I hoped Blaze wouldn't piss herself. That would make this considerably less memorable.

"Yes," Blaze squeaked.

I held my long arm out to Blaze. "Then, come. Come to me, Blaze."

Goom's hand flew to his face, and he coughed repeatedly. I knew how he felt. It was really, really hard not to bust out laughing hysterically. I had to concentrate on traumatic memories of my recent torture so as not to give us all away with great, swelling guffaws.

Blaze neared slowly. "Oh. Shoot. I'm not dressed good. I totally wasn't expecting this."

"You look fine." I took Blaze's hand and pulled her close. She cowered against my broad chest, clearly overwhelmed.

Jack raised his arms around us, speaking the sonorous, unintelligible language of his youth.

Blaze's face had drained of color. "Oh my gosh. What's he saying?"

I "translated." "He's saying, 'Blaze, for service above and beyond that of mortals, we formally induct you into Serpent Squad.' "

Serpent Squad. Where did that come from?

Blaze was shaking against me, so I tightened my grip, constricting her movement to zero. I opened my mouth wide to reveal sharp, pointy fangs. I thought I felt a tiny rivulet of my own blood run over my lower lip.

Blaze inhaled sharply. Her eyes rolled back in her head, and she went completely limp. Fortunately, I had a tight grip on her, so the surprise of her sudden weight didn't make me drop her.

Jack craned his neck and cocked his head toward Blaze. "She's out?"

I shifted my weight, bringing up a hand to gently rock Blaze's face back and forth. "She's completely out."

Goom snorted. "She fucking fainted. Great. Good work, elders."

"Uh. So what do we do now?" I looked from Jack to Goom.

Goom shrugged. "How the fuck should I know? I've never been initiated into a fucking vampire snake squad before."

Jack considered that. "Well, just bite her. She'll have a mark when she wakes up. It'll be enough."

"Hm. Okay." I tilted Blaze's head gently, revealing the brunt of her ashen pristine neck. I wondered where to stick the razor-sharp fang tips in. Maybe . . . there?

I was a hair's breadth from Blaze's neck when Jack stopped me. "Wait."

I pulled back.

He traced a line down and around Blaze's neck. "That's the jugular. You do not want to pierce that."

"Oh. I guess not."

"Unless you want to explain to the emergency room why she's dying of blood loss from a bite mark on her neck."

"No, that wouldn't be fun."

"Okay." Jack considered Blaze's exposed flesh, running his finger lightly across its surface. "Here. Put the fangs in here. Just a nibble, don't go more than a quarter inch in." He pointed to a bulge halfway up her neck.

I demurred. "Isn't that too high? Movies always show it farther down."

"I don't care what movies show. You need to hit muscle, not artery."

"Right." I took a deep breath.

Just a nibble.

— 38 —

Memorial

♀

"O keep my soul, and deliver me: let me not be ashamed, for I put my trust in thee."

A crisp wind blew through the trees and headstones of Decatur Cemetery as the pastor spoke. I had tears running down my cheeks. I stared at the urn near my feet. We had managed to secure a small plot next to our father for Ethan. His headstone read, "Taken young but always with us."

In spite of the fact I refused to believe Ethan was really gone, I felt intense grief. What would the future bring? Would I find Ethan again, his consciousness hiding deep inside his body? Or would I live a life dimorphic, using his precious body without him? I resolved to ask Jack to help me master meditation. Perhaps I could find Ethan then.

Julian stood beside me in a black suit, shirt, and tie that matched his ebony hair. He reached over and took my hand. I looked across the plot at Jack, who stood placid and unmoving in his black Mandarin suit with the silver-threaded embroidery. Goom stood beside him in a black caftan and cap. Blaze was there too, next to the pastor, in a black dress and sunglasses. Since she'd been initiated into the "cell" she wore nothing but black and constant sunglasses. The sight of her electric blue hair calmed me. I was among friends.

After the reading, we each dropped a handful of dirt on the urn in anticipation of the interment. We moved away from the plot to let the cemetary's representative do his work.

I stood next to Jack, who said, "Judith, there's talk you deserve a medal for your discoveries."

I smiled. "I was just lucky. It was General Herschel's buttons that did it. I realized they were the exact size and shape to fit in those computer boxes at the warehouse. How are they doing at finding all the bad ones?"

"They've found hundreds of them on high-ranking uniforms all over the Sun Belt. Each has a tiny sound recording device."

Goom spoke up. "I still can't believe sugarbutt figured it all out."

"You helped, you know, Goom," I said.

He grimaced. "I did?"

"Sure. With your computer magazines on miniaturization. That was what made me think of something small enough to fit inside a button."

"I can't believe this whole thing boils down to buttons. Simple, stupid buttons, breaking our national security."

Shun Yan had used his network of dry cleaners to swap the buttons out regularly. The devices then went to his server farm at the warehouse, where Jun Lo's software mined them for choice nuggets. When they found anything interesting, they sent it through the botnet to the highest bidder.

I turned to Jack. I lowered my voice so Julian, who was talking nearby with Blaze, couldn't hear. "Has Dragon been implicated?"

Jack shook his head. "No. He cannot be held responsible for the actions of Shun Yan and his consort."

"I'm sure he was behind it ultimately, though."

"Perhaps. But it is better for us if he is not dethroned."

"What happens when he goes?"

"As it stands now, Jun Lo inherits the syndicate."

"Ugh."

"Yes. As you've seen, I do not enjoy the same privilege with Jun Lo that I do with his uncle."

I shrugged. "All the same, I'm not sure how comfortable I am with some anti-American running around."

"There's no anti-American sentiment, just greed. China happened to be the highest bidder for the Predator information. If our government had offered more, it would have been different."

Julian and Blaze approached. I linked arms with Blaze and said to Julian, "Have you heard any more about the investigation?"

"Which one?"

"Well, the one about you."

Julian glanced at Jack, who was studying the ground at their feet. "Apparently it's been dropped," Julian said. "It seems someone high up realized it was a bogus claim."

Jack shifted from foot to foot. I said to him, "Is that your doing, Jack?"

He gave the barest of nods.

Julian said, "Don't think for a second that I owe you one, Colonel. It's not going to happen."

Jack shook his head. "That was not my intention."

I said, "Are you two going to play nice now? You're on the same side, you know."

Julian pursed his lips and didn't answer. Jack also remained silent. Goom snorted.

I figured that was as close to a truce as I could hope for. Julian was FBI, and Jack was Triad—it stood to reason they would be on the opposite sides of most situations. I wondered what the future would bring for the three of us. I had a vague feeling there would be a showdown between them at some point, and who would win? Not to mention the question of my own romantic allegiance. Jack or Julian? I didn't even want to think about it. Fortunately, Julian hadn't mentioned his proposal again.

The interment was over. Blaze and Goom walked toward his Mustang. Julian shook hands with everyone, then went to his government-issue SUV. Jack and I walked slowly back to the Wrangler we'd come in. I felt sad and more than a little restless.

"My house is gone. My brother is legally dead. Things aren't great."

Jack said, "We'll rebuild. And your brother is alive and well, sleeping at the bungalow."

I stopped. I took another look back at Ethan's plot. My heart sank. "Alive and well. Of course he is."

Jack reached out toward me. I hesitated, then took his hand. Together we headed away from Ethan's grave into the setting sunlight.

Afterword

Thanks for reading! Please rate and review at http://www.amazon.com. Look for more by Cy Wyss at http://www.cywywss.com. Sign up for Cy's monthly newsletter and get a free short story!

www.ingramcontent.com/pod-product-compliance
Lightning Source LLC
Chambersburg PA
CBHW070830250626
47159CB00003B/719
* 9 7 8 0 9 9 6 5 4 6 5 1 5 *

ACKNOWLEDGMENTS

I really have to thank everyone who listened to me ramble on and on about this series for months while I worked out the plot and figured out where we were going. It's a totally new genre for me. (Well, I mean except for the fact that it's still erotic romance! Let's not get carried away.) So, it took a lot of planning.

The concept came to me in the early hours of the morning in a dream when I wasn't quite awake yet. (Okay, gotta pause again here to say that "early" is a relative term. I don't do "early." Nothing in my world is actually "early." I just mean whatever time the last hour of my sleep occurred. Probably more like ten in the morning.)

In my dream, there were these scientists in a government bunker. They were studying diseases. They got sick. They had to be cryonically preserved... And from there, a series was launched. I spent a great deal of time studying cryonics and learning the difference between cryonics, cryobiology, and cryogenics--which are very different things.

I worked very hard to ensure that my terminology was correct with respect to the field of cryonics, though I obviously took a great deal of artistic liberty when reviving the preserved since alas, as far as we know, no one has been reanimated to this date.

Many thanks to Christa Soule for plotting with me when we were in the early stages, and then when we were in the middle stages, and still to this day.

Thanks to my husband and countless friends who listened to me and added their two cents.